DETROIT PUBLIC
3 5674 00584365 2
W9-BWR-987

The BOMB

CHICAGO IN FICTION
SAUL BELLOW
ADVISORY EDITOR

The BOMB

A NOVEL BY FRANK HARRIS

INTRODUCTION BY JOHN DOS PASSOS

CHICAGO & LONDON
THE UNIVERSITY OF CHICAGO PRESS

The Bomb was first published in 1909 by Mitchell Kennerley, New York. It was republished by the author in 1920.

Library of Congress Catalog Card Number: 63-22587

The University of Chicago Press, Chicago & London
The University of Toronto Press, Toronto 5, Canada

Frank Harris' Bomb

AN INTRODUCTION BY JOHN DOS PASSOS

FRANK HARRIS was an objectionable little man. He was sallow as a gypsy. He had bat ears, dark hair with a crinkle in it that grew low on the forehead, and a truculent mustache. People remarked on the richness of his bass voice. His charm was great, particularly for the opposite sex. He had the gift of gab to a sublime degree and a streak of deep scoundrelism that was the ruin of him.

A natural storyteller, tall tales so permeated his private life that his biographers were hard put to it to disentangle any facts at all from the web of fiction he spun about himself. Particularly in the twenties, when he was editing *Pearson's Magazine* in New York, there used to be considerable journalistic searching for "the real Frank Harris." One wonders now if such a creature ever existed. He wrote some good short stories. He might have developed into a first-rate novelist if he hadn't been such a damn liar.

Though at times he named Brighton, England, as his birthplace, amid other variants of his *curriculum vitae*, it seems likely that he first saw the light at Galway on the west coast of Ireland, on St. Valentine's Day in 1856, and that he was christened James Thomas Harris. His parents were Plymouth Brethren, of the most fundamentalist of Protestant sects, and were probably Welsh. His mother died when he was very small. His father was a seafaring man who had managed to work his way up in the Royal Navy from ship's boy to lieutenant in command of a revenue cutter, no mean feat in those days.

The father was always at sea. The children lived higgledy-piggledy, shifting from one small school to another as they followed their father's ports of call. Ireland was in a state of barely suppressed revolt. These were the days of the Fenian "troubles." Harris, who had been a great reader of Captain Marryat, told in later life of his bitter disappointment that his father failed to get him into the Royal Navy when he was fourteen. He always blamed his father for that.

Little Jim Harris was obviously a bright youngster, a voracious reader with a retentive memory. His father, who wanted to do what he thought best for the boy, sent him to a classical English school, which he hated with an eternal hatred. With ten pounds he managed to wangle there as a prize for scholastic attainments he ran away to Liverpool and bought himself steerage passage to America.

He must have reached New York in the early seventies. German and Irish immigrants poured off every ship. The country was in a state of intermittent boom and bust. Some greenhorns starved. Others made fortunes. Everybody talked big.

Harris became enormously Americanized. He decided his name was Frank. Like a Horatio Alger hero he started out shining shoes. Then he worked as a sandhog in the pressurized caissons they used in building the piers for Roebling's Brooklyn Bridge. He saw a man die of the bends and went back to shining shoes.

His story was that a gentleman whose shoes he was shining heard him quote some Latin and was so impressed that he offered him a job as night clerk in a Chicago hotel. If we can believe Frank Harris he was managing the entire hotel by the time he was seventeen. Some Texas cattlemen put up at his hostelry and induced him to go west with them to make his fortune.

He was physically husky, and as he told the tale, with an everincreasing abundance of detail, a great man with the ladies. He learned to ride in Texas and sopped up sagas of Indian-fighting and cattlerustling across the Rio Grande. He was developing a flair for writing. His first articles came out in frontier newspapers. Two of his brothers seem to have settled in Lawrence, Kansas, and at some point he studied for a year or so at the university there, became a naturalized citizen—so his story goes—and was admitted to the Kansas bar.

He caught the moneygrubbing fever of the time. He'd speculate in anything. When a financial crash wiped out his and his brothers' investments in Lawrence realestate, he went to work for a newspaper in Philadelphia. From then on his accounts of his meetings with the literary great become as confusing as his tales of amorous successes. He seems to have actually grasped the hand of Walt Whitman after a lecture. He told of visiting Emerson in Concord. A name was all he needed to hang a story on. He became the great namedropper of the century.

Somewhere around the time he came of age Frank Harris decided he wanted to be an Englishman instead of an American. Little malpractices, like the rumored theft of a certain judge's lawbooks, may have made it too hot for him in Lawrence, and possibly he wore out his welcome with the college professor he was sponging on in Philadelphia. He tells a fantastic tale, a little too much like Jules Verne's *Around the World in Eighty Days* to be believable, of crossing the continent to San Francisco with a highyaller paramour in his stateroom on the sleeper and sailing from the Golden Gate for Bombay and Capetown. Somehow, he did get himself from Philadelphia to Paris.

His great admiration was Carlyle. It was the Paris of the French Revolution that he saw. He hired himself a cheap room on the rue St. Jacques and learned the language by going through Hugo's *Hernani* and *Madame Bovary* with a dictionary. He attended Taine's lectures at the Sorbonne and made enough impression on that venerable critic to get a recommendation from him when he needed one.

When his money ran out he went to see his father who had retired on halfpay at Denbigh in the beautiful Welsh Vale of Clwyd. He left Denbigh in a hurry to avoid having to marry a young woman who thought herself engaged to him; and, with the help of literary friends, got himself taken on as a teacher at Brighton College. The meeting with the aged Carlyle which later became such an important part of the Frank Harris legend may have taken place in Brighton if it took place at all. Forever after he posed as an expert on poor Carlyle's marital infelicity.

As Harris told the story it was during his stay in Brighton that he speculated so successfully in Chilean bonds that he laid away twentyfive hundred pounds to finance his education. Teaching at a provincial college was not the young careerist's meat. After some kind of falling out with the college authorities Frank Harris was suddenly heard of as a warcorrespondent in Moscow for the American press, attached to the great pan-Slavist General Skobeliev in his short war against the Turks. Next he turned up in Heidelberg, listening to Kuno Fischer lecture on Shakespeare. As a writer he was planning to model himself on Carlyle. He sent Carlyle a wild west novel he was writing for his criticism. Since Carlyle was saturated with German scholarship Harris was bound he would seek his education in Germany.

Expelled from Heidelberg, so he told it, for knocking down an insulting student with his fist, he moved on to Göttingen and Berlin. He became fluent in German, read Goethe and Heine, and soaked up all the Socialist theories out of which Bismarck was building his welfare state as a bulwark for Hohenzollern autocracy. "Heroes and Hero-worship," The Iron Chancellor became his great admiration. In English Shakespeare was god.

European students in the years after the

Franco-Prussian war were obsessed with socialism and sex, the two prongs of the revolt of the intellectuals against the established order. In Vienna Freud was soon to be inciting his patients to erotic dreams. In London Marx was dissecting capitalism in the library of the British Museum. Frank Harris completed his *Wanderjahr* with a grand tour that took him to Florence and Athens and Constantinople. He never tired of talking about sex. Spouting *contes drolatiques* of cosmopolitan bedwrestling, he went back to Paris. There, by his own confession, he became the intimate friend of Guy de Maupassant. Turgenev somehow he muffed.

At the age of twentyseven, Frank Harris, tingling with lust and greed and ambition, was ready to take on the foggy capital of the Victorian world. He wrote of London as a woman "with wet draggled skirts," with "glorious eyes lighting up her wet pale face." He had somehow wangled a letter of introduction from Carlyle to Froude. It was as a poet he first showed himself. He had taken to representing himself as an American, an Irishman, or an Englishman as the occasion demanded. According to Harris' story Froude introduced him to literary society with a great dinner.

Be that as it may, by the summer of 1883 Harris had only managed to publish an occasional bookreview in the *Spectator*. His money must have run out because soon we hear of him making slim pickings as a reporter for the *Evening News.*

He had come back from Germany a Socialist. He didn't disdain to let his voice be heard at radical gatherings in Hyde Park. It was at a Socialist meeting that he first met Shaw. He told of being introduced to Karl Marx, and found the author of *Das Kapital* full of loving kindness. When Harris told him he had written the greatest book since *The Wealth of Nations*, he cried out that Harris' German was *Wunderbar.*

Socialists, Communists, anarchists were all of a heap in those days. Some Hyde Park orators were rumored to be subsidized by the Conservative party to undermine Gladstone's dominant Liberals. Kropotkin smelt the *agent provocateur* in glib young Harris and warned his disciples away from him.

Frank Harris was dragging on the shabby life of an apprentice writer in a Bloomsbury boardinghouse when suddenly he burst on Fleet Street as the editor-in-chief of the *Evening News.* It is typical of Harris' career that the most believable explanation of his sudden leap to fortune is found in a novel called *The Adventures of John Johns*, a bestseller in its day, which according to the gossip of the Café Royal, was based on Harris' career. John Johns became editor of an important London newspaper by going to bed with the publisher's wife.

He edited the *Evening News* for several years with great success. As editor he was skilful, resourceful, and ruthless. By using the sensation-mongering methods that were soon to bring William Randolph Hearst such success in America, he turned the paper from a liability into an asset for the owners in a few months. Years later he explained to some journalist friends that when he first took the sheet over his idea was to edit it as a cosmopolitan scholar of twentyeight. "Nobody wanted my opinions; but as I went downwards and began to edit it as I felt at twenty, then at eighteen, then at sixteen, I was more successful: but when I got to my tastes at fourteen years of age, I found instantaneous response. Kissing and fighting were the only things I cared for at thirteen or fourteen and these are the things the English public desires and enjoys today."

As editor of the *Evening News*, in spite of the disrepute of that scandalsheet among men of good will, Frank Harris became a figure in London society. He was dressed by the best Bond Street tailors, adopted high Spanish heels to look less pintsized, and was admitted to a number of clubs. For a man with a literary career to make the *Evening News* was a steppingstone. Though Harris had already become famous for his social agility, it was with astonishment that the English reading public discovered that this young upstart, a mere boy of thirty who had appeared out of nowhere, was to edit the *Fortnightly Review*. The *Fortnightly Review* was the most respectable literary journal in England, but respectability gave no assurance of circulation. Frank Harris was a circulation builder in the modern sense.

The eight years he edited the *Fortnightly Review* and his four years that followed as owner of the *Saturday Review* constituted the crowning period of his life. He was the center of the literary nineties. He discovered H. G. Wells. He launched Shaw as a drama critic. He encouraged Cunninghame Graham and Max Beerbohm. He published Swinburne and Oscar Wilde and Beardsley. In spite of a continuing liaison with Laura Clapton, which he publicized as the great love of his life, he married a wealthy widow with a house in Park Lane. His luncheons were notorious, in Park Lane or at the Café Royal, where he liked to seat his guests at an oval table in the center of the restaurant so that all London could overhear his gibes and indiscretions. His memory served him well. In a society appreciative of good conversation, his talk was a volcano of anecdote and paradox, laced with the scabrous revelations that so thrilled the prudish Victorians.

"Modesty," he claimed was "the fig leaf of mediocrity." He was the bounder par excellence. When he boasted to Oscar Wilde that he'd gotten himself invited to every great house in London, Wilde made the famous rejoinder "But never more than once, Frank."

He was the *arriviste* who never quite arrived. His wife soon tired of his infidelities and his cadging of her money for endless speculations on the shadier fringes of the City. Then there were freakish things about his personal habits. A colossal eater and drinker he had taken to using the stomach pump after meals as a substitute for the Roman vomitorium. Her solicitors arranged a separation.

After a purple period the forces of British respectability were gaining the upper hand again. One symptom was the trial and venomous persecution of Oscar Wilde. Another was Harris' being cashiered as editor of the *Fortnightly*. According to his account the management objected to an article which described some bomb-throwing French anarchists without condemning them and to paying Swinburne fifty pounds for a poem which they considered seditious.

The *Saturday Review* was a rearguard action. As a leader of opinion he was already slipping. Other stars of the Café Royal, Lord Alfred Douglas and Oscar Wilde, were fading into degradation and ignominy. Bernard Shaw was saved by his sense of humor and the thorough monogamy of his personal life. Wells, who kept his bohemianism quite private, was enshrined in the hearts of suburbia by his mixture of science fiction with social idealism. Licentiousness was going out of style. Harris became the man of lost causes.

He defended Wilde and Havelock Ellis. He took the unpopular side in the Boer War. He attacked British imperialism and prudishness and hypocrisy and the poems of Alfred, Lord Tennyson.

His life teemed with desperate expedients to raise money, deals with bucketshop operators, the use of his social connections to promote the sale of blue-sky securities. He had learned to live in the style of the Grand Dukes. He had become an addict of the Hotel du Cap at Antibes much frequented by the literary British in those days. Possibly hoping to cash in on the friendship, which we are assured was platonic, of the wealthy American lady who was then Princess of Monaco, he invested in a Monte Carlo hotel, then in one at Eze. He had begun to believe his own stories of his youthful success in the hotel business in Chicago. His luck had turned. Both schemes went awry.

He had to make his living by writing. His stories of the American west had always gone over when he told them from the head of the table. He started to write them down. His style was forceful and clear. He had the narrative drive. His first publications were American-type short stories. Then he tried to emulate the success of Prosper Merimée's *Carmen* by a novelette about a bullfighter which he called "Montes the Matador." Montes was a great success. George Meredith praised it because the bull's feelings were so well described. Harris' hunting with the hounds hadn't brought him the wealth and position he craved. From now on he would run with the hares.

Now, "in disgrace with fortune and men's eyes," as his beloved Shakespeare had put it, he found himself more and more siding with the exploited and the unfortunate. He would write with intent. He'd shatter the complacency of the wellheeled Victorians who were turning him down. After a hurried trip to America to refresh his memory of Chicago in 1908 he published *The Bomb*.

When on May 4, 1886, in the course of the rioting that accompanied a wave of agitation for the eight-hour day, a bomb was thrown into a group of police advancing to break up a protest meeting in the Chicago Haymarket, the British press joined the American press in intemperate denunciation of the murderous anarchists.

Frank Harris was still groping for the fourteenyearold mentality as editor of the *Evening News.* It was not till many months later that any trace of the feelings of the erstwhile Hyde Park orator appeared in its columns. Even then, though in private he seems to have doubted the guilt of the indicted anarchists, his name did not appear along with that of his friend George Bernard Shaw, or along with William Morris' or Peter Kropotkin's, on an appeal for amnesty approved by a meeting of protest in London in the fall of 1887. The Park Lane *viveur* could hardly associate himself with the grubby massmeetings of radical sectarians.

By the time Harris picked up the story the hanged men had been rehabilitated in the opinion of a large sector of American opinion. Governor John P. Altgeld of Illinois, with a rare exhibition of civic courage, pardoned the two survivors in 1892. Altgeld went further. In a careful analysis of the trial he proved, to the satisfaction of most fairminded citizens, that though the Chicago anarchists might have been guilty of inciting to riot, they were innocent of conspiracy to commit murder, or of the bomb-throwing itself. Altgeld's pursuit of justice was the ruin of his career as a politician.

The Bomb might well be classed as an early form of the "proletarian" novel.

I don't know whether Frank Harris is a "great" writer or not. He had drive and force. He had a knack for sketching characters. His writing stands up with Wells's or Kipling's as an example of the limpid English style of the period. He was very much of a precursor.

As a newspaper editor he foreshadowed the sensationalism of the cheap English press of our day. In *The Man Shakespeare* he led in the effort to save the mighty dead from the grad-grinds and the embalmers. Perhaps he loved Shakespeare "not wisely but too well." With his *Contemporary Portraits* he introduced into English with entertaining results a French strain of literary journalism. In *My Life and Loves*, and in the pornographic material he peddled pathetically from door to door in the latter part of his life, he anticipated the flood of smut that now clogs the literary market-place.

Critics have complained of historical inaccuracies in *The Bomb*. It rings true to the emotions of the time. Picking Rudolph Schnaubelt, the man who disappeared, as the bombthrower is as good a guess as any. If anybody knew who threw the bomb he has kept his mouth shut to this day. Harris fell into an anachronism in his description of the building of Brooklyn Bridge, which refers to the early seventies instead of the early eighties, but he had to work in his own experiences and recollections. Half a century after the book was first printed the reader will find the re-creation of the mood of the time singularly convincing.

Looking back on the nineteenth-century anarchists from the sixties of the twentieth century, when exploitation of aspirations and resentments has become part of the standard textbook of political careermaking, the Chicago anarchists seem as naïvely alien as the Children's Crusade. The oppressions and injustices that they protested against were real, but the notion that society could be shocked into justice and charity by the blowing up of a few policemen ranks with delusions relegated to the psychiatric ward. Out of the energy of these blind protests and deluded hatreds, of men struggling against adjustment to the changes in their lives enforced by technological revolution, we have seen terrible empires built. Perhaps the warspirit of political ideologies is losing its hold as the passions that fed the wars of religion lost their hold in the past. In any case *The Bomb* will give you a glimpse of an odd and moving and disturbing, and fortunately fairly unique, episode in Chicago's history.

Foreword

I HAVE been asked to write a foreword to the American edition of *The Bomb* and the publisher tells me that what the American public will most want to know is how much of the story is true.

All through 1885 and 1886 I took a lively interest in the labour disputes in Chicago. The reports that reached us in London from American newspapers were all bitterly one-sided: they read as if some enraged capitalist had dictated them: but after the bomb was thrown and the labour leaders were brought to trial little islets of facts began to emerge from the sea of lies.

I made up my mind that if I ever got the opportunity I would look into the matter and see whether the Socialists who had been sent to death deserved the punishment meted out to them amid the jubilation of the capitalistic press.

In 1907 I paid a visit to America and spent some time in Chicago visiting the various scenes and studying the contemporary newspaper accounts of the tragedy. I came to the conclusion that six out of seven men punished in Chicago were as innocent as I was, and that four of them had been murdered—according to law.

I felt so strongly on the subject that when I sketched out *The Bomb* I determined not to alter a single incident but to take all the facts just as they occurred. The book then, in the most important particulars, is a history, and is true, as history should be true, to life, when there are no facts to go upon.

The success of the book in England has been due partly perhaps to the book itself; but also in part to the fact that it enabled Englishmen to gloat over a fancied superiority to Americans in the administration of justice. The prejudice shown in Chicago, the gross unfairness of the trial, the savagery of the sentences allowed Englishmen to believe that such judicial murders were only possible in America. I am not of that opinion. At the risk of disturbing the comfortable self-esteem of my compatriots I must say that I believe the administration of justice in the United States is at least as fair and certainly more humane than it is in England. The Socialists in Trafalgar Square, when John Burns and Cunninghame Graham were maltreated, were even worse handled in proportion to their resistance than their fellows in Chicago.

I am afraid the moral of the story is a little too obvious: it may, however, serve to remind the American people how valuable are some of the foreign elements which go to make up their complex civilization. It may also incidentally remind the reader of the value of sympathy with ideas which he perhaps dislikes.

FRANK HARRIS

LONDON
January 1909

Chapter I

"Hold the high way and let thy spirit thee lead
And Truth shal thee deliver, it is no drede."

MY name is Rudolph Schnaubelt. I threw the bomb which killed eight policemen and wounded sixty in Chicago in 1886. Now I lie here in Reichholz, Bavaria, dying of consumption under a false name, in peace at last.

But it is not about myself I want to write: I am finished. I got chilled to the heart last winter, and grew steadily worse in those hateful, broad, white Muenchener streets which are baked by the sun and swept by the icy air from the Alps. Nature or man will soon deal with my refuse as they please.

But there is one thing I must do before I go out, one thing I have promised to do. I must tell the story of the man who spread terror through America, the greatest man that ever lived, I think; a born rebel, murderer and martyr. If I can give a fair portrait of Louis Lingg, the Chicago Anarchist, as I knew him, show the body and soul and mighty purpose of him, I shall have done more for men than when I threw the bomb. . . .

How am I to tell the story? Is it possible to paint a great man of action in words; show his cool calculation of forces, his unerring judgment, and the tiger spring? The best thing I can do is to begin at the beginning, and tell the tale quite simply and sincerely. "Truth," Lingg said to me once, "is the skeleton, so to speak, of all great works of art." Besides, memory is in itself an artist. It all happened long ago, and in time one forgets the trivial and remembers the important.

It should be easy enough for me to paint this one man's portrait. I don't mean that I am much of a writer; but I have read some of the great writers, and know how they picture a man, and any weakness of mine is more than made up for by the best model a writer ever had. God! if he could come in here now and look at me with those eyes of his, and hold out his hands, I'd rise from this bed and be well again; shake off the cough and sweat and deadly weakness, shake off anything. He had vitality enough in him to bring the dead to life, passion enough for a hundred men. . . .

I learned so much from him, so much; even more, strange to say, since I lost him than when I was with him. In these lonely latter months I have read a good deal, thought a good deal; and all my reading has been illumined by sayings of his which suddenly come back to my mind, and make the dark ways plain. I have often wondered why I did not appreciate this phrase or that when he used it. But memory treasured it up, and when the time was ripe, or rather, when I was ripe for it, I recalled it, and realized its significance; he is the spring of all my growth.

The worst of it is that I shall have to talk about myself at first, and my early life, and that will not be interesting; but I can't help it, for after all I am the mirror in which the reader must see Lingg, and I want him to feel pretty certain that the mirror is clean at least, and does not distort truth, or disfigure it.

I was born near Munich, in a little village called Lindau. My father was an Oberfoerster, a chief in the forestry department. My mother died early. I was brought up healthily enough in the hard way of the German highlands. At six I went to the village school. Because my clothes were better than most of the other boys' clothes, because every now and then I had a few Pfennige to spend, I thought myself better than my schoolmates.

The master, too, never beat me or scolded me. I must have been a dreadful little snob. I remember liking my first name, Ruldoph. There were princes, forsooth, called Rudolph; but Schnaubelt I hated, it seemed vulgar and common.

When I was about twelve or thirteen I had learned all that the village school had to teach. My father wished me to go to Munich to study in the Gymnasium, though he grudged the money it would cost to keep me there. When he was not drinking or working he used to preach the money-value of education to me, and I was willing enough to believe him. He never showed me much affection, and I was not sorry to go out into the larger world, and try my wings in a long flight.

It was about this time that I first of all became aware of nature's beauty. Away to the south our mountain valley broke down towards the flat country, and one could look towards Munich far over the plain all painted in different colours by the growing crops. Suddenly one evening the scales fell from my eyes; I saw the piney mountain and the misty-blue plain and the golden haze of the setting sun, and stared in wondering admiration. How was it I had never before seen their beauty?

Well, I went to the Gymnasium. I suppose I was dutiful and teachable: we Germans have those sheep-virtues in our blood. But in my reading of Latin and Greek I came across thoughts and thinkers, and at length Heine, the poet, woke me to question all the fairy tales of childhood. Heine was my first teacher, and I learned from him more than I learned in the class-rooms; it was he who opened for me the door of the modern world. I finished with the Gymnasium when I was about eighteen, and left it, as Bismarck said he left it, a Freethinker and Republican.

In the holidays I used to go home to Lindau; but my father made my life harder and harder to me. He was away all day at work. He did work, that is one thing I must say for him; but he left at home the girl who took charge of the house, and she used to give herself airs. She was justified in doing so, I suppose, poor girl; but I did not like it at the time, and resented her manner, snob that I was. When I had any words with Suesel I was sure to have a row with my father afterwards, and he didn't pick his words, especially when he had drink in him. I seemed to anger him; intellectually we were at opposite poles. Even when cheating or worse he was a devout Lutheran, and his servility to his superiors was only equalled by the harshness with which he treated his underlings. His credulity and servility were as offensive to my new dignity of manhood as his cruelty to his subordinates or his bestial drunkenness.

For some unhappy months I was at a loose end. I was very proud, thought no end of myself and my petty scholarly achievements; but I didn't know what course to steer in life, what profession to adopt. Besides, the year of military service stood between me and my future occupation, and the mere thought of the slavery was inexpressibly hateful to me. I hated the uniform, the livery of murder; hated the discipline which turned a man into a machine; hated the orders which I must obey, even though they were absurd; hated the mad unreason of the vile, soul-stifling system. Why should I, a German, fight Frenchmen or Russians or Englishmen? I was willing enough to defend myself or my country if we were attacked; confident enough, too, in courage, to believe that a militia like the Swiss would suffice for that purpose. But I loved the French, as my teacher Heine loved them; a great Cultur-volk, I said to myself—a nation in the first rank of civilization; I loved the Russians, too, an intelligent, sympathetic, kindly people; and I admired the adventurous English. Race-differences were as delightful in my eyes as the genera-differ-

ful tone and bustle made me feel very lonesome. When we landed I went to look for lodgings with Henschel, who was only too glad to have me with him, and, thanks to his command of English and the freemasonry of his craft, we soon found a room and board in a by-street on the east side. Next day Henschel and I started to look for work. I little thought that I was going gaily to undreamed-of misery. If I try to recall now some of the sufferings of that time, it is because my terrible experiences throw light on the tragic after-story. Never did any one go out to seek work more cheerfully or with better resolutions. I had made up my mind to work as hard as I could; whatever I was given to do, I said to myself, I would do it with my might, do it so that no one coming after me should do it as well. I had tested this resolution of mine again and again in my school life, and had always found it succeed. I had won always, even in the Gymnasium, even in Prima. Why should not the same resolve bring me to the front in the wider competition of life? Poor fool that I was.

On that first morning I was up at five o'clock, and kept repeating to myself, over and over again as I dressed, the English phrases I should have to use in the day, till they all came trippingly to my tongue, and when at six o'clock I went out into the air I was boyishly excited and eager for the struggle. The May morning had all the beauty and freshness of youth; the air was warm, yet light and quick. I fell in love with the broad, sunny streets. The people, too, walked rapidly, the street cars spun past; everything was brisk and cheerful; I felt curiously exhilarated and light-hearted.

First of all I went to a well-known American newspaper office and asked to see the editor. After waiting some time I was told curtly that the editor was not in.

"When will he be in?" I questioned.

"To-night, I guess," replied the janitor, "about eleven," with a stare that sized me up from the crown of my head to the soles of my feet. "If you hev a letter for him, you kin leave it."

"I have no letter," I confessed, shamefacedly.

"Oh, shucks!" he exclaimed, in utter contempt. What did "shucks" mean? I asked myself in vain. In spite of repeated efforts I could get no further information from this Cerberus. At last, tired of my importunity, he slammed the window in my face, with—

"Ah, go scratch your head, Dutchy."

The fool angered me; besides, why should he take pleasure in rudeness? It flattered his vanity, I suppose, to be able to treat another man with contempt.

I was a little cast down by this first rebuff, and when I went again into the streets I found the sun hotter than I had ever known it; but I trudged off to a German paper I had heard of, and asked again to see the editor. The man at the door was plainly a German, so I spoke German to him. He answered with a South German accent strong enough to skate on—

"Can't you speak United States?"

"Yes," I said, and repeated my question carefully in American.

"No, he ain't in," was the reply; "and I guess ven he comes in, he von't vant to see you." The tone was worse than the words.

I received several similar rebuffs that first morning, and before noon my stock of courage or impudence was nearly exhausted. Nowhere the slightest sympathy, the smallest desire to help: on all sides contempt for my pretensions, delight in my discomfiture.

I went back to the boarding-house more weary than if I had done three days' work. The midday meal, however, cheered me up a little; my resolution came back to me and, in spite of the temptation to stay and talk with the other lodgers, I retired to my room and began to study. Henschel had not returned for dinner, so I hoped that he had found work. However that might be, it was my business to learn English as quickly as possible, so I set myself to the task, and memorized through the swooning heat doggedly till six o'clock, when I went downstairs for tea. Our German schools may not be very good; but at least they teach one how to learn languages.

After supper, as it was called, I returned to my room, which was still like an oven, and studied in my shirt-sleeves at the open window till nearly midnight, when Henschel burst in with the news that he had got work in a great restaurant, and had wonderful prospects. I did not grudge him his good luck, but the contrast seemed to make my forlorn state more miserable. I told him how I had been received; but he had no counsel to give, no hope; he was lost in his own good fortune. He had taken ten dollars in tips. It all went into the "tronk" he told me, or common stock, and the waiters and head-waiters shared it at the end of the week, according to a fixed ratio. He would certainly earn, he calculated, between forty and fifty dollars a week. The thought that I, who had spent seven years in study, could not get anything at all to do was not pleasant.

When he left me I went to bed; but I tossed

about a long time, unable to sleep. It seemed to me that it would have been better for me if I had been taught any trade or handicraft, instead of being given an education which no one appeared to want. I found out afterwards that had I been trained as a bricklayer, or carpenter, or plumber, or house painter, I should probably have got work, as Henschel got it, as soon as I reached New York. The educated man without money or a profession is not much thought of in America.

Next day I got up and went to look for work as before, with just as little success, and so the hunt continued for six or seven days, till my first week had come to an end, and I had to pay another week's board—five dollars—out of my scanty stock of forty-five. Eight more weeks, I said to myself, and then—? Fear came to me, humiliating fear, and gnawed at my self-esteem.

The second week passed like the first. At the end of it, however, Henschel had a Sunday morning off, and took me with him on the steamer to Jersey City; we had a great talk. I told him what I had done, and how hard I had tried to get work—all in vain. He assured me he would keep his eyes and ears open and as soon as he came across a writer or an editor he would speak for me to him and let me know. With this small crumb of comfort I was fain to be content. But the outing and rest had given me fresh courage, and when we came back I told Henschel that as I had exhausted all the newspaper offices, I would try next day to get work on the elevated railways, or on the street-car lines, or in some German house where English was spoken. Another week or two fleeted by. I had been in hundreds of offices and met nothing but refusals, and generally rude refusals. I had called at every tram centre, visited every railroad depot—in vain. And now there were only thirty dollars in my purse. Fear of the future began to turn into sour rage in me, and infect my blood. Strangely enough, a little talk I had with Glueckstein on board the ship often came back to me. I asked him one morning how he intended to begin to get rich. "Get into a big office," he said.

"But how—where?" I asked.

"Go about and ask," he replied. "There is some office in New York wants me as badly as I want it, and I'm going to find it."

This speech stuck in my memory and strengthened my determination to persevere at all costs.

One fact I noted which is a little difficult to explain. I learned more English in the three or four weeks I spent looking for work in New York than in all the months, or indeed years, I had studied it. Memory seemed to receive impressions more deeply as the tension of anxiety increased. I spoke quite fluently at the end of the first month, though no doubt with a German accent. I had already read a good many novels, too, of Thackeray and others, and half a dozen of Shakespeare's plays.

Week after week slipped past; my little stock of dollar bills dwindled away; at length I was at the end of my poor capital, and as far from work as ever. I shall never be able to give an idea of what I suffered in disappointment and sheer misery. Fortunately for my reason the humiliations filled me with rage, and this rage and fear fermented in me into bitterness which bred all-hating thoughts. When I saw rich men entering a restaurant, or driving in Central Park, I grew murderous. They wasted in a minute as much as I asked for a week's work. The most galling reflection was that no one wanted me or my labour. "Even the horses are all employed," I said to myself, "and thousands of men who are much better working animals than any horse are left utterly unused. What waste!" One conclusion settled itself in me; there was something rotten in a society which left good brains and willing hands without work.

I made up my mind to pawn a silver watch my father had given me when we parted, and with what I got for the watch I paid my week's board. The week passed, and still I had no work, and now I had nothing to pawn. I knew from having talked to the boarding-house keeper that credit was not to be looked for. "Pay or get out" was the motto always on his lips. Pay! Would they take blood?

I was getting desperate. Hate and rage seethed in me. I was ready for anything. This is the way, I said to myself, society makes criminals. But I did not even know how to commit a crime, nor where to turn, and when Henschel came home I asked him if I could get a job as waiter.

"But you are not a waiter."

"Can't anybody be a waiter?" I asked in amaze.

"No, indeed," he replied quite indignantly. "If you had a table of six people, and each of them ordered a different soup, and three of them ordered one sort of fish, and the three others, three different sorts of fish, and so on, you would not remember what had been ordered, and could not transmit the order to the kitchen. Believe me, it takes a good deal of practice and memory to wait well. One must have brains to be a waiter. Do you think you could carry six soup plates full of soup, on a tray, into a room, high above your head, with other waiters running against you, without spilling a drop?"

The argument was unanswerable: "One must have brains to be a waiter!"

"But couldn't I be an assistant?" I persisted.

"Then you would only get seven or eight dollars a week," he replied; "and even an assistant, as a rule, knows the waiter's work, though he perhaps doesn't know American."

The cloud of depression deepened; every avenue seemed closed to me. Yet I must do something, I had no money, not a dollar. What could I do? I must borrow from Henschel. My cheeks burned. I had always looked on him, good fellow though he was, as an inferior, and now—yet it had to be done. There was no other way. I resented having to do it. In spite of myself, I bore a certain ill-will to Henschel and his superior position, as if he had been responsible for my humiliation. What brutes we men are. I only asked him for five dollars, just enough to pay my week's board. He lent them willingly enough; but he did not like being asked, I thought. It may have been my wounded sensibility; but I grew hot with shame at having to take his money. I determined that next day I would get work, work of any kind, and I would go into the streets to get it. I scarcely slept an hour that long hot night; rage shook me again and again, and I got up and paced my den like a beast.

In the morning I put on my worst clothes, and went down to the docks and asked for work. Strange to say, my accent passed unnoticed, and stranger still, I found here some of the sympathy and kindness which I had looked for in vain before. The rough labourers at the docks—Irishmen, or Norwegians, or coloured men—were willing to give me any assistance they could. They showed me where to go and ask for work; told me what the boss was like, the best time and way to approach him. On every hand now I found human sympathy; but for days and days no work. How far did I fall? That week I learned enough to know that I could pawn my Sunday suit. I got fifteen dollars on it; paid my bill, paid Henschel, too, and went straight to a workman's lodging-house, where I could board for three dollars a week. Henschel begged me to stay on with him, said he would help me; but the stomach of my pride would not stand his charity, so I gave him my address, in case he heard of anything to suit me, and went down—to the lowest level of decent working life.

The lodging-house at first seemed to me a

foul place. It was a low tenement house let off in single rooms to foreign workmen. You could get your meals in it or cook your own food in your room, whichever you liked. The dining-room would hold about thirty people comfortably; but after supper, which lasted from seven till nine, it was filled with perhaps sixty men, smoking and talking at intervals, in a dozen different tongues till ten or eleven o'clock. For the most part they were day-labourers, untidy, dirty, shiftless; but they showed me how to get casual light labour at docks and offices and restaurants—the myriad chance-jobs of a great city. Here I lived for months, spending perhaps three days in getting a job which perhaps only employed me for a few hours, then again finding work which lasted three or four days.

At first I suffered intensely from shame and a sense of undeserved degradation. How had I fallen so low? I must be to blame in some way. Wounded vanity frayed my nerves threadbare and intensified the discomfort of my surroundings. Then came a period in which I accepted my fate, and took everything as it came, sullenly. Usually I earned enough each week to keep me a week and a half or two weeks; but in mid-winter I had three or four spells of bad luck, when I fell even below the lodging-house to the bed for a night, hunger and hopeless misery.

It is much harder to get employment in the depth of winter than in any other season. It would really seem as if nature came to aid man in crushing and demoralizing the poor. You will say that this only applies to special trades; but take the statistics of the unemployed, and you will find them highest in midwinter. I had never experienced anything like the cold in New York, the awful blizzards; the clear nights when the thermometer fell to ten and fifteen degrees below zero, and the cold seemed to pierce one with a hundred icy blades—life threatened at every point by nature and man more brutal-callous than ever.

I had youth on my side, and pride, and no vices which cost money, or I should have gone under in that bitter purgatory. More than once I walked the streets all night long, stupefied, dazed with cold and hunger; more than once the charity of some woman or workman called me back to life and hope. It is only the poor who really help the poor. I have been down in the depths, and have brought back scarcely anything more certain than that. One does not learn much in hell, except hate, and the out-of-work foreigner in New York is in the worst hell known to man.

But even that hell of cold gloom and lonely misery was irradiated now and then by rays of pure human sympathy and kindness. How well I remember instance after instance of this. Whenever I sank to utter destitution I used at first to frequent the Battery: the swirling waters seemed to draw me, lulling my pain with their unceasing threnody. There I paced up and down for hours or swung my arms to keep warm, and was often glad that the numbing cold forced me to run about, for somehow or other one's thoughts are not so bitter when one moves briskly as they are when sitting still. One night, however, I was tired out, and sat in the corner of one of the benches. I must have slept, for I was awakened by an Irish policeman—

"Come now, get a move on ye; ye can't slape here, ye know."

I got up, but could hardly stir, I was so numbed with cold, and still half asleep.

"Get on, get on," said the policeman, shoving me.

"How dare ye push the man!" cried a husky woman's voice; "he ain't hurtin' the ould sate, anyway."

It was one of the prostitutes, Irish Betsy they called her, who regarded that part of the Battery as her own particular preserve and kept it sacred by a perfect readiness to fight for it, though its value must have been very small.

The policeman took her interference unkindly, and in consequence got the rough edge of Betsy's tongue. As soon as I could speak I begged her not to quarrel for me; I would go; and I walked away. Betsy followed and overtook me in a little while, and pushed a dollar bill into my hand.

"I can't take money," I said, handing her the bill back.

"And why not?" she asked hotly; "you nade it more than me, an' when I want it some night I'll ask it back from ye, the divil doubt me! It's loanin' it to ye, I am!"

Poor, dear Betsy! she had the genius of kindness in her, and afterwards, when times went better with me, I took her to supper as often as I could, and so learned her whole sad story. Love was her sin, love only, and like all other generous mistakes, though it brought punishment and contempt of others, it did not bring self-contempt. Betsy regarded herself as one of the innocent victims of life, and she was probably justified in this, for she kept her goodness of heart all through.

Another scene: I had gone to one place for three or four nights, where I got a bed for ten cents, and as I shivered out into the cold one morning about five-thirty, the hard Yankee who kept the place suddenly asked me—

"Have you had any breakfast?"

"What's that to you?"

"Not much; but my cawfee's hot, and if you'll have a cup, you're welcome."

The tone was careless-rough, but the glance that went with it thawed the ice about my heart, and I followed him into his little den. He poured out the coffee and put a steaming cup of it and some bacon and biscuits before me, and in ten minutes I was a man again, with a man's heart in me and a man's hope and energy.

"Do you often give breakfast away like this?" I asked him, smiling.

"Sometimes," was the answer. I thanked him for his kindness, and was on the point of going, when he added, without even looking at me—

"If you haven't got work by to-night you can come here and sleep without the dime, see!" I looked at him in astonishment, and he went on as if trying to excuse a weakness: "When a man gets up and goes out before six this weather, he wants work, and whoever wants work's sure to find it sooner or later. I like to help a man," he added emphatically.

I got to know Jake Ramsden well in a few weeks; he was harsh and silent like his native Maine hills, but kindly at heart.

How I lived through the seven months of that awful winter I can't tell; but I worried through somehow, and as the spring came on I even gathered a few dollars and went back to my old lodging-house, where I boarded for three dollars a week, and could wash and make myself decent. I had come to look upon it as a sort of luxurious hotel. That winter taught me many things, and, above all, this, that however unfortunate a man is there are others worse off and more unhappy: the misery of mankind is as infinite as the sea. And from this one learns sympathy and courage. I suppose on the whole the experiences did me more good than harm, though at the moment I was inclined to believe that they had simply coarsened my mind like the skin of my hands, and had roughened me in a hundred ways. I see now clearly enough that whatever I am or have been, I was made by that winter: for good and for evil I shall bear the marks of the struggle and suffering till I die. I wish I could believe that all the pain I had endured turned into pity for others; but there was a residue in me of bitterness.

Another scene from this period of my life, and I'll be able to tell how I came out of the abyss to air and sunlight once more. One evening in the dining-room an Englishman mentioned casually that any one could get work on the foundations of the Brooklyn Bridge. I could hardly believe my ears; I was still looking for steady employment, though scarcely daring to hope for it; but he went on: "They want men, and the pay's good: five dollars a day."

"Steady work?" I asked, in a tremor.

"Steady enough," he answered, with a scrutinizing glance at me, "but few can stick it, working in compressed air." It appeared that he had tried it and was not able to stand it; but that did not deter me. I found out from him where to apply, and next morning before six o'clock was taken on. I could scarcely contain myself for joy: at last I had got work; but the Englishman's words the night before came back to me: "It's few can do a shift, and in three months every one gets the 'bends.' " A stern joy came into me; if others could stand it, I could.

I suppose every one knows what working in a caisson on the bed of a river, fifty feet under water, is like. The caisson itself is an immense bell-shaped thing of iron; the top of it is an apartment called "the material chamber," through which the stuff dug out of the river passes on its way to the air. High up, on the side of the caisson is another chamber called "the air-lock." The caisson itself is filled with compressed air to keep out the water which would otherwise fill the caisson in an instant. The men going to work in the caisson first of all pass into the air-lock chamber, where they are "compressed" before they go to work, and "decompressed" after doing their shift.

Of course, I had been told what I should feel; but when I stepped into the air-lock with the other men and the door was shut and one little air-cock after another was turned on, letting in a stream of compressed air from the caisson, I could hardly help yelling—the pain stabbed my ears. The drums of the ears are often forcibly driven in and broken; some men not only become deaf, but have the most intense earache and sympathetic headache, attended with partial deafness. The only way to meet the pressure of the air in the ear, I quickly found, was to keep swallowing the air and forcing it up the Eustachian tubes in to the middle ear, so that this air-pad on the internal side of the drum might lessen or prevent the painful depression of the drum. During "compression" the blood keeps absorbing the gases of the air till the tension of the gases in the blood becomes equal to that in the compressed air; when this equilibrium has been reached men can work in the caisson for hours without experiencing serious inconvenience.

It took about half an hour to "compress" us, and that first half-hour was pretty hard to bear. When the pressure of the air in the lock was equal to that in the caisson, the door from the caisson into the air-lock opened by itself or at a touch, and we all went down the ladder on to the river bed and began our work, digging up the ground and passing it by lifts into the material chamber. The work itself did not seem very hard; one got very hot, but as one worked nearly naked it didn't matter much; in fact, I was agreeably surprised. The noises were frightful; every time I stooped, too, I felt as if my head would burst. But the two hours will soon pass, I said to myself, and two shifts for five dollars is good pay; in fifteen days I shall have saved the money I came to New York with, and then we shall see; and so I worked on, making light of the earache and headache, the dizziness and the infernal heat.

At length the shift came to an end, and one by one, streaming with perspiration, we passed up again into the air-lock to learn what "decompression" was like. We closed the door; the air-cocks were turned on, letting out the compressed air, and at once we began to shiver, the ordinary air was so wet and cold. It was as if a stream of ice-water had been turned into a hot bath. I had noticed when we got in that the others began to dress hastily; I now knew why. I hauled on my shirt and then my other clothes as quickly as I could; but the air grew colder and colder, damper and damper, and I began to get weak, giddy and sick. I suppose the gases in the blood were leaving it as the tension got less. At the end of an hour we were "decompressed," and we all stepped out shivering, surrounded by a wet, yellow fog, chilled to the heart.

Think of it; we had been working hard for two hours in a high temperature, and after our work we had this hour of "decompression," an hour of rapidly increasing cold and damp mist, while even the blood pressure in our veins was constantly diminishing. What with the "compression" and the "decompression," the two hours' shift lasted nearly four hours, so that two shifts a day made a very fair day's work—and such work! Most of the men took a glass of hot spirits the moment they got out, and two or three before they went home. I drank hot cocoa, and very glad I am that I did. It revived me as quickly as the spirits, I think, and took away the terrible feeling of chill and depression. Should I be able to stand the work? I could only go on doggedly, and see how continuous work affected me.

I had something to eat, and lay about in the sunshine till I got warm and strong again: but I had still the earache and headache, and felt dizzy when the time came to go to work.

The afternoon shift seemed interminable, dreadful. The compression was not so bad; I had learned how to get the air into my ears to meet the pressure, though whenever I forgot to breathe it in and keep the air-pad full, I paid at once with a spasm of acute earache. Nor was the work in the caisson unendurable; the pace set was not great: the heat comforting. But the "decompression" was simply dreadful. I was shivering like a rat when it was over, my teeth chattering. I could only gasp and not speak, and I easily let myself be persuaded to take a dram of hot spirits like the rest: but I determined that I would not begin to drink; I would bring thick, woolen under-clothes with me in the morning, all I had got. I went home exhausted, and with such earache and headache that I found it difficult to eat, and impossible to sleep.

The horror of being unemployed drove me to work next day and the next. How I worked I don't know; but I was recalled to thinking life and momentary forgetfulness of pain by seeing a huge Swiss workman fall down one morning as if he were trying to tie his arms and legs in knots. I never saw anything so horrible as the poor, twisted, writhing form of the unconscious giant. Before we could lift him on a mud-barrow and carry him away to the hospital he was bathed in blood, and looked to me as if he were dead. "What is it?" I cried. "The bends," said one, and shrugged his shoulders.

We had just come out of the air-lock into the room where we kept our clothes and food and things, and I began questioning the others about "the bends." It appeared that no one worked for more than two or three months without having an attack. It generally laid them up for a fortnight, and they were never the same men afterwards.

"Do the bosses pay us for the fortnight?" I asked.

"You bet!" cried a workman savagely; "they keep us at the Fifth Avenue Hotel, and pay us fer restin'."

"Can one only work three months, then?" I asked.

"I have worked more than that," said another man; "but you have got to take care, and not drink. Then I am very thin, and can stand it much better than any one inclined to be stout like you."

"They could make it easy enough for us," said a third; "everybody knows that if they gave us ten thousand feet of fresh air an hour in their damned caissons we could stand it all right;* but they only give us a measly thousand feet. It isn't men's work they buy at five dollars a day, but men's lives, damn them!"

I noticed then that my mates had the sullenness of convicts. It was rare that one spoke to his fellows; in silence we laboured; in silence we went to our work, and as soon as we came up into God's air and sunlight again, each man sought his home in silence. The cloud fell on me; I was not so sure as I had been at first that I should escape the common lot. After all, strong as I was, I was not so strong as that young Swiss whom I could still see, twisting about on the ground like a snake that has been trodden on. However, I determined not to think, and went to my shifts again as if nothing had happened.

I had been working in compressed air for about a fortnight when I saw a dreadful example of man's careless hardihood. A young American had been working with us for two or three days. This afternoon he wanted to get out, he said, without going through the "decompression," in order to keep an appointment with his girl, so he went up on top of the mud lift, into the material chamber and

* This workman was right. The illness of men working in caissons, which was formerly over 80 per cent in every three months when the air supplied was about 1500 cubic feet an hour, has now dropped to 8 per cent since the fresh air supply has been increased to 10,000 cubic feet an hour.—Editor's note.

so into the open air in perhaps five minutes. When we came out, an hour later, after having passed through the air-lock, we found him stretched on the floor of the waiting-room with a doctor by his side. He was unconscious, his breathing noisy and difficult, his lips puffed out, blowing froth. He died in a few minutes after we came into the room. It seemed dreadful to me; but not so dreadful as "the bends." After all, the man knew, or ought to have known, that he was running a great risk, and death seemed better to me than that excruciating physical torture; but somehow or other these two occurrences sickened me with the work. I determined to go on, if I could, till the end of the month, and then stop, and that is what I did.

Before the end of the month I began to feel weak and ill: I could not sleep, save by fits and starts, and I was practically never free from pain; still, I stuck it out for a month, and then with a hundred and forty dollars saved I took a fortnight's rest.

I spent every afternoon I could with Henschel; he had generally three or four hours free, and we went across to Jersey City or to Hoboken, bathing, or to Long Island, somewhere in the open air, and sunshine. At the end of the fortnight, I felt nearly as fit as ever, but I have still earaches and headaches occasionally to remind me of the Brooklyn Bridge. I did not go back to it; I had done my share of underground work, I thought; I would not take the risk again. Even the engineers, who had no hard manual labour to do, and earned four hundred dollars a month for merely directing, could not look on in that air for more than two hours a day. It was the men doing the hardest work who were expected to labour for two shifts a day—the hardest work, double hours, and smallest wage. With the quick rebound of youth, I soon consoled myself; after all I had done something and earned something, and after my fortnight's rest I was about again, as eager as ever to find work, but curiously soft after my fortnight's lazing.

A few days later I heard of another job, a better one this time, though it was hard work and not likely to be permanent. Still, it might be a beginning, I told myself, and hurried to the place. They were taking up a street near the docks to lay a new gas-pipe, and the work was being done by an Irish contractor. He looked at me shrewdly—

"Ain't done much work, have you?"

"Not lately," I replied; "but I will do as much as I can, and in a week as much as any man."

"Will you turn in now for half a day?" he asked, "and then we'll talk."

It was about nine o'clock in the morning. I knew he was cheating me, but I replied, "Certainly," and my heart lifted to hope. In ten minutes I had a pick in my hand, and space to use it. God, the joy of it, steady work at last in the open air! Once more I was a man, and had a place in the world. But the joy did not last long. It was the beginning of July and furiously hot; I suppose I went at the work too hard, for in half an hour I was streaming with perspiration; my trousers were wet through, and my hands painfully sore; the fortnight's rest had made them soft. One of the gang, an oldish man, took it upon himself to advise me. He was evidently Irish; he looked at me with cunning grey eyes, and said—

"You don't need to belt that pick in as if you were going to reach Australy. Take it aisy, man, and leave some work for us to-morrow."

The others all laughed. I found the advice excellent, and began to copy my fellows, using skill and sparing strength. When I returned to work after dinner my back felt as if it had been broken; but I hung on till night, and got a word of modified approval from the boss.

"For the first week I'll give you two dollars a day," he grunted; "ye're not worth more with thim hands."

I could not bargain: I dared not.

"All right," I said sullenly.

"Be here at six sharp," he went on; "if ye're late five minutes ye'll be docked half-a-day; mind that now."

I nodded my comprehension, and he went his way.

I was very tired as I walked home, but glad, glad at heart. I had the satisfaction of feeling that I had earned my living for the day, and a bit over, with pick and shovel, and surely there was enough work of that sort to be done in America. In youth one is an optimist and finds it hard to nurse bitterness; it is so much easier to hope than to hate. One week's work, I calculated, would keep me for three or four weeks, and this fact held in it a world of satisfaction.

I had a great evening meal that night, and drank innumerable cups of so-called coffee, and then went to bed and slept from about seven till five next morning, when I awoke feeling very well indeed, though horribly, painfully stiff. That would soon wear off, I told myself; but the worst of it was that my hands were in a shocking state; blisters had formed all over them and here and there had broken, and I could not use them without pain. The next day's work was excruciating, and my hands were bleeding freely before noon; but the old Irishman in the dinner hour bathed them with whiskey, which certainly dried up the wounds. I felt as if he had poured liquid fire over them, and the smart held throughout the afternoon. For the next three or four days the work was very painful; my hands seemed to get worse rather than better; but when they became so sore that I had to change tools as often as I possibly could, they began to mend, and by the end of the week I could do my day's stunt without pain or fatigue worth mentioning.

The job lasted three weeks, and when it was over the boss gave me his address in Brooklyn and told me if I wanted work he would give it me. I was the only man he picked out in this way. My heart rose again. I thanked him. After all, I said to myself as I went home, it's worth while doing a bit more than other men; one gets work easier.

My new job was road-making, and I was only one of a hundred men employed. At the end of a few weeks the boss said to me suddenly—

"Shure, you ought to be ashamed to work wid your hands, and you an edjicated man! Why don't you take a sub-contract?"

"How can I get a sub-contract?" I asked.

"I'll give you one," said he. "See here now; I get five dollars a yard for this road, and the stone found me; if you want to take fifty yards or a hundred yards I'll give them to yez at four dollars a yard; a man must make a little on a contract," he added cunningly, "and your profit'll be big."

I was very grateful to him, I remember, just as grateful as if he had been trying to do me a kindness, which was certainly not the case.

"But how am I to pay men?" I asked.

"That's your business," he replied indifferently. I hesitated a little, but next day I contracted to take a hundred yards and went to work to find labourers. Strange to say it was hard to get men; I could only find casuals —here to-day and gone to-morrow—and they were anything but energetic. I made up for their laziness by working double hours, and by the end of the week I had got five or six fairly good men working for me. After I had completed the first fifty yards of work I was astounded at my profit. I had to pay about a hundred dollars for labour, and had a hundred dollars for myself.

Naturally I wanted as much of this work as I could get, and the boss let me have two hundred yards more; but now I had worse luck. It was the end of October, and we had heavy rains, then it froze hard and snow fell. I soon found that I should have to drive the men or scamp the work, or be content with little or no profit. I hardly made as much over the next two hundred yards as I had made over the first fifty. Still, my month's work had yielded over a hundred dollars net profit, and with that I was content.

One day, talking with the old Irishman who had worked with me on my first job, and who was now working for me, I happened to say that if the frost held I should lose money.

"Hwat's that ye say?" he asked suspiciously.

"It costs me four dollars a yard, now," I explained ruefully.

"An' you gettin' six an' sivin," he retorted with derision.

"Four," I corrected.

"Thin you've bin chated," he concluded; "the ould un's gettin' eight."

I thought he was simply talking loosely, and paid no further attention to him. Still I tried to get a little better contract out of the boss; I failed, however, completely; it was four dollars a yard, take it or leave it, with him.

I took another two hundred yards at this price; but now luck ran dead against me. It froze all through that wretched December and January, froze hard, and when we tore up the road to lay the stones one day, we had to do the work all over again the next day.

At the end of the month's work I had lost fifty dollars, though I myself had worked sixteen hours a day. I remonstrated with the boss, told him it was not good enough to keep on at such a rate; but he would not let me have a cent more than my contract price, and swore by all his gods that he was only getting five dollars himself, and could not afford to allow me a cent more for the weather. "We have all to take the scats with the good spuds," he said.

Now that I knew exactly what the work cost, I could not believe him, so I took a day off and went with the old Irishman to find out if he was telling the truth. A few drinks in an Irish saloon, a talk with a captain of Tammany, and I soon discovered that the contract was given to the boss at ten dollars a yard; ten, though it could have been done profitably for five. I found out more even than that. My boss had sent in a claim for extra money because of the bad weather, and had been allowed three dollars a yard on the work I had done in the last two months. Then I understood clearly how men get rich. Here was an uneducated Irishman making ten thousand dollars a year out of the city contract. True, he had to give something to the Tammany officials in bribes, but he always "made a poor mouth," as they said, pretending to be hard up, and in the year, I am certain, never disbursed more than five hundred dollars in palm oil.

I found all this out in one forenoon. I thanked the old Irish labourer, and treated him, and then went off to call on Henschel and spend the afternoon with him. He, too, wanted to see me. He had got to know the editor of the "Vorwaerts," he told me, the Socialist paper in New York, and he asked me to go up and see Dr. Goldschmidt, the editor.

I was in the right humour. I could not bear to think of going on working for that swindling Irish contractor; nor could I make up my mind to take the advice of the old Irishman, who said, "Now you have the truth, force the swindling old baste to give you sivin dollars a yard, or threaten him wid the papers you'll write to; that'll frighten him."

I didn't want to frighten the boss, nor would I take any part in his thieving. I merely wished to be quit of him and to forget the whole sordid story. After all, I had two or three hundred dollars behind me now, and my experiences cried to be given form and to be set out in print.

I went with Henschel to see Dr. Goldschmidt, and found him to be a pleasant man, a Jew, of good education, and with a certain kindliness in him that attracted me. He asked me what I proposed to write about. I said I could give my experiences as an out-of-work or as a day-labourer with pick and shovel, or I could write on the Socialism of Plato. I had had this subject in mind when I first visited the newspaper offices months before. Now Plato and his Republic sounded ridiculous in my ears; I had fresher fish to fry. Goldschmidt was evidently of the same opinion; for he laughed at the suggestion of Plato, and as he laughed, it suddenly became clear to me that I had gone a long way in thought during my year in New York. All at once I realized that my experiences as an emigrant had made a man of me; that those twelve or fifteen months of fruitless striving to get work had turned me into a reformer if not yet into a rebel.

"Let me write on what I have gone through," I said finally to Goldschmidt. "After all, the pick and shovel are as interesting as sword and hauberk, and the old knights who went forth to fight dragons had nothing to meet so fearful as compressed air."

"Compressed air?" he caught me up. "What do you mean? Tell me about that."

He had certainly the journalist scent for a novelty and sensation, so I told him my story; but I could not talk merely about my work in the caissons. I told him nearly everything I have set down here, and, worst of all, I gave him the lessons first, and not the incidents, in my serious German way; told him that manual work is so hard, so exhausting in the American climate, that it turns one into a soulless brute. One is too tired at night to think, or even take any interest in what is going on in the world. The workman who reads an evening paper is rare. The Sunday paper is his only mental food; on week days he labours and eats and then turns in. The conditions of manual labour in the States are breeding a proletariat ready for revolt. Every man needs some rest in life, some hours of enjoyment. But the labourer has no time for recreation. He dare not take a day's respite; for if he does he may lose his job, and probably have more leisure than he wants.

My view of the position seemed to strike the doctor as interesting; but my experiences in the caissons clinched the matter.

"Write all the out-of-work part," he said, "and end up with your days in the caisson. I know something about that job. The contractors are to get sixty million dollars for it, and I suppose it'll not cost twenty; but I'll look it all out and back your story up with some hard facts."

"But does any one make two hundred per

cent on a contract?" I asked, forgetting for the moment my Irish boss who wanted at least a twofold profit and as much more as he could get by lying.

"Certainly," replied Goldschmidt. "There are only a few competitors, if any, for a big job, and the two or three men who are willing and able to take it on, are apt to open their mouths pretty wide."

Bit by bit, it was being forced in on me that our competitive system is an organized swindle.

I went off determined to write a telling series of articles. While talking to Goldschmidt I had made up my mind not to go back to the road-making; it was all brainless, uninteresting, stupefying to me, and the corruption in it horribly distasteful. An hour's talk with an educated man had turned me against it forever. I hated even to meet that lying boss again. I would not meet him. I ached to get back to my books and clean clothes and studious habits of life.

I took rooms up town, but on the east side, very simple rooms, which cost me, with breakfast and tea, about ten dollars a week, and went to work with my pen. I soon found that labour with the pick and shovel in the bitter weather had made it almost impossible for me to use the pen at all. My brain seemed tired, words came slowly, and I soon grew sleepy. Thinking, too, is a function that needs exercise, or it becomes rusty. But in a week or two I wrote more freely, and in a month had finished a series of German articles embodying my experiences as a "tenderfoot," and sent them to Goldschmidt. He liked them, said they were excellent, and gave me a hundred dollars for them. When I received his letter I felt that at long last I had come into my own and found my proper work. The articles made a sort of sensation, and I got two hundred dollars more for them in book form. For the next three or four months it was easy enough by going about New York and keeping my eyes open to get subjects for two or three articles a week. I didn't earn much by them, it is true; but, after my experiences, twenty to twenty-five dollars a week were more than enough for all my needs.

Moreover, I felt that I had solved the problem. I could always earn a living now one way or another by pick and shovel, if not by pen. I was to that extent at least master of my fate.

One day going into the office of the "Vorwaerts," whom should I run across but Raben. Of course we adjourned immediately to a German restaurant near by, and ordered a German lunch, and many Seidels of German beer. He had been working steadily, it appeared, ever since he left the ship, but at low rates. He wanted to go to Chicago, he told me, where the pay was better, only he had a wonder of a girl whom he could not bear to leave. She was a perfect peach, he added, and I noticed for the first time that his lips were sensual, thick.

While he was speaking it came to me that I should like to go West, too, and break fresh ground. Those accursed months when I tried vainly to get work had left in me a dislike of New York. Deep down in me there was a fund of resentment and bitterness.

"I should like to go to Chicago," I said to Raben. "Could you give me an introduction to any one?"

"Sure," he said, "to August Spies, the owner and editor of the 'Arbeiter Zeitung.' He is a first-rate fellow, a Saxon, too, a Dresdener. He would be sure to take you. All you South Germans hang together."

I called for pen and paper, and got him to write me a letter of introduction to Spies then and there.

The same evening, I think, I went to see Dr. Goldschmidt, and asked him if I might write him a weekly letter from Chicago, about labour matters, and he arranged that he would take one a week from me, at ten dollars a letter; but he told me that I must make it a good two columns—two or three thousand words for ten dollars—the pay was not high; but it ensured me against poverty, and that was the main thing. On the morrow I packed my little trunk, and started for Chicago . . .

Chapter II

THE long train journey and the great land spaces seemed to push my New York life into the background. I had been in America considerably over a year. I had gone to New York a raw youth, filled with vague hopes and unlimited ambitions; I was leaving it a man, who knew what he could do, if he did not know yet what he wanted. By the by, what did I want? A little easier life and larger pay—that would come, I felt —and what else? I had noticed going about the streets of New York that the women and girls were prettier, daintier, better gowned than any I had been accustomed to see in Germany. Many of them, too, were dark, and dark eyes drew me irresistibly. They seemed proud and reserved, and didn't appear to notice me, and, strange to say, that attracted me as much as anything. Now that the struggle for existence left me a little breathing space, I would try, I said to myself, to get to know some pretty girl, and make up to her. How is it, I wonder, that life always gives you your heart's desire? You may fashion your ideal to your fancy; ask for what eyes and skin and figure you like; if you have only a little patience, life will bring your beauty to the meeting. All our prayers are granted in this world; that is one of the tragedies of life. But I did not know that at the time. I simply said to myself that now I could speak American fluently, I would make love to some pretty girl, and win her. Of course I had to find out, too, all about the conditions of labour in Chicago, for that was what Goldschmidt wanted in my weekly articles, and I must learn to speak and write American perfectly. Already in my thoughts I had begun to call myself an American, so strongly did the great land with its careless freedom and rude equality attract me. There was power in the mere name, and distinction as well. I would become an American, and—my thoughts returned on themselves—and a girl's face fashioned itself before my eyes, dainty-dark, provocative, wilful. . . .

My year's work in the open air had made me steel-strong. I was strung tense now with the mere thought of a kiss, of an embrace. I looked down and took stock of myself. I was roughly, but not badly dressed; just above the middle height, five feet nine or so; strongly built, with broad shoulders; my hair was fair, eyes blue, a small moustache was just beginning to show itself as golden down. She would love me, too; *she* . . . the blood in me grew hot; my temples throbbed. I rose and walked through the car to throw off my emotion; but I walked on air, glancing at every woman as I passed. I had to read to compose myself, and even then *her* face kept coming between me and the printed page.

I reached Chicago late in the evening, after a forty hours' journey. I was not tired, and in order to save expense I went at once in search of Spies, after leaving my baggage at the depot. I found him at the office of the "Arbeiter Zeitung." The office was much smaller and meaner than Dr. Goldschmidt's; but Spies made an excellent impression on me. He was physically a fine, well set up fellow, a little taller than I was, though perhaps not very strong. He was well educated, and spoke English almost as fluently as his mother tongue, though with a slight German accent. His face was attractive; he had thick, curly brown hair, dark blue eyes, and long moustaches; he wore a pointed beard, too, which seemed to accentuate the thin triangle of his face. I found out, bit by bit, that he was very emotional and sentimental. His chin was round and soft, like a girl's. His actions were always dictated by his feelings at the moment. He met me with a frank kindliness which was charming; said that he had read my articles in "Vorwaerts," and hoped I would do some work for him. "We are not rich," he said, "but I can pay you something, and you must grow up with the paper," and he laughed.

He proposed that we should go out and sup; but when I told him I wanted lodgings he exclaimed: "That fits exactly. There is a Socialist, George Engel, who keeps a toyshop between here and the station. He told me he wanted a lodger. He has two good rooms, I believe, and I am sure you'll like him. Suppose we go and see him." I assented, and we set off, my companion talking the while with engaging frankness of his own plans and hopes. As soon as I saw Engel I knew we should get on together. He had a round, heavy, goodnatured face; he was perhaps forty-five or fifty years of age; his brown hair was getting thin on top. He showed me the rooms, which were clean and quiet. He was evidently delighted to talk German, and proposed to take my checks and bring my baggage from the depot, and thus leave me free. I thanked him in our Bavarian dialect, and his eyes filled with tears.

"Ach du liebster Junge!" he cried, and shook me by both hands. I felt I had won a friend, and turning to Spies said, "Now we can sup together."

Though it was getting late, he took me off at once to a German restaurant, where we had a good meal. Spies was an excellent companion; he talked well, was indeed, on occasion, both interesting and persuasive. Besides, he knew the circumstances of the foreign workers in Chicago better than perhaps any one. He had genuine pity, too, for their wants and faults, sincere sympathy with their sufferings.

"Whether they come from Norway or Germany or South Russia," he told me, "they are cheated for the first two or three years by every one. In fact, till they learn to speak American freely they are mere prey. I want to start a sort of Labour Bureau for them, in which they can get information in their mother tongue on all subjects that concern them. It is their own ignorance which makes them slaves—pigeons to be plucked."

"Is the life very hard?" I asked.

"In winter dreadfully hard," he replied. "About thirty-five per cent of working men are always out of employment; that entails a sediment of misery, and our winters here are terrible. . . .

"There are some dreadfully unfortunate cases. We had a woman last week who came to our meeting to ask for help. She had three young children. Her husband had been employed in Thompson's cheap jewellery manufactory. He earned good wages, and they were happy. One day the fan broke and he breathed the fumes of nitric acid. He went home complaining of a dry throat and cough; seemed to get better in the night. Next morning was worse; began to spit thin, yellow stuff. The wife called in a doctor. He prescribed oxygen to breathe. That night the man died. We got up a subscription for her, and I went to see the doctor. He told me the man had died of breathing nitrous acid fumes; it always causes congestion of the lungs, and is always fatal within forty-eight hours. There the wife is now, destitute, with three children to feed, and all because the law does not compel the employer to put up a proper fan. Life's brutal to the poor. . . .

"Besides, American employers discharge men ruthlessly, and the police and magistrates are all against us foreigners. They are getting worse and worse, too. I don't know where it'll all end," and he went silent for a time. "Of course you're a Socialist," he resumed, "and will come to our meetings, and join our Verein."

"I don't know that you would call me a Socialist," I replied; "but my sympathies are with the workmen. I'd like to come to your meetings."

Before we parted he had taken me round,

and shown me the lecture-room, which was quite close to his newspaper office, and given me a little circular about the meetings for the month. He left me finally at Engel's door, with the hope that we might meet again soon.

It must have been nearly midnight when I got into the house. Engel was waiting up for me, and we had a long talk in our homely Bavarian dialect. I told him it was my rule never to speak German; but I could not resist the language of my boyhood. Engel, too, had read my articles in "Vorwaerts," and was delighted with them; he was entirely self-taught, but not without a certain shrewdness in judging men; a saving, careful soul, with an immense fund of pure human kindness at the heart of him—a clear pool of love. We parted great friends, and I went to bed full of hope and had an excellent night.

Next morning I went about looking at Chicago; then I paid a visit to the "Arbeiter Zeitung" for some statistics which I wanted for my New York article, and so the day drifted by.

I had been in Chicago a week when I went to the first of the Socialist meetings. The building was a mere wooden shanty at the back of some brick buildings. The room was a fairly large one, would seat perhaps two hundred and fifty people; it looked bare and was simply furnished with wooden benches and a low platform on which stood a desk and a dozen plain chairs. Fortunately the weather was very pleasant, and we could sit with open windows; it was about mid-September, if I remember rightly. The speakers could hold forth, too, without being overheard, which was perhaps an advantage.

The first speaker rather amused me. He was presented by Spies as Herr Fischer, and he spoke a sort of German-American jargon that was almost incomprehensible. His ideas, too, were as inchoate as his speech. He believed, apparently, that the rich were rich simply because they had seized on the land, and on what he called "the instruments of production," which enabled them to grind the faces of the poor. He had evidently read "Das Kapital" of Marx, and little or nothing more. He did not even understand the energy generated by the open competition of life. He was a sort of half-baked student of European Communism, with an intense hatred of those whom he called "the robber rich."

Fischer probably felt that he was not carrying his audience with him, for he suddenly left off his sweeping denunciations of the wealthy, and began to deal with the action of the police in Chicago. In handling the actual he was a different man. He told us how the police had begun by dispersing meetings in the streets under the pretext that they interfered with the traffic; how they went on to break up meetings held on lots of waste ground. At first, too, the police were content, he said, to hustle the speaker from his improvised platform, and quietly induce the crowd to move on and break up; lately they had begun to use their clubs. Fischer remembered every meeting, and gave chapter and verse for his statements. It was not for nothing that he had worked as a reporter on the "Arbeiter Zeitung." He had evidently, too, an uncommonly vivid sense of fairness and justice, and was exasperated by what he called despotic authority. He spoke now in the exact spirit of the American Constitution. Free speech to him was a right inherent in man. He declared that he for one would never surrender it, and called upon his audience to go to the meetings armed and resolved to maintain a right which had never before been questioned in America. This provoked a tempest of cheers, and Fischer sat down abruptly. His argument was unimpeachable; but he did not realize that native-born Americans would claim for themselves rights and privileges which they would not accord to foreigners.

The next speaker was a man of a different stamp, a middle-aged Jew called Breitmayer, who spoke in favour of subscription for Spies' Labour Bureau. He told how the labourers were exploited by the employers, and pointed his discourse with story after story. This sort of talk I could appreciate. I had been exploited, too, and I joined heartily in the applause which punctuated the speech. To Breitmayer humanity was separated into two camps—the "Haves" and the "Have-nots," or, as he put it, the masters and the slaves, the wasters and the wanters. He never raised his voice, and some of his talk was effective; but even Breitmayer could not keep off the burning subject. A friend of his had been struck down by a policeman, in the last meeting; he was still in hospital, and, he feared, permanently injured. What crime had Adolph Stein committed, what wrong had he done, to be maltreated in this way? Breitmayer, however, ended up tamely. He was in favour of passive resistance as long as possible (some hissing); "as long as possible," he repeated emphatically, and the repetition provoked cheer upon cheer. My heart beat fast with excitement; evidently the people were ripe for active resistance to what they regarded as tyrannical oppression.

After Breitmayer sat down there was a moment's pause, and then a man moved forward from the side, and stood before the meeting. He was a slight, ordinary, nondescript person, with a green shade over his eyes. Spies went up beside him, and explained that Herr Leiter had been injured in a boiler explosion a year before; he had been taken to the hospital and treated; had been discharged two days ago, almost totally blind. He had gone to his former employers, Messrs. Roskill, the famous soap manufacturers, of the East Side, who had two thousand hands, and asked for some light job. They would give him nothing, however, and he now appealed to friends and brother workmen for help in his misfortune. He could see dimly at two or three yards. If he had a couple of hundred dollars he could open a shop for all sorts of soap, and perhaps make a living. At any rate, with the help of his wife, he would not starve, if he had a shop. All this Spies told in an even, unemotional voice. A collection was made, and he announced that one hundred and eighty-four dollars had been collected. One hundred and eighty-four dollars from that small gathering of working-men and women—it was splendidly generous.

"I dank you very mooch," said Herr Leiter, with a catch in his voice, and retired on his wife's arm to his seat. The helpless, hopeless pathos of the shambling figure; the patience with which he bore the awful, unmerited disaster, brought quick, hot tears to my eyes. Mr. Roskill could spare nothing out of his millions to this soldier broken in his service. What were these men made of that they did not revolt? Had I been blinded down there under water at Brooklyn I would have found words of fire. Roskill had done nothing for him. Was it credible? I pushed my way to the platform and asked Leiter in German: "Nichts hat Er gethan—Nichts? Nichts gegeben?" ("Did Roskill do nothing? Give you nothing?")

"Nichts; er sagte dass es ihm Leid thaete." ("Nothing; he said that he was sorry.") My hands fell to my sides. I began to understand that resignation was a badge of servitude, that such sheepish patience was inherited. In spite of reasons, my blood boiled, and pity shook me; something must be done. Suddenly Breitmayer's words came back to me, "passive resistance as long as possible." The limit must be nearly reached, I thought. I could not stay on at the meeting. I had to get by myself to think, with the stars above me, so I made my way to the door. Blind at six and twenty, and turned out to starve, as one would not turn out a horse or a dog. It was maddening.

To judge by the speeches, the working-men in Chicago were even worse off than the working-men in New York. Why? I could not help asking myself: why? Probably because there was not so much accumulated wealth, and an even more passionate desire to get rich quickly.

"Blind and no compensation, no help," the words seemed to be stamped on my brain in letters of fire. It was the thought of Leiter that made me join the Socialist Club two days later.

I had arranged with Spies to go about visiting the various workmen's clubs, and I went to several of them for the sake of that weekly article to New York, and found what I expected to find. The wages of the working-man were slightly higher than in New York, but wherever it was possible to cheat him he was cheated, and the proportion of unemployed was larger than it was on Manhattan Island.

After finishing my article on Leiter that week for "Vorwaerts," I went down theMichigan Boulevard and walked along the Lake Shore. The broad expanse of water had a fascination for me, and I liked the great boulevard and the splendid houses of brown stone or brick, each standing in its own grassy lawn. After I had walked for an hour, I returned by the Boulevard and had an interesting experience. A hired brougham had run into a buggy, or the buggy had run into the hired carriage, which was turning out of a cross street; at any rate, there was a great row; the buggy was badly broken up and a couple of policemen were attending to the horses. A crowd gathered quickly.

"What is the matter?" I asked of my neighbour, who happened to be a girl. She turned. "I don't know; I've only just come," and she lifted her eyes to mine.

Her face took my breath away; it was the face of my dreams—the same dark eyes, and hair, the same brows; the nose was a little thinner, perhaps, the outlines a little sharper, but the confident, wilful expression was there, and the dark, hazel eyes were divine. Feeling that confession was the best sort of introduction, I told her I was a stranger in Chicago; I had just come from New York; I hoped she'd let me know her. It was so lonely for me. As we turned away from the crowd she said she thought I was a foreigner; there was something strange in my accent. I confessed I was a German, and pleading that it was a German custom to introduce oneself, I begged her to allow me to do so, adding in German fashion, "My name is Rudolph Schnaubelt." In reply she told me her name, Elsie Lehman, quite prettily.

"Are you a German, too?"

"Oh, no!" she said; "my father was a German; he died when I was quite little," and then she went on to say that she lived alone with her mother, who was a Southerner. I hoped I might accompany her to her house; she accepted my escort with a prim, "Certainly."

As we walked we talked about ourselves, and I soon learned a good deal about Elsie. She was a typewriter and shorthand writer, and was engaged during the day with Jansen McClurg and Company, the booksellers, but was free every evening after seven o'clock. I seized the chance; would she come to the theatre some night? She replied, flushing, that she'd be delighted; confessed, indeed, that she liked the theatre better than any other amusement except dancing, so I arranged to take her to the theatre the very next night.

I parted with her at the door of the lodging-house where she and her mother lived; she asked me in to make her mother's acquaintance, but I begged her to let me come next night instead, for I was in my working clothes. I can still see her standing at the top of the steps as she said "good night" to me—the slight, lissom figure, the provocative dainty face.

As I went away I wondered how she managed to dress so well. She looked a lady; she was both neat and smart. How could she do it on her wages? I did not know then as I knew afterwards that she had a natural gift for whatever was at once becoming and distinguished, but the provocative beauty of her ran in my blood like wine, and before I went home I bought a couple of papers in order to see exactly what theatre to select. I suppose because I am a German and sentimental, and born with an instinctive respect for women, I picked out the most proper play I could find; it was "As You Like It," with a distinguished actress as Rosalind.

Next evening I dressed myself as well as I could in dark clothes with a silk tie in a loose bow, and went round to fetch Elsie at seven o'clock. I had been thinking of her the greater part of the day, wondering if she liked me as I liked her, wondering if I might ever kiss her, catching my breath at the thought, for the divine humility of love was upon me, and Elsie seemed too dainty precious for possessing.

It was her mother who met me when I called, a washed-out little woman, with tired, dark eyes, and white linen things at her neck and wrists, and a faintly querulous voice. She told me that Elsie would be down "right away," that she had "only just got back from the store," and was "fixin' up."

We sat down and talked, or rather she drew me out, perhaps without object, about myself and my prospects. I was quite willing to speak, for I was rather proud of my position as a writer. She seemed to have no illusions on the subject; writing, she said, "was right easy work," but she guessed it didn't pay very well, for "there was a writer in the boarding house where we lived before who used to borrow round from everybody and never paid anybody back. He did meetings and things": from which I gathered he was a reporter. While we were still chatting about the impecunious and unscrupulous reporter, Elsie came in and took my senses captive.

She was dressed in a sort of light corn-coloured tussore, and had a crimson rose in her dark hair, just above the ear. She had thrown on a scarf of a deeper yellow as head-dress—she had the colouring, and all the dainty grace of a flower. I told her the dress was like a daffodil, and she bowed to the compliment with smiling lips and eyes. It was quite fine and warm, so we walked to the theatre. Once or twice my arm touched hers as we walked, and new pulses came to life in me.

What an evening we had! I had read the play, but had never seen it, and it was all enchantment to me. Between the acts Elsie told me that she was enjoying it too; but she objected to Rosalind's dress. "It wasn't decent," she said, "no nice woman would wear it," and she scoffed at the idea that Orlando could take Rosalind for a boy. "He must have known her," she declared, "unless he was a gump; no man could be so silly." She did not like Jacques particularly, and the court in the forest seemed to her ridiculous.

Before the evening was over she had made on me the impression of a definite, strong personality. Her beauty was fragile, flower-like, appealing; her nature curiously masterful-imperious. To me she has always since been touched with something of the magic of Rosalind; for Elsie, too, was hardly used by fortune, and I liked her the better because she was far stronger than Rosalind, far more determined to make her own way in this rough world.

She liked the lights and the crowd and the pretty dresses, and showed perfect self-confidence.

"I love the theatre," she cried. "What a pity it is it's not real, not life."

"More real," I said, in my didactic German way; "it should be the quintessence of life."

Elsie looked at me in astonishment.

"Sometimes you're funny," she said, and

laughed out loud, I could not make out why.

As we came away after the theatre was over, we passed a tall, dark girl, not nearly so good-looking as Elsie, with a row of magnificent pearls round her neck.

"Homely, wasn't she?" said Elsie to me, as we went out. "But did you see her pearls and that lovely dress?"

"No," I replied, "I didn't notice it particularly."

She described it to me, said she would like such a dress; she just loved to imagine she was rich. "When I see a pretty dress," she went on, "I fancy I am wearing it for the rest of the day, and I'm quite happy. Happiness is half make-believe, don't you think?"

"A good part of it," I replied, wondering at her wisdom. "And make-believe is great fun," I went on, "but a little hard to practise as one grows older."

"You talk like Methuselah," she retorted, "but you're not more than twenty."

"Oh yes, I am," I shot back; but I didn't tell her how near she had come to the truth.

When we got to her door the house was all dark; but her mother, she said, would be sure to be sitting up for her. Quite naturally, as we said "good night," she lifted up her face to me. I put my arms round her eagerly and kissed her on the lips. I made an appointment for the next evening to take her for a walk, and went home with the feeling of her body on my arms, and hands, and the fragrance of her warm lips on mine.

Engel had not gone to bed; he never did go to bed till all hours. I could not talk to him about Elsie, so I told him a little about the play, and then hastened to my room. I wanted to be alone, so as to re-live the strange, sweet sensations. Again and again I put my arms round her slender, supple waist, and kissed her lips; they were silken-soft; but the imagining only set my blood aflame, and that was not needed. At last I got a book and read myself to sleep.

From time to time after that first night Elsie and I met. When the evening was fine we took long walks; her favourite walk was Michigan Boulevard, or the Park. "There," she said, "life was graceful and beautiful." I learned many things from her. I think she showed me the aristocratic view of life; she certainly taught me how to speak American like an American. In some way or other she increased my desire to become an American. She excited my ambition, too; wanted to know why I did not write for the American papers instead of for the ugly little German papers that no one cared anything about. In all cases she was on the side of the prosperous and the powerful, against the dispossessed and the poor.

But she liked me, and we were boy and girl together, and sometimes we got beyond the sordid facts of existence. She used to let me kiss her, and as she got accustomed to going out with me, she yielded now and then for a moment or so, at least in spirit, to my desire. I had not known her for a week when I wanted to become engaged to her, *verlobt*, after the serious German fashion, and I thought I chose my time for the proposal very cunningly. We were on a bench looking out over the Great Lake, silence about us, and the sunlight a golden pathway on the waters. We had been seated side by side for some time. At length I grew bolder and gathered her in my arms: as I kissed her she seemed all mine.

"I want to get an engagement ring for you, dear," I said. "What would you like?" She straightened herself up and shook her dark curls rebelliously.

"Don't be crazy," she said; "you have nothing to marry on, and I have nothing. It's just silly. Now we will go home," and in spite of all I could say, she started off for the Boulevard and home.

I suppose the sense of difficulty increased my ardour; at any rate, I remember, in a week or two she was the rose of life to me, and every moment lived away from her was tedious-flat.

It was Elsie who first taught me love's magic, the beauty that never was on earth or sea. She transfigured life for me, and made even the garment of it adorable. When I was with her I lived to a higher intensity—my senses inconceivably keen and quick—and all the while the witchery of her was in the air and sunlight as well as in my blood. When she left me I was dull and lonely-sad; all the vivid world went grey and sombre. As I met her frequently the glamour became charm, and passion grew more and more imperious. She met my desire in a way that delighted me: often a glow of responsive heat came in her cheeks and lips; but her self-control puzzled me. She did not like to yield to the sensuous spell or even to be forced to acknowledge its reality. At first I put her resistance down to her regard for convention, and as I was frightened of losing the companionship that had grown dear to me, I did not press her unduly. To hold the beauty of her in my arms and kiss her lips was intoxicating to me, and I could not risk offending her. But when her lips grew hot on mine I would try to kiss her neck or push up her sleeve and kiss her arm in the tender inward that was like a flower, an ivory white petal all freaked with violet tracery.

"No, you must not," she cried; "I like you, like you very much; you're good and kind, I'm sure; but it's wrong; oh yes, it is, and we're too poor to marry, so there. You must behave, Boy." ("Boy" was her pet name for me.) "I like your blue eyes," she went on meditatively, "and your strength and height and moustache" (and she touched it, smiling.) "But, no! no! no! I'll go home if you don't stop."

Of course I obeyed, but only to begin again a minute or two later. My desire was uncontrollable; I loved Elsie; the more I knew of her the more I loved her; but while the affection and tenderness lay deep, passion was on the surface, so to speak, headstrong and imperious; it was not to be bridled, whipped to madness as it was by curiosity. My only excuse was my youth, for I could not help wanting to touch her, to caress her, and my hands were as inquisitive as my eyes.

As soon as my desire became too manifest she checked me; as long as it seemed unconscious she allowed me almost complete freedom. When away from her I used to wonder whether it was real modesty which moved her, or shyness of the palpable, dislike of the avowed.

I quickly found that if I made her share my fever, induced her to abandon herself even for a moment to her feelings, she was sure afterwards to punish me for this yielding and close the passage by leaving me in a pet.

"No, sir, don't come with me. I can find my way home, thank you. Good-bye," and the imperious beauty swept away, and I was punished.

Left in this way one evening, I turned and walked down to the lake shore. Elsie did not like the shore, it was bare and ugly, she said; no grass would grow there and no trees; it was desolate and wild, too, and only hateful, common people walked there; but the illimitable prospect of the waste of water always drew me, so now I followed my humour.

I had not walked over half a mile when I came upon a great meeting. A man was speaking from a cart to a crowd that must have numbered two or three thousand persons. The speaker was a tall American and evidently a practised orator, with a fine tenor voice. He interested me at once: his forehead was high; his features well cut; his dark moustache waved up a little at the ends. There was something captivating in the man's picturesque speech and manifest sincerity. He seemed to have travelled a good deal and read a good deal, and when I came to the outskirts of the crowd I found every one hanging on his lips.

"Who is it?" I asked. I was told at once

that he was a man called Parsons, the editor of "The Alarm," a Labour paper. He was speaking about the Eight Hour Bill, which the Labour party hoped to get passed that Session, and he was contrasting the lot of the rich yonder on Michigan Boulevard with the lot of the poor. He spoke well, and the crude opposites of life were all about him to give point to his words. There, a couple of hundred yards away, the rich were driving in their carriages, with costly wraps about them, and servants to wait on them, and round about him and before him the producers, the workmen who could hardly be sure of their next meal; the text was splendidly illustrated.

"You workmen make the carriages," he cried, "and the rich drive in them; you build the great houses and they live in them. All over the world workmen are now preparing delicacies for them; dogs are being bred for them in China and goldfish in Cuba. In the frozen North men with frost-bitten fingers are trapping animals so that these worthless lazers may drive in furs; in sun-baked Florida other men are raising fruit for them; your children go hungry and half-naked in the bitter winter, while they waste fifty thousand dollars on a meal and keep footmen to put silk stockings on toy dogs."

He had certainly a gift of rhetoric, and he

tried to reason as well. He called this "the age of machinery," and declared that through machines the productive power of the individual had been increased a hundredfold in the last century. "Why, then, is the producer not paid a hundred times as much?" he shouted. "Eight hours of work now produce as much wealth as hundreds of hours a century ago, why shouldn't the employer be satisfied with eight hours a day, and leave the workman the possibility of a human existence? He would be satisfied were he the employer and not the exploiter. . . .

"Think of the injustice of it all," he cried. "We men are gradually winning a mastery over nature. The newest force, electricity, is also the cheapest and the most efficient. First comes the scientist who discovers the law or the new power; then the inventor who puts it to use; then the greedy brute who by law or force or fraud annexes the benefits of it. The poor here in Chicago are as poor as ever; many of them will die this winter of cold and destitution; but the rich grow richer continually. Who ever heard a century ago of a man making a million of dollars in his own lifetime. Now we have our Rockefellers and others with fortunes of a hundred millions. Did they *make* those huge sums?" he asked. "Of course they didn't, they stole them, and they are only able to steal such enormous amounts because the brains of the scientist and the inventor have made labour tenfold more productive than it was before we compressed steam to our service and harnessed the lightning to our use. But are all the benefits of man's wisdom and labour always to go to the greedy few; to be lost, so to speak, in lakes and cisterns, and never to spread in fertilizing showers over the whole land? I refuse to believe it. I have another vision in my mind," and he proceeded to sketch a sort of workingman's paradise. . . .

The appeal was effective; the murmurs in the crowd showed that. Several times Parsons puzzled me; he talked of Socialism and Anarchy as if they were one; but certainly he talked with passion and enthusiasm. All at once I noticed a man on my left; he had come up after me. He was dressed like a workman, but neatly. I noticed him because he turned aside from something the speaker had said with a certain contempt in his look. I remarked quite casually—

"You don't seem to agree with Parsons."

Suddenly our eyes met; it was as if I had had an electric shock, the gaze was so piercing, so extraordinary, that involuntarily I braced myself to meet it.

"A little florid," the man replied.

I was nettled at the contempt, but spoke again, mainly in order to see the eyes fairly, and find out the secret of their strange power.

"There is surely a good deal of truth in what he says, and he says it splendidly."

Again his eyes met mine, and again I had the same shock.

"Oh yes!" he assented, looking out over the lake, "it's the shallow water has the lace-foam on it," he added, and turned quietly away.

I could not help looking after him as he went. Were his eyes grey or black? I could not tell. I could see him still, he was only about middle height, but squarely built, and he walked with a lithe speed and ease, as of great strength. I was never so impressed in my life by any one; yet he had scarcely said anything. Though I did not know it then, I had spoken for the first time to Louis Lingg, the man who was to shape my life.

CHAPTER III

ABOUT this time I began to realize that the struggle between the employers and the employed in Chicago was becoming dangerously bitter, and was envenomed by the fact that nine out of ten native-born Americans were taking sides with the masters against the workmen on the ground that the workmen were foreigners and interlopers. The agitation for an eight-hours' day was looked upon as a foreign innovation, and denounced on every hand.

Acting on Elsie's advice, I had gone to the great American papers in Chicago and tried to get work. When asked what I could do, I handed the editors an English translation of the best of my articles in "Vorwaerts." After many disappointments, I had a talk with the editor of "The Chicago Tribune," who accepted my paper on working underground in New York on condition that I would cut out all that "socialist poppycock."

"It won't go down here," he said, smiling; "it's Limburger cheese to us, see! Good in its own way, I've no doubt; but a little too strong. You catch on, eh?"

At the same time he gave me a cheque for twenty-five dollars for the article. I could not let such an opportunity slip. I told him I knew German even better than English, and should like to act as his reporter in the labour troubles.

"O.K.," he replied; "but don't go tootin' about for the foreigner. We're Americans every time and stand for the star-spangled banner: understand?"

I said I would confine myself to the facts, and I did so more or less successfully on several minor occasions. At last something happened which seemed to me at the time significant and which later I saw marked a new departure. There was a strike on the East Side. It was in December or January, bitter winter weather, fifteen or twenty degrees below zero. Snow was falling slowly, the afternoon closing in. The operatives in some machine shops had come out, and were holding a meeting on a vacant lot near the factory. A thousand workmen or so attended, and perhaps a hundred women and boys. The speeches were for the most part in German, and were dull to a degree. The main complaint was that the employers were cutting down wages, and increasing fines, because they had too large a stock, and wanted to diminish expenses in winter while trade was at its worst. The work, too, was such that any workman could do it, and so the masters had every advantage.

There we stood in the bitter wind and driving snowflakes, while these poor wretches talked and decided to picket the neighbourhood to prevent new men taking on their jobs in ignorance of the situation. I went among the crowd studying the strikers. Most of the faces were young, strong, intelligent; hardly any wastrels among them, the average of looks far higher than one would see in Hamburg or Munich; but care and anxiety were to be read on nearly every countenance. Many faces, too, seemed bitter, a few were sullen, or hard. The fight for life was evidently terrible in this town, where the workmen were weak—disunited through differences of race and speech.

The gloomy day was darkening to night; the snow was falling more heavily. I had drawn a little away from the crowd, and was thinking about getting home to write up my notes, when I heard the tramp of feet, and saw a strong force of police, perhaps one hundred in all, marching down the street. At once I was at my keenest. The police drew up at the lot, and Captain Bonfield, a big, powerful fellow, who had won to command through sheer strength and courage, thrust the crowd asunder, and, with a dozen of his men pushed his way to the centre. "Come down," the police cried to the speakers, calling at the same time to the crowd about them to disperse: "break up, there! break up!" was the cry, and the strikers began to obey with sullen murmurs of discontent.

At first it looked as if high-handed authority would triumph once more; but there came a fateful pause, and at once the police seemed to lose their tempers. I pressed into the crowd to see what was going on. Bonfield was talking to one of the speakers, a man whom I afterwards knew, called Fielden, an Englishman, a middle-aged, dark-bearded man, the essence of good-nature, but stolidly determined. He kept repeating now—

"We are not interfering with anybody. Who are we interfering with? We are harming nobody."

Bonfield had his club in his hand. He suddenly seemed to lose self-control. Perhaps he was pressed against by the crowd. I can't tell. But of a sudden he struck Fielden in the stomach with his club, and knocked him backwards off the cart, which was serving as a sort of extemporized platform. At once a man thrust himself forward in front of Bonfield, shouting some gibberish that I could hardly distinguish, and using wild gestures. It was Fischer, the Communist reporter. He was evidently beside himself with angry excitement, and his German-English jargon was wholly unintelligible to the police. Bonfield looked at him for a minute, and thrust him back with his left hand. As Fischer pressed forward again, gesticulating, Bonfield thrust him back again, and then clubbed him savagely on the head. Fischer fell senseless, and that was, as it were, the signal for the row to begin. In one moment the police were lost, pulled down, and trampled under foot by the surging crowd of men. Immediately I turned and began to push through the crowd to get out in order to see what would take place. The police on the outskirts had already drawn their clubs, and were using them on every one. The crowd began to ravel away at its edges before the fierce attack. I struggled out of it somehow, and got to the pavement, and from there I saw the police bludgeoning every one they could. Most of the crowd were already running away. While trying to escape men and women were brutally struck down. It was a butchery. My blood was boiling; but I had no weapon, and could do nothing. I was standing just at the corner of the street and the vacant lot, when a policeman near me ran after a boy. The boy could not have been more than thirteen or fourteen years of age. He got almost to my side, and then as the policeman caught up to him and lifted his club, I think I shouted in horror. But some one passed me like a flash, and before the policeman's club had fallen, indeed, while he was in the very act of striking, he was struck himself, under the jaw, and with such speed and force that I gasped with amazement at the way he went down, his club whirling in the air a dozen feet away. The next moment his assailant turned and strode past me down the street. It was the man whose gaze had made such an impression on me a short time before at Parson's meeting on the Lake shore.

A moment later I called after him, but, in the meantime, several of the strikers had rushed between us, and when I followed him he had disappeared.

I wrote the account of the police attack, as I have told it here, and took it to the office of the "Tribune"; but before going I took care to get together some facts to corroborate my statements. Thirty-five strikers had been taken to the hospital, all of them severely wounded, two of them dangerously; while not one policeman was injured sufficiently to come under the doctor's hands.

When the editor had read my article, he put it down frowning. "It may be as you say, Schnaubelt," he said; "the admittances to the hospital make your story look probable. But you are up against America in this matter, and I am not going to take sides against my own people. 'Yankee Doodle' is our tune every time, and don't you forget it!" he added assertively.

"I have taken no side," I explained; "I am telling simply what I saw."

"That's the worst of it," he admitted. "D—n it. I believe it is the truth; but, anyway, I can't and won't publish it. You foreigners are trying to make an eight-hour day, and we are not going to have it. I will write a little 'par' myself, just saying that Bonfield was needlessly energetic."

"Well," I said, "if you won't take this strike stuff of mine, perhaps you will keep me on still about the fires and anything of that sort."

"Yes, yes," he said. "You do it very well. You go to every fire, and our American reporters get too cunning. They write up accounts without having been there. Yes, I'll take the fire stuff all right; but you keep off this strike business. It's going to be bad weather for some of those Poles and Germans, I can see—mighty bad weather."

The editor was right; it was bad weather for the foreign workmen all through that savage winter and spring, for the editor of the "Tribune," like all the other American editors, put in no part of the truth. He forgot even to say in his leading article that Bonfield was needlessly energetic, as he had promised. What he did say was that the thirty-five foreigners in the hospital would perhaps serve as a warning to the rest that any attack on the police would be vigorously repressed. Hard weather, indeed, and worse to come for the foreign workmen!

I was no longer employed to go to the strikes. I saw them, and hundreds of American eye-witnesses are still living who can prove that the police went on from brutality to brutality. Every month their actions became more indefensible, till at length they did not even summon the crowds to disperse, but used their clubs at once, indiscriminately upon strikers and lookers-on and casual passers-by, like madmen.

But I am getting ahead of my story. After that talk with the editor of the "Tribune," I went to see Spies. He was delighted to have my description of the police attack for his paper; introduced me to Fielden, the Englishman, who had already given him a rough account of it; and who told us that Fischer was lying ill at home. He had had a terrible blow, it appeared. The whole side of his face had been crushed in; he was suffering from concussion of the brain, and would not be able to get about again for months. The dreadful affair seemed to have excited Spies's courage and strengthened his resolution. "Shameful, shameful," he kept on saying. "For the first time in America orderly meetings on vacant lots are dispersed by force. Thoughts are met with police bludgeons." He was almost beside himself with excitement and anger.

On my way out I stopped in the outer office to say a word or two to the cashier, and as I went into the outside waiting-room I met Raben.

"What!" I cried, "you here in Chicago?"

He told me he had been in Chicago some time.

"Come out," I went on, "and let me give you a German meal like the one you gave me in New York. Do you remember? There's a lot to talk about."

"There is," he said. "You people in Chicago are making history. I have been sent by 'The New York Herald' to write up these strikes of yours." His air of triumph was amusing. His connection with the well-known paper increased his self-importance.

As we went out together I noticed with some satisfaction that my accent in American was now better than his. I spoke like an

American, whereas any one could see that he was a German. Elsie had done me a lot of good. Besides, my reading of the English writers and the articles I had already written in English had given me a larger vocabulary and a greater control of English than he could pretend to.

We were soon seated in a restaurant at a good meal, and I learned to my astonishment that Raben had been ten days or a fortnight in Chicago.

"I heard of you," he said, "and expected to run across you any day."

"But have you been about?" I asked. "It is curious I have not seen you." The fact, of course, being that I had been out with Elsie nearly every evening, and so had not been in the way of meeting many Germans.

Half in self-defence, I added, "I have been in the 'Arbeiter Zeitung' twice in the last week."

"Oh," he said, "that 'Arbeiter Zeitung' is nothing important. The revolutionary force in Chicago is the 'Lehr and Wehr Verein.'"

I repeated the words, "'Revolutionary force . . . 'Lehr and Wehr Verein'—I have never heard of it."

"You come with me to-night," said Raben, with the intense satisfaction of a Columbus, "and I'll show it to you. Anarchists, my boy; men who'll do something; not your meek Socialists who will talk and let themselves be clubbed to death without resisting." Raben, I had noticed already, lived to astonish people. His excessive vanity had dramatic ambitions; he wanted to be a Cassandra and Jeremiah rolled into one.

"Good God!" I cried, "are there really Anarchists in Chicago?" The mere word seemed terrible to me.

Raben gloated over my amazement and awe. "You come with me," he said, "and I will show you Chicago. Though I have only been here a fortnight, I know more of it than you who have been here for months. I don't let the grass grow under my feet," and he pursed his lips in perfect self-satisfaction.

After the meal we set off for the Anarchist club, and he took me out to the East Side, to the outskirts of the town, in the centre of the foreign, cheapest quarter. There we went into a German saloon, and he introduced me to Herr Michael Schwab, who was an assistant editor on the "Arbeiter Zeitung," and whom I had seen with Spies, a bespectacled German professor, thin, angular, sallow, with black hair and long, black, unkempt beard. Raben told Schwab in German who I was and what my sympathies were, and Schwab said yes, he would take us upstairs. He led the way through the back of the saloon and up a narrow staircase into a bare, empty room, where there were perhaps thirty men and three or four women. There was a long table down the centre of the room, round which the audience sat, and a small plain deal table at the end of the room for the speakers. Our appearance caused some stir; every one looked at us. Apparently the meeting had not yet begun. As soon as I entered the room I was struck again by seeing the man who had knocked the policeman down, and whom I was so curious to know. As I was about to ask Raben to get Schwab to introduce me, Raben turned to me and said—

"Oh, there she is. I must introduce you to the prettiest Anarchist in the world," and he pulled me in front of a tall, handsome brunette, who had begun to talk to Schwab. "Allow me," he said in American, "Miss Ida Miller, to present to you a friend of mine, Mr. Rudolph Schnaubelt."

She smiled and held out her hand. Raben told her how he had persuaded me to come to the meeting, a real Anarchist meeting, though I didn't believe there was an Anarchist in Chicago. "He's a South German, you know," he added almost contemptuously. Something in Miss Miller's expression attracted me greatly, and almost before I knew it we were talking sympathetically. Her eyes were fine, and she interested me, appealed to me, indeed, as a child might appeal. Suddenly I remembered.

"There is one man here whom I must know, Miss Miller. I wonder if you know him?"

"What's he like?" she asked.

I described his eyes, the impression he had made on me at the first meeting, and then told of his extraordinary defence of the boy, the speed and power of his attack, and the cool way he turned and disappeared down the street.

"That must be Louis," cried Ida, "Louis Lingg. Just think of it! he never said one word to me about it, not one word."

I repeated the words after her, "Louis Lingg. Is he French, then?"

"Oh no," she said: "he is a German from Mannheim. That's him over there at the end of the table. He is the founder of this society—a great man," she went on, as if to herself.

"Of course you think him great," said Raben; "that is only natural."

Miss Miller turned and looked at him.

"Yes," she repeated, "it is only natural. I am glad of that. Those who know him best, think most of him."

"I'd like to know Lingg," I said.

"He'll be glad to know you," she replied. As we turned aside she went on, in a low voice, "He is always glad to know any one who wants to learn or help," and the next moment she had called him, "Louis!" and had introduced me to him. His eyes met me now fairly; but I had no shock from them. They were dark grey, with black pupils and lashes; in expression curiously steady and searching; but not lambent-wonderful, as I had thought them at first. Yet I was to see the unearthly power in them often enough in the future. While I was still looking at Lingg, trying to fix his features in my mind, trying to understand wherein lay the abnormal and extraordinary in his personality, Miss Miller began reproaching him for not having told her what he had done.

"I did nothing," he said, very quietly and slowly.

"Yes, you did," she cried enthusiastically; "you knocked down the policeman and saved the boy, and then walked away as if nothing had happened. I can see you doing it. Mr. Schnaubelt has been telling us all about it. But why didn't you tell me?"

He shrugged his shoulders, and said simply, "Perhaps we had better get on with the meeting."

At this moment there was an interruption.

Schwab came round making a collection, "For Mrs. Schelling," he said.

"Who? What for?" I asked.

Lingg seemed glad of the interruption. He answered my questions courteously.

"A case at our last meeting, a case of lead poisoning. Mrs. Schelling is a widow with one rickety child. She's finished, I'm afraid; she can't last long."

"Really!" I exclaimed. "Is lead poisoning frequent here?"

"Very frequent," he said, "among house painters. You must have heard of 'wrist-drop'—paralysis of the nerves of the wrist?"

"No," I said; "but are women employed as painters?"

"Not as painters, but in manufactories of white lead and in type foundries," said Lingg. "The worst of it is that women are much more liable to plumbism, and suffer much more than men. It kills them sometimes in a few weeks."

"Good God!" I exclaimed, "how awful!"

"Lead poisoning has one good result," he went on bitterly; "married couples seldom bear children; miscarriages are frequent, and the few children there are usually die of convulsions in babyhood, or as idiots a little later."

"Shocking!" I cried. "Why isn't a substitute found for white lead?"

"There is a substitute," he answered, "zinc white. The French Chamber wants to prohibit the use of white lead altogether, and substitute zinc white; but the Senate won't. Characteristic, isn't it? Of course, the democratic American Government pays no attention to such matters; the health of workingmen doesn't concern it."

"Is the pain great?" I asked.

"Horrible, sometimes. I have known young girls blinded, others paralysed, others go mad and die." He broke off. "We are always glad to have a little money in hand for real need; but you must not feel compelled to subscribe—the giving is voluntary," and saying this he led the way to the little table at the top of the room. Raben followed him.

Everything Lingg said impressed me. He brought me into a new atmosphere, a new life.

Still trying to find a reason for my admiration of him, I took a seat beside Miss Miller at the long table. There was a little stir, and then a man got up and gave in English a very good description of the fight between the police and the strikers. I was astonished at the restraint of his speech, and the unimpassioned, detached way in which he described what had taken place. I felt Lingg's influence on him. When he sat down there was a little murmur of applause.

After him Louis Lingg got up, and said he was sure the meeting was grateful to Mr. Koch for his account; the meeting would now listen with pleasure to Professor Schwab.

The bilious doctrinaire Professor made what seemed to me a rambling, ineffective speech. He knew political economy from one end to the other, as only a German can know a subject; knew the English school and the American school, and the French and German schools, all of them, with encyclopædic exactness; but his own ideas seemed to have come from Lasalle and Marx, with a tincture of Herbert Spencer. One thing he was quite clear about, and that was that individualism had been pushed too far, especially in America and England. "There is no pressure from the outside," he said, "on these countries, and so the atoms that constitute the social organism tend to fall apart. Here and in England we have individualism run mad." And then he quoted Goethe with unction—

"Im Ganzen, Guten, Schoenen,
Resolut zu leben."

His assumption of authority, his great reading, something flabby in the man, annoyed me. I did not want a sea of words to wash away my memory of the terrible things I had seen; the tempest of pity and anger which had carried me away that afternoon. Something of this I said to Ida Miller, and she immediately said, "Go up and speak; say so. Truth will do us all good."

So I stood up and went to the table. I asked Lingg might I speak, and then sat down waiting. He immediately got up, and said formally the meeting would have pleasure in listening to Mr. Schnaubelt. I began by saying it seemed to me wrong to say that America suffered from too much individual freedom when we were being clubbed to death for speaking our minds in an orderly fashion. Americans cherished the right of free speech, but denied it to foreigners, though we were Americans, too, with just as good title to the name as the native-born who had only preceded us into the country by a generation or two.

"I don't know," I went on, "whether equality is possible or not. I came to this Lehr Verein, or teaching club, in order to find out whether any one can tell me anything new about the possibility of equality. I can see no equality in nature; no equality among men in gifts and powers; how can there be equality in possessions? But there may be fair play and equal rights, it seems to me," and I bowed and went back and took my place again by Ida.

"Splendid! splendid!" she said; "that will draw Louis."

Lingg got up at once, and asked whether there was any one else who wished to speak, and there came a general murmur, "Lingg, Lingg." He bowed to the call, and then said quietly, in the tone of familiar conversation—

"The last speaker doubted the possibility of equality. Complete equality is of course unthinkable; but ever since the French Revolution there has been an approach towards equality, an endeavour after equality. Vanity is as strong a passion in man as greed," he said, evidently thinking aloud. "Before the French Revolution it was considered nothing out of the way for a nobleman to spend a hundred thousand or two hundred thousand livres a year on his dress. I think the professor will tell you that there were noblemen at the French Court whose mere clothes represented the yearly earnings of hundreds of workmen.

"The French Revolution did away with all that. It brought in a dress for men more suited to an industrial civilization. We are no longer dressed as soldiers or dandies, but as workmen, and the difference between one man's dress and another's is a few dollars, or a few score of dollars a year. The man now who would wear a lace shirt or diamonds in his shoes that cost him a hundred thousand dollars, would be regarded as a madman; these extravagances have become impossible. Why should there not be another revolution, and a similar approach towards equality in payment for services? I look forward, not to equality, which does not seem to me either possible or desirable; but to a great movement towards equality in the pay of individual work."

At this moment a note was passed to him. He asked the permission of the ladies and gentlemen present to read it. He was curiously courteous, this man, always. He read the note, and then went on in the same slow, quiet tone—

"I said," he began, "all I wanted to say; but I have a request here from one of our Society to speak on the police attack to-day." He suddenly moved forward to the end of the table, and as he looked down it a thrill went through all of us who caught his eye. Then he looked down again.

"I do not know what to say. One hopes that such an outrage will not be repeated. I will say no more to-night, though"—and his words dropped slowly from his lips like bullets—"though our Society is for defence as well as education." There was a menace in his voice I could hardly account for or explain. He looked up sombre, and the words seemed to repeat themselves in our awe-stricken ears.

"One can't meet bludgeons with words," he went on, "nor blows by turning the other cheek. Violence must be met with violence. Americans should surely know that action and reaction are equal and opposite; oppression and revolt equal and opposite also."

He suddenly stopped, bowed to us, and the meeting broke up into talk—quick chatter about the table, in an endeavour, it seemed to me, to get rid of the effect of Lingg's speech upon us and his astonishing personality. For the first time in life I had come into the presence of a man who was wiser than I had imagined possible, who brought new thoughts into life at every moment, and whose whole being was so masterful and intense that one expected greater things from him than from other men.

I turned enthusiastically to Miss Miller.

"Oh, you are right," I said; "he is a great man, Louis Lingg, a great man. I want to know him well."

"I am glad," she said simply; but her face lighted up at my praise. "Nothing easier. If he has nothing to do this evening you could come home with us."

"Do you live with him?" I asked, in my amazement utterly unconscious of what I was saying. Without any false sentiment she answered me—

"Oh yes; we do not believe in marriage. Louis thinks moral laws are simply laws of health; he regards marriage as a silly institution, without meaning for men and women who wish to deal honestly with each other."

Evidently this evening I was to go through shock upon shock. I stared at her, scarcely able to believe my ears.

"I see you are astonished," she said, laughing; "but we are Anarchists and rebels. You must get accustomed to us."

"Anarchists!" I repeated, genuinely shocked; "really?"

How the meeting broke up I do not know; but it did break up at last. We had a glass or two of beer all round, for the good of the house, and then we dispersed; but not before Lingg had given me his address, and told me he would be glad to see me on the morrow, or whenever I liked to call.

"I have read some of your work," he said, "and I like it. There's sincerity in it."

I got crimson in spite of myself; no compliment ever pleased me so much. I went off with Raben, and wanted to know all about Lingg; began, indeed, to talk about him enthusiastically; but found Raben not at all enthusiastic, and soon discovered that he knew little or nothing about Lingg, was much more interested in Miss Miller, and looked upon Lingg's liaison with her as a very bad thing for the girl. That night I felt as if Raben dirtied everything he touched. I bade him "good night" as soon as possible, and hurried home to get my own thoughts clear, and to digest the new ones which Lingg had put into my head, and, above all, the new spirit that he seemed to have breathed into my being. Could one man stand against the whole of society, and defy it? How——?

Chapter IV

THERE now began for me a period of forced growth; growth of mind through intercourse with Lingg; growth of emotions and knowledge of life, knowledge of myself and of women, through intimacy with Elsie Lehman. For months and months I met Lingg continually, often spent the whole day with him; yet in all that time I never met him once without learning something new from him. Again and again I went to him, feeling sure that he could not have anything new to say, but at some time or other in the conversation a new subject would be touched on, and immediately new ideas, a new view, came from him. At the time, I remember well, this astounded me, for I myself loved ideas, any and every bold generalization, which like a golden thread would string together a hundred pearls of fact. I was fairly well equipped, too, in the wisdom of the schools, and in books, before I met Lingg. I had read a good deal of Greek and Latin, and the best authors in French, German and English. The amazing part of it to me at first was that Lingg had read very little.

Again and again when talking on social questions I had to say, "Oh, that's Heine's thought, or "Goethe's." His eyebrows went up; they were his thoughts, and that was enough for him. He seemed to think where other thinkers left off, and if I were to attempt to set down here in cold sequence all the fruitful ideas and brilliant guesses which came from him naturally in the heat of conversation, or sprang like sparks from the cut and thrust of dialectic, I should be painting a prig, or a thinking machine, and Louis Lingg was neither of these; but a warm-hearted friend and passionate lover. There were in him all sorts of contradictions and anomalies, as there are in all of us; but he seemed to touch the extremes of life with a wider reach than other men. He was a peculiar nature; usually cool, calculating, self-concentrated, judging men and things absolutely according to their value, as a realist; the next moment all flame and emotion, with an absolute genius for self-sacrifice.

To show the insight in him, the power and clearness of his intellect, I must give another of his speeches at the Lehr Verein. When I heard it, it seemed to me so wise, fair, and moderate as to be convincing.

Lingg began by saying that the chief evils of our society showed themselves first towards the end of the eighteenth century. "This period," he went on, "was made memorable by the invention of the spinning jenny and by the use of steam as a force, and by the publication of 'The Wealth of Nations,' in which individualism was first preached as a creed. Just at the time when man by using natural laws began to multiply tenfold the productivity of his labour, it was proposed to leave everything to the grab-as-grab-can principle of individual greed. Now, consider the consequences of this mistake in a concrete form; the roads of the country had always been regarded as national property; they were made as cheaply as possible at the public cost, and maintained by the local authorities; but the railroads were made and owned and maintained by individuals or rather by groups of individuals. The land, too, in every country, had been leased to the individual by the State on some sort of payment, and from one-third to one-half of it reserved as common land; now the land was given in freehold to the individual. At once the social organism began to suffer. It grew rich quickly; but the poor grew poorer; the workhouses filled; the modern contrast of extravagant riches and extreme destitution came into being. . . .

"Socialism, or Communism, is now being preached as a remedy for all this; let us take everything from the individual, Marx cries, and all will be well. But that's surely an experiment. Civilization, as we understand it, has been founded on individualism; cannot the individual be restrained without subverting the social structure? I agree with Professor Schwab, we are suffering from too much individualism; the problem is how to limit individualism, how far socialism should come into life? The answer, to my mind, is clear; the individual should be left with all those departments of industry which he is able to control: his activity should not be limited in any honest direction; but all those departments of labour which he is not able to control, in which he has given up his freedom in order to join with other men in Joint Stock Companies, and so increase his power to plunder the community—all such industries should be taken over by the State, or by the Municipality, beginning, of course, with those which are most necessary to the welfare of the body politic.

"I take it, too, that the land of a country should belong to the people of the country, and should be rented out to cultivators on easy terms, for country life produces the strongest and most healthful citizens. All the railways and means of communication should be nationalized; the water companies, the gas and electric lighting companies, banks and insurance companies, and so on. If you consider the matter, you will find that it is just in and through these great industries, directed by Joint Stock Companies that all the evils of our civilization have shown themselves. These are the hot-houses of speculation and theft where the lucky gambler, or daring thief, to give him his proper name, has won millions and demoralized the public conscience.

"If you had here in America, beside the landed population, an industrial army managing the railways and canals, the lighting and water companies, with fair wages and absolute security of employment pending good behaviour, you would have lifted the whole scale of wages of the day labourer, for if the individual employer who could not give such security did not offer higher wages than the state he would not get the best men."

As he spoke light dawned on me; this was the truth if ever it was heard from human lips; the exact truth struck in the centre. The individual should be master of all those industries which he could control unaided, and no more. Joint Stock Companies' management was worse even than State management; every one knew it was more inefficient and more corrupt. All my reading, all my experience, leaped to instant recognition of Lingg's insight, to instant agreement with him. What a man he was!

Of course this statement as it stands compressed here gives a very imperfect idea of Lingg's genius; it is all set down boldly, without the vivid, living flashes of humour which made his talk inimitable; but still, the truth is there, the wine of thought, though gone a little flat. That evening was made doubly memorable to me by another experience.

A workman was introduced suffering from "phossy jaw"; he had worked as a "dipper," it appeared, at a match manufactory on the East Side. The "composition" into which the heads of the matches are dipped is warm and moist, and contains about five per cent of white phosphorus. The fumes of the phosphorus can be seen rising above the composition. Of course fans are used; but fans are not sufficient to protect a workman with bad teeth. This man had good teeth at the beginning; but at length a tooth decayed in his lower jaw, and at once phosphorus necrosis set in. He was strangely apathetic; so powerful a motive is vanity that it almost seemed as if he were proud of the extraordinary extent to which his jaw was decayed.

"I'm pretty bad," he said; "the doctor says he has never seen a worse case. Look here," and he put his fingers in his mouth, and broke off a long sliver of jaw-bone. "Bad, ain't it? . . . I've been twelve weeks out of work; I'm rotten," he confided to us, "that's what I am—rotten. I stepped down off the sidewalk into the street and—crack! my thigh bone snapped in two — rotten! I wouldn't care if it weren't for the missus and the kids. It don't hurt, and there's lots worse off; but twelve weeks is a bit long. I guess they could get a substitute for that phosphorus if they wanted to." *

No rage over his ruined life, no resentment. I was appalled. We collected nearly a hundred dollars for him in a full meeting, and he seemed grateful; though confident that nothing could cure him.

A few days after this meeting at the Lehr and Wehr Verein, I called on Lingg in his rooms, and got to know him pretty well. He had a bedroom and sitting-room on the second floor in a comparatively quiet street on the East Side; the sitting-room was large and bare; the corner near the window, which was hidden by the opening door, was furnished with

[*The workman was right. The Belgian Government has since offered a prize for a harmless substitute, and one was found almost at once, in the sesquisulphide of phosphorus, which is now generally used. Think of the hundreds of deaths, of the human misery that might have been avoided if some government had seen this obvious duty forty or fifty years sooner: but of course no government cared to interfere with the blessed principle of *laissez faire*, which might be translated, "Am I my brother's keeper?"—Note of Editor.]

broad pine shelves, and the many bottles gave it the look of a laboratory, which, indeed, it was. Lingg was not in when I called; but Ida was, and we were soon talking about him. I told her how his words had stuck in my head, and how much he had impressed me and interested me.

"I'm glad," she said; "he needs a friend."

"I should be proud to be his friend," I assured her warmly, "he's a great man; he attracts me immensely."

"How true that is," she said; "I always think great souls draw us more strongly than small ones, don't you?"

I agreed with her; I was struck by the phrase; it seemed to me like a thought of Lingg's.

I think it was on this first visit, or soon after, that she showed me a side of her character which I should never have divined. She was of equable temper, and not lightly to be thrown off her balance; yet she kept breaking off the conversation to listen for Lingg's step, in a fever of suspense. When I rallied her about this unwonted excitement I found there was no special reason for it; she admitted simply that she was anxious. "If you knew him as well as I do, you'd be anxious too." And again she held her breath and listened.

She was always willing to talk about Lingg

with me, for she recognized, I think, at the very beginning with a loving woman's intuition that I, too, would become devoted to him, and so bit by bit I gathered from her nearly all Lingg's history. When a mere boy of fifteen, in the first year, indeed, of his apprenticeship to a carpenter at Mannheim, his widowed mother lost all her little income through a death. The boy, it appears, had chosen his trade himself and would not give it up; he simply redoubled his efforts and spent all his spare time at work in order to keep his mother and himself. He worked so hard that the master-carpenter proposed to give him a small weekly wage, which he increased again and again of his own accord. "Young Lingg," he used to say, "was worth three men to him, and half a dozen apprentices." The mother, it seems, had this praise of Herr Wuermell always on her lips.

As soon as Lingg was out of his time and had saved some money, he announced his intention of emigrating, and in spite of a dozen good offers to stay in Mannheim, for some reason or other he shook the dust of Germany off his feet, and came to New York with his mother. A few months later he brought her from New York to Chicago, for her lungs, it appeared, could not stand the moist sea-air of Manhattan Island. In Chicago at first she seemed to rally; then caught cold, and grew rapidly weaker. Lingg did everything he could for her; tended her day and night during her illness; was nurse and son in one. Like most strong and lonely natures he gave his confidence to few, and his affection gained in intensity through concentration. He was devoted to his mother, would not leave her bedside, even to go out with Ida, and when she died he seemed to take a dislike to life, and gave himself over to melancholy brooding.

Ida had been seduced by a rich young clubman, and when deserted had fallen to the streets. There she met Lingg, who was struck with her misery and beauty, and gave her love and hope; saved her, as she used to say, from hell. Ida spoke of her connection with Lingg quite as a matter of course, in a detached sort of way, as if there were nothing unusual in it, nothing to be explained, much less excused. I think her love for him was so engrossing, her affection so tender and self-absorbed, that she could not think of herself apart from him. After the death of his mother she came to live with him. The truth is the two were devoted to each other, and united in curiously intimate fashion. When Ida spoke you heard Lingg's phrases continually. I do not mean that she aped him; but the very tone of his mind had infected her thought and speech. Perhaps this was a result of their isolation, and the contempt the foolish American world has for people living, as they lived, outside convention. I have heard Lingg say in fun, "There's no union like the union of pariahs; wild dogs even pack, only the tame brutes live in civilized selfishness, each for himself alone!"

But now, after a long period of happy intimacy, Ida had begun to grow anxious about Lingg. "He's taking these strikes to heart," she told me, "and any bullying or tyrannical use of strength drives him mad . . ." and she looked at me, I suppose, to see if I divined her meaning. At the time I did not understand; but in the calm light of memory I see it all clearly. Lingg, though infinitely stronger and more resolute than Shelley; indeed, partly because of his immense strength and resolution, resembled the English poet in one essential. He, too, was

> ". . . . . .the nerve o'er which do creep
> The else unfelt oppressions of mankind."

And Ida's heart shrank with tragic apprehension of what might happen; or did she know, even then, with the sad prescience of love? I think she did; but whether I am right or wrong in this, at least I myself was wholly blind, altogether in the dark, and beyond being vaguely affected by her fears was completely at my ease.

A little later, after I had got to know Lingg well, I met him one day in court: Fischer had brought an action against Bonfield, the policeman, for injuries; I was one of the witnesses; there were three or four of us. We all swore the same thing, that Fischer did not touch Bonfield; but simply remonstrated with him for striking Fielden. Eight or nine policemen, however, one after the other, got up and swore that Fischer had struck Bonfield, and though they admitted that he had no weapon, still, the jury chose to believe that Bonfield had been struck first and that he had only bludgeoned an unarmed man in self-defence. The verdict for the police was hailed with an unanimous cheer that came as from one throat. They cheered a lie, all those hundreds in the court, cheered it with one voice, and at the same time, cheered the brutality of the police —giving the brute, Bonfield, license to go on and do worse.

I do not know what effect that cheer had on others; but it roused hell in me, and I turned and glared at them—they were trying to make outlaws of us. At this moment I caught Lingg looking at Bonfield with that flaming regard of his; I saw that Bonfield was uneasy under it. The next moment Lingg looked down and a little later we came out of the court together.

"An infamous, infamous verdict," I cried.

"Yes," Lingg agreed, "the prejudice is very strong; things will get worse before they get better."

The words conjured up the great room, the exultation of the police, the contempt in the faces of the bystanders for us poor foreigners who were simply trying to get justice.

I walked on with Lingg; his quiet was ominous. "Damn them!" I cried despairingly. "What can we do?"

"Nothing," was the answer. "The time is not come yet."

I stared at him, while my heart beat so loudly I could hear it. "'Yet,'" I echoed. "What do you mean?" He looked at me searchingly.

"Nothing," he said; "let us talk of something else. Have you seen Parsons lately?"

"No," I replied, "I have not; but tell me something. Parsons and the rest take it for granted that wealth is merely another name for robbery, and they deny the rich, or robbers, even ability. Is that your view of it?"

He turned to me: "Moderate wealth is often honestly earned; still, riches always represent greed rather than capacity. If a man has real capacity he must want twenty other things besides money, some of them probably more than money, mustn't he? Nearly all the rich men I've known, have been cunning and mean, but nothing more. No one except some fortunate inventor ever made a million honestly."

"But why are we all suffering so? Can the poverty and misery be mended?" I asked.

"A great deal of it," he replied; "Germany is far healthier and happier than America."

"That's true," I cried; "but why?"

"The worst fault in our civilization here," said Lingg, "is that it is not complex enough. It holds up one prize before all of us—riches. But many of us do not want wealth; we want a small competency without care or fear. We ought to be able to get that as employees in some department of State. That would remove us from the competition, and tend to increase the wages of those who live in the whirl of competition. Some of us, too, are born students, want to give ourselves to the study of this, that, or the other science; there ought to be chemical laboratories in every street; physical laboratories in every town with posts attached at small pay for those who would give their lives to the advancement of knowledge; studios, too, for artists; State-aided theatres. Life must be made richer by making it more complex. By not reserving whole fields of industry to the State, by giving everything to the individual, we are driving all men into this mad race for riches; hence suffering, misery, discontent, the ill-health of the whole organism. The brain and heart have their own rights, and should not be forced to serve the belly. We turn flowers into manure."

While he was talking of greedy desire as the method of fulfilment, I was thinking of Elsie, and I suppose he saw that I was not following very closely what he said, for he broke off, and the talk between us became lighter and more detached for some little while.

We reached his rooms, and I picked up a book from the table; it was on chemistry, and dealt, not with elementary chemistry, but with quantitative and qualitative analysis. I was not a little astonished. I picked up another book treating of gas analysis and explosives, and this was well-thumbed.

"My goodness, Lingg," I exclaimed, "are you a chemist?"

"I have been reading it a little," he replied.

"A little," I repeated; "but how on earth did you get as far as this?"

"Any one who can read to-day has the key," was his answer.

"I don't know so much about that," I said.

"I'd hardly know how to go to work to make myself a master-chemist; I should break down over some difficulty in the first month."

Lingg smiled that inscrutable smile of his which I was beginning to know.

"Yet I have had all the advantages," I went on. "I was properly taught Latin and Greek, and elementary mathematics, and science, and shown how to learn. Our education can't be worth much."

"Your education helps you to learn languages, I think; you know American better than I do."

At the time I accepted this statement as a very obvious fact; but later I had reason to doubt it. Lingg took no colour from his surroundings; he spoke American with the strongest South German accent, but he knew the language astonishingly well; knew words in it that I did not know, though he had less control of it in speech, perhaps because his vocabulary was larger. But at the time I accepted his statement. A moment later Ida came into the room, and I took up the subject of books again.

"Astonishing thing, books; the greatest pleasure in one's life is reading. And quite a modern pleasure. Three or four centuries ago only the richest had half a dozen books. I remember a princess of the Visconti in the sixteenth century leaving a large fortune and three books in her will. To-day the poorest can have dozens of masterpieces."

"A questionable good," said Lingg. "The greatest piece of luck in my life was that when my mind began to open I had no money to get books. I had to work all day at carpentering, and a good part of the night, too, to get money to live, and so had no time for reading. I had to solve all the problems which tormented me for myself. Our education leans too much on books; books develop memories, not minds."

"Would you do away, then," I asked, "with Latin and Greek, and all the discipline of the mind which they afford?"

"I have no right to speak," he said, "as I know nothing about them except in translations; but I certainly should. Did the Greeks study dead languages? Did the study of Greek help the Romans to make their language better? Or did it hurt them? We live too much in the past," he said abruptly. "All our lives the past and its fears impede and lame us. We should live in the present and in the future. I do not know any poetry but there is one line of poetry which has stuck in my memory—

> '. . . .Our souls are to the future set,
> By invisible springs'

How ignorant that education in mere language leaves us, ignorant of all the important things of life. We start in life at eighteen or nineteen with no knowledge of our own body, and with little or no knowledge of our passions and their effects. We should all be taught physiology, the rules of health, of waste and decay—that is vital. We should all know some chemistry, some physics. The romantic ones among us should be taught astronomy and the use of the telescope, or else the infinitely little and the use of the microscope. We should study our own language, German, or English. My God! What a heritage those English have got, and how they neglect their world-speech for a smattering of Greek and Latin. . . .

"But let us come into the air, for to-morrow I go to work again on a new job. Won't you put on your things, Ida; our holiday time is nearly over."

"Was this your holiday task, then?" I asked, touching the book on gas analysis. Again the inscrutable regard; he nodded.

"But why do you want to analyse gases?" I went on. "I should have thought that would have been too special for you."

"Oh no," he said lightly; "my idea is that you should know something about everything, and everything about something. Till you push the light of knowledge a little forward into the night you've done nothing."

I gasped. Lingg spoke of widening the demesne of knowledge as if that were easy; yet why not? We went out into the sunlight; it happened to be one of those clear, sun-bathed days in an American winter which are so enjoyable. We walked along the lake shore for miles and miles, but I did most of the talking with Ida. Then we had lunch and came back home.

I noticed for the twentieth time Lingg's unusual strength; I could not help speaking of it once; he took up a heavy chair and handed it to me over the table as if it had been a fork or a spoon; it astonished me; his body was like his mind, of extraordinary power.

"It's very natural," cried Ida. "He runs for a mile or so every morning, and comes in drenched with perspiration."

On our return it was growing dark; they both pressed me to go to a theatre and see a German play that was being given, a comedy by Hartleben, I think; but I could not go. I had something better to do, so I said "Good evening!" to Ida and Louis at their door and hurried off to Elsie.

On my way to her, I began to puzzle myself, "What does Lingg mean?" In Spies's office, at Parsons's meetings, I had heard vague threats, but I paid no further attention to them. I knew that Parsons let off all his steam in talking and Spies in writing, but when Lingg said, "the time is not come yet," that "yet" was fraught with menace—was awful. My heart beat fast as I recalled the quiet, slow words and quieter tone. Then the chemistry books, and those pages on modern explosives—every formula underlined. By God! if—I felt as if I were in the presence of a huge force and waiting for an extraordinary impact.

"Sleep-walking, are you?" cried a voice. I turned and found Raben beside me. "I saw you in the court," he said; "but you and Lingg were on the other side of the room, and you disappeared after the verdict; I looked for you, but you had vanished. A silly case, wasn't it?"

"I don't know what you mean," I said; "I thought it was a just case, and a disgraceful verdict."

"You didn't surely expect an American jury to give a verdict against the police and in favour of an epileptic like Fischer, did you?"

"Yes," I replied, holding on to myself. "I expected an honest verdict."

"Honest," he repeated, shrugging his shoulders. "The jury believed ten American policemen in preference to four foreigners honestly enough."

"Then I'm a liar?" I turned to him hotly.

"My dear Schnaubelt," he said, "even you can be mistaken; the affirmative, too, is always stronger than a negative; the policemen say they saw Fischer strike Bonfield. You can only say you did not see it; but he may have struck him without your seeing it."

What was the use of arguing; the man knew better. I tried to turn the conversation.

"Are you working for 'The New York Herald,' still?"

"Yes," he replied, "and they like my stuff. I had a 'scoop' to-day on that verdict; I wired it before the police had finished testifying; I knew how it would be." He turned to me abruptly. "May I speak openly to you?" he asked.

"Of course," I replied. "What is it?"

"Well," he began slowly, "don't go about so much with that fellow Lingg; he's badly looked upon; there are fishy stories about him, and he's mad with conceit."

I was about to break out again; but I would not give him the paltry satisfaction of thinking he had stirred me.

"Really," I said gravely; and then, "his disease is not catching, is it?" and I laughed —genius not being infectious.

I caught a gleam in Raben's eye, and felt certain of his spite.

"All right," he remarked coolly; "remember I warned you. You know, I suppose, that Miss Ida was seduced by Lingg and sent on the streets by him—a pretty couple!" His tone was more infamous even than his words.

The blood grew hot in my temples; but I held to my resolves to show nothing, to give the venomous creature no satisfaction.

"I know all I want to know," I said carelessly; "but now I must bid you 'good-bye,'" and we parted.

"What a vile snake!" I thought to myself, and then wondered was Raben jealous, or what was the matter with him; I did not know then that envy and wounded vanity would lead a man to worse than slander. I gave up the riddle; Raben was vile by nature, I decided; but if I had known how vile—perhaps it's better that we should not see beyond our noses.

. . . .

I had promised to meet Elsie; we had arranged to meet at least three times during the week, and we generally spent the whole of Sunday together. It was one of my griefs that though I had introduced Elsie to Ida and Lingg she would not become friendly with them; she disliked Ida for calling herself Miss Miller while living openly with Lingg.

"If she called herself Mrs. Lingg, I should not mind so much," she used to say. Elsie was always conventional, and was certain to be found on the side of the established order. Everything exceptional or abnormal seemed to her erratic, and in itself evil. Ida, for example, never wore corsets; Elsie wore them always; though her lithe figure, little round breasts, and narrow hips would have looked better unsupported than Ida's more generous outlines.

I often tried to explain to myself this conventionalism in Elsie, but without result. She had as much brains as Ida; sometimes I thought her cleverer; she had certainly more temperament—was it distrust of her own passionate feelings that made her cling to accepted rules?

In any case, it was the shock of contradictories in her which made her so eternally new and attractive to me; the passionate impulses in her, beating wave-like against her immutable self-control, lent her an infinite enchantment. Had she been cold, I should never have cared for her; had she given way to passion I should have loved her; but never admired her, and even my love perhaps would then never have been whipped to ecstasy as it was by her perpetual alternation of yielding and denying. I had to conquer her afresh every time I met her; but this talk of Lingg's about the power of mere desire to get its own way, influenced me unconsciously, I think, when I was with her.

There was no wilful purpose of seduction in me; that I think is often assumed without reason; the natural desire is there blindly seeking its own gratification; men and women are the playthings of nature's forces.

But whatever the cause I seemed to be gradually making way with Elsie. Since I had written for the American papers I had been earning more money, and this extra money enabled me to take her out to dinner and the theatre, and to drive her home afterwards, which was a special delight to her. One night I had had a private room; we had dined together and then sat before the fire talking. She came and sat on my knees. After she had been in my arms for perhaps an hour her resistance seemed to be melting. Suddenly she stopped me and drew away. I could not help reproaching her.

"If I were rich, you would not leave me."

"If you were rich," she said, facing me, "everything would be easy; it's always easy to yield to love." She flushed and stared into the fire. A moment later she went on, as if speaking to herself—"How I hate poverty; hate it, hate it! I have been poor all my life," she said, sitting on the arm of the chair and looking me straight in the eyes. "You don't know what that means."

"Don't I, indeed?" I interjected.

She went on—

"No, you don't know what it means to a girl to be poor, mean poor—cent poor, not dollar poor—to go to school in winter through the snow with icy feet because your boots are old and patched, and can't keep out the wet; to wake in the night and see your mother trying to mend 'em, and crying over 'em. By poor, I mean cold always in winter, because bread and drippin' and coffee don't keep you warm."

She paused again; I waited patiently, my heart hurting me in pity.

"I was always hungry as a child, always, and cold every winter. That was childhood to me. When I grew up and saw I was pretty and fetched men, do you think I didn't want to go to swell restaurants and wear pretty frocks?"

"I haven't done it because of my mother, who's a darling; but is she always to be poor? No, sir, not if I can help it, and I'm going to, you bet," and she cocked her little round chin defiantly. "I'd just die for her, right now;

she lives for me. I want to get everything nice for her now she's getting on.

"You mustn't think badly of me; girls want money and little comforts more than men; we're not so strong, I reckon. I've known boys to like fightin' the cold and hunger. I never knew a girl who did. I hate 'em both. . . .

"I've seen boys, big boys, men, proud of dirty old clothes; put 'em on and like 'em. I never saw a girl proud of an ugly old frock, never. We want to be nice and dainty and comfy more than men."

She looked so tantalizingly pretty that I could not help taking her in my arms, and kissing her, and saying to her—

"But I'll get you all that, and much more, and it will be heaps more fun getting it bit by bit."

"And suppose you don't get it? Never get it?" said Elsie, holding me away from her. "We girls don't want risks. I hate ups and downs. I want a comfy house, and nice things, always, sure, sure."

"Are you afraid to risk it?" I asked.

"It isn't the risk, even of being poor," she said. "How do you think I'd feel if I pulled you down? Oh yes, some time or other the strain on you might be too much. You might get out of work or times would be hard, and you'd be shut out, and then—I should feel I'd made it harder for you. And my mother? No, sir. Love's the best thing in the world, the honey of life; but poverty is the worst, the vinegar, and a little vinegar soon takes away the taste of the honey. I won't be engaged, and I won't yield, for that would be the same thing, and you mustn't be a tiny bit hurt."

I was not hurt: to be with her was a perpetual intoxication; but I went back to kissing her and praising her, as the drunkard goes back to his drink, the opium-smoker to his pipe, to find life in a higher expression, an intenser reality.

It must not be thought that all this courting was merely sensuous; the spirit always counted as much as the body. Often and often I would sit and recite German poems to her, translating them into English as I went along; little bits of Heine; folk songs, the pearls hidden in the rough life of the common people, words that spring from the heart and are of universal appeal. I remember one day making her cry with those simple four lines of Heine, which hold in them all the heart-ache of life, distilled into pure beauty:

"Es ist eine alte Geschichte
Doch bleibt Sie immer neu,
Und wem Sie just passieret
Dem bricht das Herz entzwei."

There we sat holding each other like two children, while the tears of the world's sorrow flooded our eyes.

In telling the story of my idolatry, the tenderness and affection, the passion of admiration, all the fibres of spiritual attachment are difficult to bring into the proper perspective, because they were always present, and I should only give the effect of monotony if I dwelt on them, it seems to me, where there was no monotony.

My passion, on the other hand, was full of incidents, and always new. The first time I ventured to kiss her neck (it makes me flush still to think of it) marks an epoch in my life; every liberty gained was an intoxication, so that it may seem in telling the story as if I gave undue place to passion.

I don't know why, but her figure awakened in me a sort of insane curiosity. Her hands were so slim and pretty; I wanted to see her feet, and was delighted when I found them slim, too, and arched, with tiny ankles. But then she drew away from me.

"That's mean of you, Elsie," I complained. "If you deny the one thing, you ought to give me as much as you can—please." The argument was irrefutable, but another had more weight.

"You are perfectly beautiful, I know, but

you hide yourself as if you were ugly—please let me, please. Let my eyes have pleasure, too, please." The compliment and the pleading persistence together triumphed, and sooner or later I caught a glimpse, or was permitted a glimpse of the slim round limbs. She was beautifully made, what the French would call a *fausse maigre*; small bones, perfectly covered, a slight lissom figure. All my senses grew quick, my blood hot; but I knew by this time that the cooler I appeared, the more unconscious, the further she would yield.

Half an hour afterwards she pushed me from her suddenly, and rose up and went in front of the glass.

"Look how my face is blazing, sir, and my hair is all coming down; we must not meet any more. No, I mean it. This must be the last time."

Oh, I knew the words by heart, the terrible words which seemed to clamp my heart with fear and turn me into a blind beast rage. Whenever she felt intensely, had been made to feel against her will, she always threatened not to come again. I was always in dread of losing her, always in greatest dread when I had most nearly brought her to complete self-surrender; she seemed to avenge her own yielding on me, and, poor fool that I was, I resented this as unfair. But somehow or other before parting we nearly always made it up again; nine times out of ten through my humble submission. I am proud to think now that, at any rate, I had sense enough to know that yielding and being humble, was the only way to complete triumph over my proud, imperious beauty.

It was very hard for me to tell whether I was winning her or not. Over a period of three months, however, I saw that I had made great advances, that what was not permitted at first was allowed to me now without question; but often from day to day the waves of her submission seemed to ebb.

One thing was certain, I was falling more hopelessly in love with her week by week; every meeting made me more devoted to her, more and more her slave, or was it the slave of my own desire? I could not separate them; Elsie was to me desire incarnate.

As summer came she grew prettier and prettier; the light, thin dresses moulded her; she was like a Tanagra statuette, I said to myself, as beautiful as one of the swaying figures on a Greek vase. And I carried the fragrance of her lips, and the slim roundness of her limbs with me from meeting to meeting.

Chapter V

MY memory now of the sequence of events is perhaps not so good as it might be; but having no wish to mis-state the facts, and no power of getting at the newspapers which might vivify or perhaps distort my memory, I shall simply set down my impressions. It seems to me that about this time there was a certain slackening, both in the revolutionary current of feeling, and in the brutality of repression. A strike of street-car employees, which occurred about this time, did not lead to anything; these employees were for the most part American, and the police never attempted to interfere with their public meetings, or to limit their freedom of speech. This wholesome respect of the police for people of their own race, naturally caused some indignation among us foreigners who had never been treated fairly by the authorities; but not much. Young men, and most of the foreign workmen were young men, are so inclined to hope, that we at once assumed that the police had learned wisdom and self-control, and that there would be no more bludgeonings, no more brutalities, and so our talks at the Lehr and Wehr Verein assumed immediately a somewhat academic tone.

One discussion was of my making, and I recall it because it shows in what a masterly way Lingg's mind worked even when he was at every disadvantage. I had talked to him one afternoon about the Gorgias of Plato. I had always thought that the argument of Callicles about laws was the furthest throw of Plato's thought, the wisest hypothesis on the subject which had come out of antiquity. Lingg asked me to set it forth at length that evening at the meeting of the Lehr and Wehr Verein, and I consented. The argument is very simple. Socrates demolishes adversary after adversary with ease, till at length he comes to Callicles, whom Plato pictures as a sort of well-bred man of the world. Socrates as usual tries to fly away from the argument on a rhetorical statement about the sacredness of laws, the same theme which he developed later in the Crito, when he declared that the laws on this earth are but faint reflections of the eternal, divine laws which obtain throughout the universe, and throughout eternity, and which, therefore should be obeyed. Callicles throws a new light on the subject; he says that laws are merely made by the weak for their own protection. The strong man is not allowed to knock down the weak one and take away his wife or his goods, as he would do in a state of nature. The laws are a sort of sheepfold; walls put up by the weak in their own interest and for their own protection against the strong; mere class defences which are purely selfish, and therefore have nothing whatever to do with right and wrong, and are in no sense sacred or divine.

An interesting debate followed, but nothing of weight was said on the subject till Lingg got up. His very method of speaking had a strange individuality about it; he scarcely ever used an adjective; his sentences were made up of verbs and nouns, and the peculiar slowness with which he spoke was due to the fact that with a very large vocabulary he was resolved upon picking the right word.

"The argument of Callicles is foolish," he said; "how can the weak make defence against the strong, the sheep against the wolves. Furthermore, laws are not for the protection of persons, primarily, as they would be if the weak made them; but for the protection of property, which is the appanage of the strong. Even in this Christian town you can knock a man down savagely, injure him for life, and go and plead excitement or rage, and pay five dollars and a quarter, and you are held to have purged the offence. But take five dollars from his person, even without injuring him, and you will probably get six months' imprisonment, and the prosecution will be conducted by the State. Laws are made for the protection of property; they are made by the strong in their own interest; the wolf wants to be assured peaceable enjoyment of his 'kill.'"

Once again the man made a sensation; but this time Raben got up and tried to dissipate the impression. He talked the usual vapid nonsense; laws protected both the weak and the strong, and were good in themselves. He even quoted a verse of Schiller beginning—

"Sei im Besitz....."

—a sort of poetic rendering of the common American saying, "Possession is nine parts of the law," without seeing that Schiller was speaking ironically No one, however, paid any attention to him or answered him, which, of course, enraged him, for he attributed our silence to a conspiracy of envy.

I could not help asking Lingg to explain how he hoped for any improvement if it was indeed the strong who made the laws in their own interest. He answered me at once, having perhaps thought the matter over long before, for in no other way could I explain the clear precision of his statement.

"At all times," he said, "some of the wolves have taken the side of the sheep; partly out of pity, partly out of an intimate conviction that they must first lift up the poor if they themselves would reach a higher level of existence. It even seems to me probable," he went on slowly, "that men are gradually being drawn upwards and humanized by a power working through them, for more and more of the strong are taking the part of the weak, through an inborn sense of justice and fair play. A man's work produces ten times as much now as it did before we knew how to use steam and electricity; it seems to us that the labourer has a right to a part of this extra product. And so even those who could take it all from him are inclined to leave him a little of what he has created."

He ended up splendidly, as he often did, by appealing to the heart. "There is an intimate conviction in all of us," he said, "that justice is better than injustice, even when we seem to profit by the wrong; generosity is its own justification."

Raben sneered; but Raben was, perhaps, the only person who sneered. Mommsen's "Cæsar" had had an extraordinary effect upon me when I read it as a boy, and when Lingg was speaking my thoughts went back at once to Cæsar. He spoke with strange authority, and with a still nobler spirit than Cæsar's ; but it was the same spirit, the spirit which induced Cæsar to pass a law letting off all debtors with a payment of three-quarters of their indebtedness, and preventing their persons being sold for debt.

It was from this time on that I began to realize how great a man Louis Lingg was. Whatever the question might be, if he spoke at all, he spoke as a master. At the end of the debate Raben came up to us and was very pleasant; he made himself particularly agreeable to Lingg; it struck me as disloyal and false of him, and it hurt me that Lingg should receive his advances, or appear to receive them, in his usual courteous way.

When we got out of the meeting, and were on our way home together, Lingg turned to me with the question—

"Why do you bring that man Raben to our meetings? Are you such a friend of his?"

I immediately put him right—

"Raben brought me to the meeting of the Lehr and Wehr Verein first of all. He told me he was a great friend of yours."

"I met him," said Lingg, "only once before I saw him there with you in the meeting; he came to me as a reporter of 'The New York Herald'; I answered his questions, and that was all."

I then told him all I knew of Raben, and something foolishly good-natured in me made me paint the man better than he was, paint him in high lights and leave out the shadows which existed, as I had already reason to know. When I think of my folly I could kill myself; if I had only told Lingg then the bare, simple truth about Raben, things might have turned out very differently; but I was foolishly, feebly optimistic, sentimentally desirous of praising the damned creature because he was a German, or I thought he was because he spoke the language—as if a viper has a nationality! And all the while Lingg's deep eyes rested on me, searching me, reading me, I am sure, rightly.

When we got home, I went up with them as usual for half an hour's talk before going back to my rooms, when suddenly Lingg began again.

"You regard Raben as true?"

"Surely," I exclaimed, "he is with us, I suppose?"

"Did you notice how he spoke to-night?" asked Lingg. (I nodded.) "I mean that jargon of American and German which he uses. Did you remark how he kept repeating two or three words, which serve him as adjectives for everything? 'Awful' is one, in English, 'schaendlich—shameful' is another; he immediately translates the German epithet into English."

I nodded my head, wondering what was coming.

Suddenly Lingg produced a piece of paper. "Here is an anonymous letter I got. I do not propose to read it, but here are four lines in it, and in the four lines there is 'schaendlich—shameful' twice, and 'awful' twice. A letter denouncing you as a traitor to the cause and throwing dirt at me; the man is too malignant to be effective."

He squeezed the letter into a small ball in his hand while he spoke, opened the stove door and threw it in. As he straightened himself he looked me full in the face.

"Raben wrote that letter. Be on your guard against him."

"Good God!" I cried. "What do you mean?"

Suddenly the icy-calm seemed to break up—

"I mean," and again that menace was in his voice, "that he is envious of us, of all of us, of you, of me, of our good faith, of our liking for one another. Look at the thin mean face of him, the washed-out hair and eyes; something feeble and assertive in the whole creature! Let us talk of something else."

And not one word more did he ever say on the subject. Thinking it all over, of what I had let Raben say to me about Lingg and about Ida, my cheeks blazed with shame. I could have killed the foul-tongued snake; I wish now that I had.

All this time Ida said nothing; but her tact soon smoothed over the sore place, and brought us back to kindly feelings, though she, too, felt compelled to say that she had never liked Raben, that she felt that Raben was not with us, but against us.

"From now on," I said, "I will take care, you may be sure." And so the matter dropped. . . .

The lull in the political storm did not last long. Almost immediately after the events I have talked about, I think some time in March, there came a strike among the pig packers. Nine out of ten workmen in these establishments were Germans and Swedes, officered by Americans. The foremen and speeders-up, that is, were nearly all Americans, and these foremen took small part in the strike.

The very first meeting of the foreign workmen on strike was dispersed by the police, and there was some passive resistance on the part of the strikers. The police were led by a Captain Schaack, who seemed to have modelled himself on Bonfield. These strikers were not quite ordinary workmen; they were not only young and strong; but they had learned the use of knives, and they were not minded to be clubbed by the police like sheep. Parsons threw himself into the strike with his accustomed vigour, and so did Spies. In his weekly paper, Parsons called on American workmen to stand by their foreign brothers and resist the tyranny of the employers. The fighting spirit grew in intensity from hour to hour, and the flame of revolt was no doubt fanned by "The Alarm" and "Die Arbeiter Zeitung."

I find in reading over what I have already written that I have not differenced Parsons and Spies sufficiently, though they were in reality completely different personalities. Parsons was a man of very ordinary reading, but with really great oratorical powers; arguments to him were but occasions for rhetoric, and he made mistakes in his statements and in the sequence of his reasoning, but he had genuine enthusiasm; he believed in the Eight Hours' Bill for working-men, and a minimum wage, and all the other moderate reforms which commend themselves to the average American workman.

Spies, on the other hand, was an idealist; far better read than Parsons and a clearer thinker, but emotional and optimistic to an extraordinary degree. He really believed in the possibility of an ordered Socialist paradise on earth, from which individual greed and acquisitiveness should be banished, and in which all men should share the good things of this world equally. Blanc's phrase was always on his lips, "To each according to his needs; from each according to his powers."

Both Parsons and Spies were in the main unselfish, and both spent themselves and their substance freely in the cause of labour. Parsons was the more resolute character; but both of them soon became marked men, for at length that happened which from the beginning might have been foreseen.

A meeting was called on a waste space in Packerstown, and over a thousand workmen came together. I went there out of curiosity. Lingg, I may say here, always went alone to these strike meetings. Ida told me once that he suffered so much at them that he could not bear to be seen, and perhaps that was the explanation of his solitary ways. Fielden, the Englishman, spoke first, and was cheered to the echo; the workmen knew him as a working-man and liked him; besides, he talked in a homely way, and was easy to understand. Spies spoke in German and was cheered also. The meeting was perfectly orderly when three hundred police tried to disperse it. The action was ill-advised, to say the best of it, and tyrannical; the strikers were hurting no one and interfering with no one. Without warning or reason the police tried to push their way through the crowd to the speakers; finding a sort of passive resistance and not being able to overcome it, they used their clubs savagely. One or two of the strikers, hot-heads, bared their knives, and at once the police, led on by that madman, Schaack, drew their revolvers and fired. It looked as if the police had been waiting for the opportunity. Three strikers were shot dead on the spot, and more than twenty were wounded, several of them dangerously, before the mob drew sullenly away from the horrible place. A leader, a word, and not one of the police would have escaped alive; but the leader was not there, and the word was not given, so the wrong was done, and went unpunished.

I do not know how I reached my room that afternoon. The sight of the dead men lying stark there in the snow had excited me to madness. The picture of one man followed me like an obsession; he was wounded to death, shot through the lungs; he lifted himself up on his left hand and shook the right at the police, crying in a sort of frenzy till the spouting blood choked him—

"Bestie! Bestie!" ("Beasts! Beasts!")

I can still see him wiping the bloodstained

froth from his lips; I went to help him; but all he could gasp was, "Weib! Kinder! (Wife, children!)" Never shall I forget the despair in his face. I supported him gently; again and again I wiped the blood from his lips; every breath brought up a flood; his poor eyes thanked me, though he could not speak, and soon his eyes closed; flickered out, as one might say, and he lay there still enough in his own blood; "murdered," as I said to myself when I laid the poor body back; "murdered!"

How I got home I do not know; but I told the whole story to Engel, and we sat together for hours with tears in our eyes, and rage and hate in our hearts. That night Engel came with me to the Lehr and Wehr Verein. Already every one knew what had happened; the gravity of the occurrence weighed upon all of us. One after the other we went through the saloon and took seats upstairs, saying very little. After we had almost given them up, Lingg and Ida came in. To my astonishment he moved briskly, spoke as usual, called the meeting together in his ordinary tone, and asked who would speak; evidently he knew nothing of the shooting.

Every one seemed to look at me; it was plain that they had heard I was an eye-witness, so I got up, and read an account out of a Chicago evening paper. The paper travestied the facts. "Three or four men have been killed, and fifteen or sixteen dangerously wounded while resisting the police with knives." One policeman, it appeared, had had a cut on his arm sewn up—one policeman, that was the extent of the resistance. I added to the newspaper account a brief report of what had taken place. There had been passive resistance; but no active resistance till men were being clubbed, then I did see one or two knives drawn; but immediately, before they could be used, the police drew their revolvers and shot down unarmed men. "They were foreigners," I said, "that was why they were shot down. We Germans, who have done our share in the making of this country, are not to be allowed to live in peace in it. These men were murdered," and I took my seat, blazing with indignation and rage.

Raben was not present at this meeting; indeed, after his somewhat futile attempt to correct Lingg about the laws, he seldom put in an appearance at any of our gatherings. I think I remember he came once for a few minutes. After I sat down Lingg got up, and made an extraordinary speech. I wish I could report it word for word as he delivered it, gravely, seriously, to those grave and serious men who were being driven to extremity.

"Resistance to tyranny is a duty," he began. "The submission preached by Christ is the one part of His teaching which I am unable to accept. It may be that I am a pagan; but I do not believe in turning the other cheek to the smiter. I remember a phrase of Tom Paine, who was the leading spirit of the American revolution; he said that the English race would never be humanized till they had learned in England what war was, till their blood had been shed on their own hearthstones by a foreign foe. I do not believe the insolent strong will ever refrain from tyranny till they are frightened by the results of tyranny."

Professor Schwab seemed to be thrown off his balance by Lingg's words; every one felt that there was something fateful in them; this impression was so strong that it seemed to have shaken the professor out of all self-control. He got up and made a rambling speech about the impossibility of doing anything in a democracy; the tyrant was hydra-headed; we had overthrown kings and set up the people, and King Log was worse than King Stork, so he counselled patience and education, and sat down. Lingg would not have this, and took up his speech again—

"No one should imagine that society is able with impunity to do wrong; *tout se paie* —every evil is avenged; though it does look as if a large community could commit wrongs which would put an end to the existence of a smaller body. . . .

"But surely the true lesson of history is the growth of the individual as a force. Every discovery of science," he went on, with a thrill of triumph in his strong voice, "strengthens the individual. In the past he had one man's life in his hand; a single oppressor could always be killed by a single slave." The whole meeting seemed to shiver with apprehension. "But now the individual has the lives of hundreds in his hand, and some day soon he will have the lives of thousands, of a whole city, then they will cease to do wrong, the tyrants, or cease to exist."

He had not raised his voice above the usual tone; his speech was even slower than usual, yet I remember certain of his words as if I heard him speaking now. There was an extraordinary passion in his speech, an extraordinary menace in his whole person, a flame in the deep eyes. The words of this man seemed like deeds; frightened one like deeds.

Chapter VI

A MORNING or two later I was surprised by a little letter from Ida Miller, in which she asked me to come and see her some morning soon, "if possible on Wednesday next; he will be out then; I want to consult with you. Say nothing to any one of this."

What did it mean? I asked myself in wonder. What could Ida want to see me about, and why did she want to see me while Lingg was away? I puzzled my brains in vain; but the cares and anxieties of the day and hour absorbed me, and I forgot the letter for the moment; I just noted on my almanac that I was to call on her the next Wednesday at noon.

In truth, weightier matters would have been put out of one s head by the growing excitement in the city. It really seemed to us as if the American population had gone mad—or were we perhaps misjudging the people because of the newspapers? No one could deny that the newspapers were hysterically insane; they went on whipping up the passions of their readers day after day, hour after hour. If one had not known that newspapers increase their circulation in troubled times and periods of general excitement, one could not have understood the ape-like malevolence they displayed. When they were not bragging and attributing the highest virtues to themselves, they were running down foreigners and foreign workmen as if we had been of a lower race. The fond imaginings of the journalists were the reverse of the truth, and this fact contained in itself the seed of danger. The foreigners were outnumbered six to one, and disunited by differences of race and religion and language; but whatever original political thinking was done in the town was done by them. Intellectually they were the superiors of the Americans among whom they lived. It was brute force against brains, the present and the oppressors against the dispossessed and the future. It was the intellectual honesty and clearsightedness of the foreigners which gave them strength and made them a force to be reckoned with. Day by day they won adherents among the American workmen; day by day they grew in power and influence, and the understanding of this was what maddened the authorities against them.

It was Spies who really ended the strike, and at the same time concentrated public attention on himself, and incidentally on Parsons. He published an article in the "Arbeiter Zeitung" in German, written by a German workman, which contained almost incredible tales of dirt and filth of the pork-packing establishments. "The workers were always above their soles in blood," he wrote, "and this blood was swept off the floors down shutes and utilized in sausages." The account was made up of such details; but it had little effect till Parsons got it translated into English, and published it in "The Alarm." I did the translation, and I went out for Parsons immediately and interviewed five or six more of the strikers, and put in their accounts, by way of corroboration. One fact which I discovered was quoted everywhere as horror's crown. It had come under my notice in one of my visits to a pork-packing establishment. As their throats were cut the pigs were plunged into a bath of very hot water in order to loosen their bristles, so that they could easily be scraped off. Thousands of pigs passed through this boiling bath daily; long before midday it was fetid, stinking with blood and excrement; but no one paid any attention; the carcasses fell into the revolting mixture and were supposed to be washed clean by the contact with nameless filth. At any rate, that was all the washing they ever got; they were hacked up at once into flitches, hams, sides, and so forth, and thrown steaming into the brine barrels, ready for sale. But even this was not the worst of the matter. Fresh water was supplied each day; but the baths themselves were only cleaned out when the accumulation of filth in the bottom and round the sides made a clearance imperatively necessary. So long as only the food suffered, and the health of the workmen, nothing was done. The baths stank for weeks in summer, and no one paid any attention to the fever-breeding filth. "Pork-packing ain't a perfumery store," was the remark of a millionaire packer, who thought the matter could be disposed of in that comforting way.

The American newspapers could not afford to leave us this field; they, too, sent out reporters, who supplied them with other details of the way food was being prepared, sickening details, incredibly revolting, and soon the town was ringing with the scandal. The better American sheets called upon the Government to see that the inspectors did their duty and protected the consumers; but there is no doubt in my mind that the publication of the facts brought the strike to an end quicker than anything else could have done. The employers saw that it was more profitable to yield to the demands of the strikers than lose their sales through the exposure of their filthy, careless methods.

All this led to a discussion in the Lehr and Wehr Verein, in which Lingg took the ground that the mediæval laws against the adulteration of food and of many other things, would have to be brought into force again. "There is far too much individual liberty in America," was his text. "Professor Schwab has already given us the scientific reasons for it; but this freedom of the individual must be restrained, when it comes to giving us soda instead of wheat for bread, filth from the floors instead of wholesome meat. We shall have to restrain the ruthless competition in a hundred ways."

We were all agreed that there should be a minimum wage established by the State, an eight-hour day, and even the right to work; Lingg insisted that the workman who claimed this right should be paid by the municipality or by the State the minimum wage, what he called a living wage. Government work, too, he declared, should come as little as possible into competition with work directed by the individual; Government work should be for the welfare of all—the extension of roads, afforestation of waste places, and so on. I only mention this to show the man's innate moderation and practical wisdom.

As soon as the strike was over everyone

seemed to wipe it from memory; nobody cared for the three or four people killed, or the twenty poor foreigners who had been wounded.

On the Wednesday morning I went to Lingg's rooms. Ida met me at the door; I was quite cheerful. We talked for a few minutes the usual nothings; but all the time there was a constraint in her; she was talking, as it were, from the lips outwards, not saying what she meant; at last I faced the music.

"What is the matter, Ida?" I asked. "Why did you send for me?"

She looked at me at first, and did not answer; she seemed troubled, and wanted sympathy, wanted me perhaps to divine the answer; but though sympathetic, I could not guess her secret. I pressed her to tell me what was the matter.

"Our anxieties are always greatest," I said, "when we do not talk about them. Once talked about they grow less. Tell me what it is."

"There is nothing certain," she said; "that is, I cannot convince you that there is any imminent danger; but there is. You know Louis is against marriage; talks of it as an invention of the priesthood, a means of filling their pockets, like all the other sacraments. The other night when we came home after your account of the shooting, Louis told me that in the present state of things he was wrong; he thought we ought to get married at once."

She looked at me with appealing eyes; her lips were trembling; I saw she was overwrought; I almost smiled; it did not appear to me to be very serious one way or the other; but she went on—

"It frightened me; he has not altered his opinions, nor changed in any way; he was thinking of me, and wants us to be married at once. Don't you understand? At once! That is because he feels that soon he will be no longer here. Oh, Rudolph, I'm frightened half to death; I can't sleep for fear," and the sweet face quivered pitifully.

"What do you mean?" I cried. But even while I spoke I began to fear she was right. Of course I tried to cheer her up; tried to show her that her fears were exaggerated; but I did not convince her, and bit by bit her fears infected me, began to give shape and meaning to my own vague dread.

"Perhaps," I said to myself, "Lingg's words seem like deeds, have the weight of deeds, because they are closely related to deeds, because he means to make good. That would explain everything"; and as the conviction struck me, I shivered, and we looked at each other, a nameless fear in both our minds.

Suddenly, as if unable to control herself any longer, or perhaps excited by my sympathy, she burst out, her long white hands accentuating her words—

"Oh, if you knew how I love him, and how happy I've been in his love. It's nothing to say 'I am his.' I am part of him; I feel as he feels, think as he thinks; he has given me eyes to see with, and courage to live or die with him; but not without him. If you knew where I was when he met me. Ah, what a man! I had been fooled and deserted, and didn't care what became of me, and he came, and oh, at first I scarcely dared hope for his love, and he gave like a king, without counting. How kind he is and strong. . . .

"You know men and women are much alike; we women at any rate all pretend not to feel any sex-attraction save towards the man we love; but in reality we often feel it. We love a man for instance who is quick and passionate and virile, but when we meet a man who is slow and strong and domineering our soft flesh feels the force in him, and we cannot restrain our liking. The flesh is faithless in woman as in man; though we control it better. But since I met Lingg my flesh even has been faithful to him. I desire nothing but him, my body is as loyal to him as my soul. He is my soul, the vital principle of me. I cannot live without him. I will not...

"I am so happy, I hate to give it all up. I know it's vile and base of me: I ought to think of those others who suffer while we enjoy; but love is so sweet, and we are so young; we might have each other a little longer, don't you think? Or is that very selfish of me?" And the luminous, lovely, wet eyes appealed to me. I had never been so shaken. I could not say, "You are exaggerating." I could frame the words, but could not utter them. She was so sincere and so certain that she lifted me to truth. I could only look in her face with unshed tears, and nod my head. At times life is appalling--more tragic than any imagining.

"We must trust him," I said at last. Out of my sympathy with her the words came, and at once they seemed to help her.

"Yes, yes," she cried, "he knows how a woman loves love; he will not be hard on me, but he is very hard on himself," she added with trembling lips, "and that is the same thing."

"Life is not gay for any of us," was all my wisdom found; "you are rarely lucky ever to have found such complete love, such perfect happiness."

Again I had struck the right note by chance. She nodded her head, and her eyes cleared.

"I wish I could have one day," I went on, "like the months you have had."

"With Elsie?" she asked, smiling, and as I was about to say "Yes," Lingg came into the room. He shook hands with me, showing no trace in his manner of astonishment, embarrassment, or misgiving.

"It is good to see you," he said simply as he went over to the table, and put down some books that he had brought in. "Did Ida send for you?" and his eyes probed mine a moment. "I mean," he went on more lightly, "there is a sort of coincidence in the matter, for I wanted to see you to-day. It is such a fine day, and I have been working very hard. Why not let us go out and have a holiday? Take something to eat with us, German fashion, sausages, beer, bread, and a potato salad, *echt Deutsch*, eh? and eat in a boat on the lake."

He seemed in a radiant good-humour, strangely light-hearted. Looking at him, all my fears vanished, and I immediately backed up the project with all my heart. I, too, had been over-working, and wanted a holiday; so we began to get the things together, packing up the eatables in a little hamper. Lingg allowed me to carry the basket, I noticed, though it was his usual custom to carry everything himself. He would walk apart from us, too, though he usually walked between us. Why do I remember all these things so clearly, though I do not think I remarked any of them at the moment?

We went down to the lake shore and engaged a row-boat, and the man who hired us the boat wanted to come with us, or to send a boy with us; but Lingg would not hear of it.

"Give us a good safe boat," he said, "your broadest, safest boat; put in a good life-belt, too, because we are unused to the water, and we want to enjoy ourselves without being afraid of capsizing."

The American laughed at us, thinking we were silly Dutchmen, and gave us the boat we asked for, a broad, heavy barge of a thing. Lingg told Ida to go and sit in the stern-sheets and steer, and then put me on the after-thwart to row a pair of sculls, and went with a pair of sculls himself into the bow. He left a thwart between us unoccupied. That, too, I remember distinctly, though at the time I did not notice it.

When we pushed off and began to row, I thought that Lingg meant to get half a mile or so out, perhaps a mile, and then eat; but he rowed on steadily. At last, I turned round to him—

"Look here, Lingg, I want something to eat. When are we to have dinner?"

He simply smiled.

"When we can no longer see the city," and bent to the oars again. We must have rowed for two hours and a half, must have made seven or eight miles out into the lake, before I put down the sculls and said—

"I say, Lingg, do you want to row across the Lake? Or do you call this pleasure to work us like slaves, and give us nothing to eat?"

At once he came back to me on the after-thwart, and we had our meal, and I tried to make merry; but Lingg was always rather silent, and to-day Ida was silent, too, and nervous; she upset things, and was evidently overwrought. When we had finished the simple meal, and put away the things, I proposed to row back, but Lingg said "No," and then got up on the after-thwart and stood there looking towards Chicago. When he stepped down again he said—

"Not a thing to be seen except this"; and he took a sort of boy's catapult out of his pocket.

"What on earth's that for?" I asked.

"To try this," he answered, and he took a little ball of cotton-wool out of his trousers pocket, and, stripping the cotton off, discovered a round ball, about the size of a walnut.

"What may that be?" I asked laughingly; but as I laughed I caught a glimpse of Ida's face, and again the fear came back, for she was leaning forward staring at Lingg with parted lips, and all her soul in her wide eyes. He said—

"That is a bomb, a small bomb, which I am going to try."

"Good God!" I exclaimed, astounded so that I could not think or feel.

"I want the catapult," he went on, "to throw it some distance from the boat, because I think that if I threw it with my hand it might wreck the boat, and we might have to try to swim back to shore. Whereas, this catapult will throw it twice as far as I could, and we shall see the results of it, and be able to gauge them pretty accurately."

I do not suppose I am more of a coward than other men; but his quiet words terrified me. My heart was in my mouth, I could not breathe freely, and my hands were cold and wet. I said—

"Do you mean it, Lingg?"

The inscrutable eyes rested on me, searched me, judged me, and against their condemnation my pluck seemed to come back to me, and my blood began to flow again. That was the terrible thing about Louis Lingg: he judged you by what there was in you; he liked you, or admired you, for the qualities you possessed, and absolutely refused to attribute to you qualities which you did not possess. To know him was a perpetual tonic. I would not let him see I was afraid, I'd have died sooner.

I am honestly trying to tell exactly what went on in me, because in comparison with Lingg I look upon myself as merely an ordinary man, and if I did things that ordinary men do not do and cannot do, it is because of Lingg's influence on me.

As the spirit came back to me, and the blood rushed through my veins in hot waves, I could see that his eyes were kindlier; they rested on me with approval, and I was intensely proud and lifted up in soul because of it.

"Shall we try the bomb," he said, "or are you frightened that we may have to swim?"

"I will trust your judgment," I said carelessly. "I expect you know about what it will do. But when did you make it?"

"I began working a year ago," he said, "when the police began to use their clubs, and I have gone on ever since." In a flash I remembered the chemistry books, and all was plain to me.

"I had no business to bring you with us," he said, turning to Ida. "It will be too much for your nerves?" he questioned gently.

She looked at him with all her love in her shining eyes, and shook her head.

"I have known about it for months past," she said—"months. You made it two months ago in your little shop by the river."

And these two strange beings both smiled. The next moment Lingg had put the bullet in the catapult, and drawn the india-rubber out to arm's length and let go. The eyes followed the black bullet in its long curve through the air. As it reached the water there was a tremendous report, a tremendous shock; the water went up in a sort of spout, and even at thirty or forty yards distance the boat rocked and almost capsized. For minutes afterwards I could not hear. I began to be afraid I was permanently deaf. How could so small a thing have such enormous force? The first thing I heard was Lingg saying—

"If we had been standing up we should have been thrown down; as it was I had to hold on to the side of the boat."

"Surely," I said, "the noise will have been heard in the town?"

"Oh, no," said Lingg, "the explosion is rapid, the blow very quick, so that it does not carry so far as the slower pushing blow of powder; the high explosive gives a greater shock near at hand; but the blow does not spread over nearly so large an area."

"It was dynamite, wasn't it?" I asked, after a little reflection, when the deafness was beginning to wear off.

"No," Lingg answered; "a much more powerful agent."

"Really!" I exclaimed. "I thought dynamite about the strongest."

"Oh, no," Lingg replied, "dynamite is nothing but nitro-glycerine mixed with Kieselguhr, in order to allow it to be handled easily; nitro-glycerine mixed with nitro-cotton is called blasting gelatine, and is much stronger than dynamite. But the percussion of a small quantity of fulminate of mercury embedded in nitro-glycerine produces an enormously greater effect than the explosion of either substance by itself. And there are more powerful explosives than nitro-glycerine. My little bomb," he went on, as if talking to himself, "is as powerful as fifty times its weight of dynamite."

"Good God!" I exclaimed; "but what was it made of?"

"All high explosives," he said, "contain a lot of oxygen and some nitrogen . . . but do let's talk of something else," he broke off, "it's too long a story. . . ."

Suddenly Ida said to Lingg—

"I want to throw the first bomb, Louis."

He shook his head. "It's not woman's work," he said, "and I still hope there will be no bomb-throwing needed."

Now what prompted me to speak, I cannot tell; I suppose it was vanity, or rather a desire to gain Louis Lingg's approval. I suddenly heard myself saying—

"Let me throw the first bomb."

Lingg looked at me, and again my blood warmed under the kindly approval of his gaze.

"It is a terrible thing to do," he said. "I am sure a woman would break down under it; I am afraid you would break down too, Rudolph."

"But you?" I asked.

"Oh," he replied carelessly, "I think I have always known that I was born to do something of this sort. There is a passage in the Bible which struck me when I first heard it as a boy, which has always lived with me. I did not read much of the Bible, and I did not pay much attention to what I did read. The Old Testament seemed to me poor stuff, and only the Gospels moved me much; but that word has always lived with me. It is something like this: 'It is expedient that one man should die for the people . . . .'

"We Germans dream too much, and think too much; for a generation or two we should act. We are far ahead of the rest of the world as thinkers; it now remains for us to realize our thoughts and to show the rest of the world that in deeds, too, we can surpass them.

"I had a dreadful childhood; perhaps I will tell you about it some day," he went on. "They heat the steel in the furnace and then plunge it in icewater in order to make a sword-blade. I think I was subjected to extremes of pain and misery—for some purpose," he added the last words slowly. In spite of its clearness, his mind just touched mysticism. He felt a purpose in things—his star and fate one with the whole. He seemed lost in thought for a moment, and then resumed in his accustomed clear way—

"The only good thing in your offer, and it is a great offer," he smiled at me, "is that it would multiply the effect of us both tenfold. I could save you, too, the first person to throw a bomb, and reserve myself for the second when there will be no saving. You see, one bomb is an accident; two show sequence, purpose; suggest a third and fourth —are terrifying. I know the fat tradesmen; they'll hide under the beds with fear."

Again the man terrified me, again I heard myself talking, assenting, felt myself grinning; but my senses were numbed, paralysed, by the awful reality of the talk, or the unreality of it, whichever you please; my thinking and feeling faculties all seemed dead; the shock had been too great for me. I moved as in a dream; in a dream, when he went to his thwart and took up the sculls, I went to mine and took up the sculls too, like an automaton, and in almost complete silence we rowed back to Chicago. . . .

The short spring day was over, the sun went down before we got back; night came with her shadows, her merciful, shrouding shadows, and hid us as we rowed up to the wharf. As the Yankee received the money, something in his quaint, sharp accent recalled me to reality; but I had no wish to talk, I was drained of emotions, and I accompanied the others home in a sort of waking dream. At the door Lingg sent Ida upstairs, and turned to walk with me towards my rooms.

"Put all this out of your head," he said to me; "it has overstrained you. Perhaps the troubles will settle down, perhaps the police will come to some sense of humanity. I hope so. In any case, I do not take your offer seriously. I need not say I trust you; but it is not well to try to do more than one can do," and he smiled at me with loving-kindness in the deep eyes. From that moment we were intimates. I felt that in some strange way he knew my weakness as well as I knew it, and would never ask me for more than I could give, and this filled me with loving gratitude to him; but I felt also that same wild exhilaration in the heart of me, knowing well that I was always willing to give more than he asked, more than he expected.

Chapter VII

ALL these experiences in the strikes and with Lingg had not only taken me away from Elsie, prevented me spending much time with her, but they had alienated me from her to a certain extent. We had gone on meeting two or three times a week, but I was always occupied with the events of the social war, with the emotions and sensations which the wild struggle called to life in me, and with the demands the incidents made upon my time and thought. Before this period came to an end, I noticed that my position with Elsie had improved. As I seemed to draw away from her and to be a little less her slave, she became kinder to me, less imperious, and as soon as I noticed this a tinge of contempt mingled with my love for her. Was she indeed like all the other girls whom I had read of who ran away if you ran after them, and who ran after you if you ran away? I was not like that, I reflected; I desired her above everything in the world; but then the thought would not be denied that when she was imperious and difficult she attracted me most intensely. There is not a pin to choose between us, I reluctantly admitted; human nature in man or woman is not differenced widely.

But the fact that self-possession, self-mastery did me good in Elsie's eyes and strengthened my influence over her enormously, was perhaps the real gain in the somewhat casual intercourse of these few weeks. The last time I had seen her she had flushed with pleasure when we met, and when we parted she kissed and clung to me as if she wished to show her passion. "You will come to-morrow, won't you?" she asked. This called to life a sort of mocking contrary devil in me, and I answered with careless courtesy—

"I will come on Saturday and take you for a walk—if I possibly can," I added.

"I will wait in and be ready," she replied quickly.

That Saturday afternoon was bright and hot, I remember, and our steps turned naturally towards the lake shore, for the asphalt was soft, and the smell of it overpowering. One would almost have done anything to avoid those hot shafts of light reflected from the pavement and buildings; they blinded one. I did not wonder that Elsie said pettishly—

"I hate walking. To-day is the day for a drive."

I had intended merely to go into the park and lie about; but the moment she said this I thought of the boat, and it gave a purpose to me.

"I am going to take you for something better than a drive," I said.

"What is it?" she asked, her eyes sparkling.

"I will tell you within quarter of an hour," I said, and she walked on towards the boating place, chattering of all she had done in the past fortnight. She was delighted, it appeared, for the manager had made much of her, was pleased with her work, and had given her a rise in wages. I was a little jealous, I remember, vaguely jealous though pleased for her sake that she had got a better position. The unworthy spirit soon vanished, however, for her provocative, saucy beauty had a warmth of tenderness about it that thrilled me with delight, bathed my heart in joy, and banished all thought of rivalry.

In a few minutes we came to the landing-stage, and before the Yankee had time to ask me what I wanted, Elsie cried out in wild excitement—

"It's just lovely of you! I'd like a row on the cool water better than anything."

"Let us have a broad, safe boat," I said, and the Yankee picked us out a tub of a thing.

"You'll find it hard rowing in that, if you

want to go far," was his remark, "though it ain't so hot on the water as on land, by a long way; but the boat's safe as a barge."

I did not intend to pull as far as I had pulled with Lingg, so I took the boat he offered me, and after settling Elsie in the stern-sheets and showing her how to use the steering lines, I rowed out into the lake for half an hour or so, and then went and threw myself in the bottom of the boat at her feet. She looked at me half shyly, with love's confession in the eyes that hardly dare to meet mine.

"Isn't it rather strange?" she said to me. "A month ago I made up my mind again and again not to meet you: said I wouldn't: told you I wouldn't. And when I was away by myself I used to begin by saying, 'I don't think we ought to go on meeting; it's not right, and I'm not going to, anyway.' But 'it's not right' simply meant, I think, 'I don't want to very much,' for now when you haven't come once or twice I have just wanted you ever so bad; now, don't be conceited, or I'll not tell you another thing."

Naturally at this avowal I slipped my arm round her hips and looked up in her face. Her eyes still avoided mine. At first Elsie liked me, I think; but love came with companionship, and she was now as much in love as I was, lost in the transfiguring glamour.

"We are alone here, aren't we, Boy," she went on, "more alone than in a room or anywhere; just our two selves between sky and sea."

I agreed with her, and she went back to her original theme.

"I didn't want to go on meeting you, because I thought I did not care really, and that you did care, and now it seems as if I had grown to care more, and so, just as I used to reason against you, now I am always reasoning for you. Isn't that strange?" And the divine eyes lifted shyly for a moment.

I put my face up to her and her lips drooped on mine: her tender abandonment was simply adorable.

"Love calls forth love, Elsie," I said, "as 'deep calls unto deep.'"

"Besides," she began, with a quick change of mood, "you have altered a great deal, you know. When we first met you were, oh, so German; you spoke American comically, and you had all sorts of little German ways, and now you speak American as well as I do. You seemed a little soft then, and very—sentimental; now you are stronger, more resolute. . . .

"You are very well educated, aren't you? Much better even than our college boys. You ought to get on, you know," and she looked quite excited and eager; but another wave of reflection swept over her, and her lips drooped pathetically.

"But to get on far will take ten or twelve years, and what shall I look like in ten years? I shall be an old hag. Fancy me twenty-nine! and if I married you now, you'd never get through. I'd keep you poor. Oh, I'm afraid, I'm afraid! . . .

"You mustn't, Boy! Please don't or I'll get cross," she broke in, for I had begun kissing her arm with little slow kisses which left flushes like roseleaves on the exquisite skin; but in return for my imploring look she bent down and kissed me, as she alone could kiss.

Then we began talking of this and that, forming little plans of what might be, plans which would bring us together. I used to be the castle-builder; but lately Elsie had begun to build castles, too, or rather, cosy little houses, which seemed nearer than my castles, and certainly more enticing. But now I talked with some certainty of a secure post on an American paper, for Wilson, the editor of the "Post," was willing to give me a steady berth, where I could reckon on earning at least eighty dollars a month, and that was surely enough for all of us; but she shook her prudent little head, till I drew her down from her seat into my arms, and there we sat with our arms round each other and lips given to lips. After a while she drew herself away again.

"Oh, we ought not to meet," she said; "we ought not to meet like this. You smile, you bad boy, because I'm always saying that; but I mean it this time. When I said it before, we didn't care really; but now it's different. Oh, I know. . . . Each time we meet, you want me more, and as you want me more and more, I find it harder to refuse and deny myself to you. Every time, too, the joy of yielding tempts me more and more, and I'm beginning to get afraid of myself. If we go on meeting and kissing, some day I'll yield; it's human nature, Boy, or girl's nature, and then I'd just hate myself and you, too; I'd kill myself, I think. I hate giving way, bit by bit, out of weakness, and doing something I don't want to do; it humiliates me!"

All this time I let her talk, and went on kissing and caressing her. Something of Lingg's steady purpose had got into me. Speech is often a veil of the soul, and my patience and persistent desire drew us together more surely than any words. Day by day I was more masterful, and Elsie was more yielding than she had been, nearer to complete self-surrender.

I simply went on kissing her, therefore, till of a sudden again she drew away resolutely, and threw her little head back and took a long breath.

"Oh, you bad boy! Why do you tempt me?"

"You don't care for me much," I said, looking in her eyes with dumb appeal, "so you needn't talk of temptation; you don't care enough for me to yield a little bit."

"More than you think, Boy," she said, giving herself to me for a moment in a look; but the next instant she got up, nevertheless, with proud resolution, shook her skirts out with a rueful pout at the way the muslin was crushed and tumbled, and sat down again in the stern-sheets.

I let her go. After all, what right had I to tempt her, or to go on caressing her? What right? At any time Lingg might call on me, and I felt sure I should respond, and all hope of love and a happy life with Elsie were blotted out in one black gulf of fear. No, I would restrain myself; and I did on that occasion, though it cost blood.

I had already noticed that every caress, innocent though they were for the most part, was a permanent advance. She had let me catch a glimpse of her limbs once; she could not refuse me the next time. In truth, it was harder and harder for her to refuse me anything, for love was on her, too, with its imperious desire. In spite of my determination not to go any further, certainly not to compromise her in any way, we seemed to be on a fatal slope; every little movement took us further down, and it was impossible to go back. I do not know whether Elsie realized this as clearly as I did; sometimes now I am inclined to believe that she understood even better than I whither the road led.

But that day, I am glad to think, I put the bridle on myself resolutely, and yielded no whit to the incessant tormenting desire. And if Elsie had rewarded me for my self-restraint by showing me increased tenderness, perhaps I should have persevered in the narrow, difficult way. But she did not; she seemed to think I had taken offence at her resolution, so she sulked a little in reply to my unwonted coldness, and that I simply could not stand, so I kissed her into a good humour and thanked goodness that the April sun had almost run his short course, and compelled us to seek the shore.

On our way to the boarding-house, Elsie repented of her coolness, and was delightful to me; kissing her as we parted, I could only promise to visit her as usual, and give her more time than I had lately been able to afford.

It looked as if my good resolutions were likely to be put to a severe test.

When I was alone and had time for cool reflection, I took myself earnestly to task. God knows I did not wish to harm the woman I loved; yet each time that Elsie and I met seemed to bring us nearer to the moment when there would be no retreat for us, when the last veil would fall of itself, and the irremediable would happen. All my half-hearted efforts to resist the current that was sweeping us along only served to show how strong the current was, how irresistible. At length I made up my mind and on next Saturday night I wrote to her that I could not see her on the Sunday; "we ought to be prudent." Before I was out of the house, next morning I received a pathetic little note, asking me to visit her some time during the day. If I were busy would I come to supper, or even after supper, or later, just to say "Good night." It would make the day so happy to know that I was coming; the hours would be so long and lonely-miserable if I stayed away. . . .

Of course, I yielded. I sent back at once to say that I would put off the work which I was required to do, and take her and her mother for a drive and a lunch out somewhere instead.

I thought of her mother simply as a protection, and, of course, she was a shield to me; but I am inclined to think that the companionship and the complete freedom tempted Elsie to show her love for me a little more freely than she would have done if we had been alone together. All day long she was unspeakably delightful—provocative, wilful, imperious, as always, with an undercurrent of appeal and abandonment. The contrasts in her, the quick changes, were simply bewitching.

I took them out to the little German restaurant where I had gone with Lingg, and the whole place was lighted up by Elsie. She tried all the German dishes, fell in love, if you please, with Sauerkraut, declared that it was excellent; wanted to know how to make it; would have the recipe; flattered the German waiter so that he blushed all over his white face, and almost set his straw-coloured hair on fire.

After lunch we went for a walk, and found a knot of trees making a grateful shade, where we sat and chatted. Every now and then I could not resist the temptation to touch Elsie, and I thrilled from head to foot at the contact; and every now and then she touched me, and the second or third time this happened I saw that she, too, touched me on purpose. The thought was intoxicating.

We drove back along the lake shore, with the dying sun shooting long crimson arrows, fan-like, over the western sky. The colours were all reflected in the water, with a sort of sombre purple magnificence. I shall never forget that drive. We had put a rug over our knees, and I was sitting opposite Elsie, and of course our feet met, and held one another. The peace and hush of the dying day seemed to envelop us. That was the happiest day of my life, for it ended well, too.

Mrs. Lehman insisted on my staying to supper, and we all had supper together in the boarding-house. After supper Elsie put on her hat and came with me, and then I saw her back home again and by this time the stars had come out, and a little sliver of moon, a baby moon, was shining over the lake. As we said "Good night" at the door her arms went round my neck naturally, and our lips clung together. Feeling her yield, and overpowered by desire, I drew her inside the dark passage: "I love you," I said, "you darling! I love you," and went mad. "My own boy," she sighed back to me, and her supple, warm beauty gave itself to my desire. . . .

But the place was impossible; in a minute or two there came footsteps on the stairs; footsteps, too, outside. I could only hold her to me in one long, passionate, quick kiss and set her free, when one of the boarders came in and discovered us. Elsie, of course, greeted him with perfect courtesy and unconcern. I, too, tried to look at my ease; but there were a thousand pulses beating in me, and the blood was rioting through my veins, and my voice, when I spoke, was strange in my ears. Still, the stolen sweetness of it all was deathless; it is as honey in my memory; whenever I think of it, I taste life's ecstasy again at the springing fount, as I had never tasted it before.

The best day of my life, I said to myself, as I went back to my lodgings, and the thought was more exactly true than I imagined. The best day! I still see her as she stood when the door opened—the mutinous face and the great eyes with the curling lashes, and I hear the cool words with which she dismissed the intruder. . . . Ah me! how long ago and beautiful it all seems now!

. . . .

All the incidents of the late spring of that year are bathed in my memory in golden light; there is about them the evanescent loveliness of April sunshine. The weather helped this illusion; there had been floods of rain early in the month; now we had a sort of summer of St. Martin in midspring. The dreadful, harsh winter had passed away beyond recollection, and the whole city turned to enjoyment; there were parties and excursions in all directions, and for a time the mutterings of social war died out, and we heard, on every hand, the laughter of children. My new resolve to restrain myself with Elsie threw me more and more with Lingg and Ida. Besides, as my work for the "Post" became more and more important, I needed to consult oftener with Lingg. It was seldom I could use his opinions; they were neither obvious nor popular; but he always forced me to think; and now instead of looking at me and shrugging his shoulders when he disapproved, he gave himself the trouble of showing me the steps by which one reached new thoughts.

Now, too, I began to realize his infinite kindness of nature; in spite of a cold and somewhat formal manner, he was singularly considerate and sympathetic to every form of weakness. Ida suffered periodically from shocking, nervous headaches; while they lasted Lingg moved about the sick-room with his cat-like, noiseless step, now bringing eau-de-Cologne for her forehead, now mitigating the sun-glare, now changing a hot for a cool pillow—indefatigable, quiet, helpful. And when the crisis was past, he would plan some excursion; forty miles on the cars, and then a whole day in the woods with our meals at some farmhouse.

I remember one excursion which I know fell about this time. Having thrown off the headache, Ida was at her brightest, and Lingg and I spent the whole noontide finding and bringing her masses of spring flowers which she tied into posies. We dined at the Oeslers' farm at one o'clock, and about three we went back to the forest, as to a temple. Our train did not start till seven, and Herr Oesler had promised to pick us up with a spring-wagon and fast team at six, so that we might have tea before starting for the depôt. At first, we lay about talking idly and laughing, disinclined for any exertion by the untimely heat; but as the sun slid down the sky, and cool airs began to make themselves felt, a more strenuous spirit came over us.

I had long wanted to know why Lingg called himself an anarchist, what he meant by the term, and how he defended it; and accordingly I began to question him on the subject. I found him in a communicative mood, and, strangely enough, he showed that day an idealistic enthusiasm which seemed foreign to his nature, which a mere acquaintance would never have attributed to him.

"Anarchy is an ideal," he said, "and like

all ideals is of course full of practical faults, and yet it has a certain charm. We want to govern ourselves, and neither govern others nor be governed by them; that's the beginning. We start from the truism that no man is fit to judge another. Was there ever such a ludicrous spectacle, even on this comic earth, as a judge pronouncing sentence on his fellow! Why, in order to judge a man at all, one must not only know him intimately, but love him, see him as he sees himself; whereas your judge knows nothing about him, and uses ignorance and a formula instead of intimate sympathy. And then the vile, soul-destroying punishments of the prison—bad food, enforced idleness, or unsuitable labour, and solitary confinement, instead of elevating companionship. . . .

"Suppose there are persons suffering from incurable moral faults; if there are any, they must be few indeed; but let's suppose there are such people: why punish them? If they have incurable physical faults such as elephantiasis, we take care of them in splendidly equipped hospitals; we give them the best of air and food, cheerful books, regular exercise; we provide, too, charming nurses and good doctors. Why not treat our moral patients as well as we treat congenital idiots? Since Christ, with His pitying soul, came upon earth, we recognize in some dull, half-hearted way that these deformed or diseased people are the scapegoats who bear the sins of humanity; 'they are wounded for our transgressions, and with their stripes we are healed.' . . .

"Let us sweep away both hospitals and prisons, and substitute lethal chambers for them, as our pseudo-scientists would have us do; or let us treat our moral lepers at least as well as we treat our cripples and our idiots. As soon as humanity understands its own self-interest it will make an end of prisons and judges, as more poisonous to the soul than any form of crime. . . .

"I see a thousand questions on your tongue," he went on, laughing; "resolve them all for yourself, my dear Rudolph, then they'll do you good; but don't put them to me. Each of us must construct the kingdom for himself, the Kingdom of Man upon Earth. This one will make it a fairyland; that one will make it a sort of castle of romance, with machicolated turrets, and set it in a meadow of blowing daffodils and lilies; I would have a modern city with laboratories at every street corner, and theatres and art studios and dancing halls, instead of drinking saloons; and at another moment I would build it with tent-like houses, after the fashion of the Japs, which could be taken up and carried off and reconstructed in a night, for 'here we have no abiding city,' and the love of change—change of air, change of scene—is in my blood. But why shouldn't we have both; the stable working city and the fleeting tents of joy? . . .

"There were two beautiful ideas in what we stupidly call the dark ages: the idea of purgatory, which is a thousand times more suitable to mankind than either hell or heaven, and the idea of service. Think of it, a nobleman would send his son as a page to the house of some famous knight to learn courage and courtesy and consideration for others, especially for the weak or afflicted. There was nothing menial in such service; but the noblest human reverence—that's the anarchic ideal of service, free and unpaid . . ." and he broke off, laughing heartily at the surprise in my face.

I had never seen him let himself go with such abandon: he even quoted poetry—a verse of a parody which he had seen in a paper and applied to some Chicago millionaires—with huge delight:

"They steal the lawns and grassy plots,
They grab the hazel coverts,
They mortgage the forget-me-nots
That grow for happy lovers."

He laughed boyishly over this for some time, but soon the graver mood came back.

"All true progress," he said, "comes from

the gifted individual; but in my view a certain amount of Socialism is needed to bring a wider freedom to men, and with completer freedom and a stronger individualism I dream of a State industrial army, uniformed and officered, employed in making roads and bridges, capitols and town halls, and people's parks, and all sorts of things for the common weal, and this army should be recruited from the unemployed. If the officers are good enough, believe me, in a year or two, service in the State army at even a low rate of wages would carry honour with it, as our army uniform does now. Don't forget that our dreams, if beautiful enough, are certain to be realized; the dreams of to-day are the realities of tomorrow. . . .

"There are three manifestations of the divine in man," he went on, as if speaking to himself; "beauty in girls and boys, the bodily beauty and grace of youth, which we hide and prostitute, and which we should exhibit and admire in dances and public games, for beauty in itself humanizes and ennobles. Then there is genius in men and women, which is for the most part wasted and spent in a sordid conflict with mediocrity, and which should be sought out and put to use as the rarest and most valuable of gifts. And then come the millions of the toil-weary and dispossessed

—each of them with a spark of the divine and a right in human pity to a humane life. Oh, there needs no saviour of men from among the gods," he cried; "but a saviour of God, of the Divine, among men . . ." and again he broke off suddenly, smiling with inscrutable eyes.

There surely never was a more interesting talker, and I was soon to find that as a man of action he was even greater. That day was our last day of joy and happiness together. In an hour or so the farmer came and gathered us, and Ida smiled as we all three went hand in hand, flower-crowned, to the wagon.

. . . .

My resolution not to let myself go with Elsie, or tempt her any further, held for some two or three weeks, and then it broke down again, broke down more completely than ever. I had taken her out to dinner, and she had put on a low-necked dress. The day had been very warm, and the night was close and sultry. We dined together in a private room in a German restaurant, and afterwards we sat together, or rather she sat on my knees, with my arms round her, and I began to kiss her beautiful bare shoulders—flower-like, cool and fragrant.

I don't know what possessed me; I had been working hard all day, had written a couple of good articles, had made a little extra money, and saw my way to make more. I was excited, happy, and therefore, perhaps, a little more thoughtless, and a little more masterful than usual. Success is too apt to make one imperious, and so I took Elsie in my arms and began kissing her and caressing her, with a thirst for her that I cannot describe. The very first kiss gave me the intensest sensation, made my senses reel, in fact, and when she stopped me I was enraged; but she drew away from me, and stood by herself for a minute or so, then she turned to me.

"You don't know how you tempt and try me," she cried, and then after a pause: "How I wish I were beautiful!"

"Why do you talk like that?" I said; "you are beautiful enough for anything, and you know it."

"Oh, no, I'm not," she replied. "I'm just pretty, very pretty, if you like, on my days; but beautiful, extraordinary, never. I'm not tall enough," she went on, meditatively, "only just middle height" (two inches below that standard, I thought, with a smile, for the repulse had awakened a sort of sex-antagonism in me), "and sometimes undistinguished, almost plain."

She turned to me and spoke passionately:

"If I were beautiful I'd yield to you at once. Yes, I would, for then I could win through anyway, but, as it is, I'm afraid. You see, I could not win through if anything happened, and it would just break mother's heart; so you must not tempt me, Boy, please!" and her eyes besought me.

I took her in my arms again, almost ruthlessly, in spite of her soul-revealing frankness, and again began kissing and caressing her—as a thirsty man drinks. For a moment she yielded, I think, and then she broke away again, and when I asked her why, she said hurriedly, as if afraid to trust herself—

"I must go now; I must go home."

"Oh, no, no!" I cried. "If you do not care for me, what does it matter, and it is too early to go home yet. I'd have the whole long evening before me to call myself names in."

"I ought to go," she repeated.

"There's no risk for you," I retorted sulkily; "you are always completely mistress of yourself."

"Oh," she exclaimed, "how blind you are, and unkind! . . . I'd like to go on just as much as you: I should. Why do you make me say such shameful things? But they are true. I am trembling now from head to foot. Just feel me. Ah!" and she came over to me, and slipped into my embrace again, and slid her arms round my neck. "Don't make it too hard for me, Boy," and her lips gave themselves to mine.

Almost I had taken her then. If she had not made the appeal I should have. But the appeal suddenly recalled me to the terrible edge of the abyss on which I was standing, and I felt chilled to the bone. No, I had no right to. No, I would be a man now and control myself; and so, gathering her in my arms and drawing her head back to kiss her throat, "Darling mine!" I cried, "I won't make it hard for you. We two will make it easy for each other always, won't we—as easy as possible?"

Again her lips sought mine with a little contented sigh. From that time on, I think the resistance in her was completely broken, and I could have won her whenever I liked, but I dared not. All my regard for her, all my admiration of her beauty and frankness and provocative charm came back, and helped me again and again to restrain myself. I would not yield, and the less would I yield now that there were no barriers between us; for after this day, when she found that I meant to restrain myself, she did not attempt to restrain me, but gave herself to my desire. I could do what I would with her, and this freedom, the power given to me, held me back as nothing else could. I fought with myself, and every time I conquered, Elsie was sweeter to me, and made the next self-conquest harder and easier at the same time. I cannot explain the tangled web of my feelings, nor how the tenderness for her triumphed over my passion; but the passion was always there, too, watching its opportunity and trying to make it. But from that night on I held it by the throat, though it twined snake-like round all my body and nearly conquered at the last.

Chapter VIII

AND now, like those who have sown the wind, we came, at length, to the reaping of the whirlwind. For a moment there was a lull in the storm; the gale, so to speak, taking breath for a final desperate effort. There are those who profess to find a crescendo in the awful business from beginning to end. We who lived at the storm-centre did not remark that—perhaps because we had other and more important things to do and think about. You see the position: on this side intolerant, greedy Americans, satisfied with their steal-as-you-can or competitive swindling society; on the other side bands of foreign workmen with ideas of justice, right and fair play in their heads, and little or nothing in their bellies. These poor foreigners were systematically overworked, and underpaid; they had no compensation for injuries incurred in their work; they were liable for the most part to be discharged at a moment's notice, the longest notice accorded being a week, and that notice was usually given on the approach of winter, in order that the honest employer might weed out the worse workmen and force down to starvation limit the wages of the best. On the side of the Americans, the authorities, the law-courts, the police; the whole vile paraphernalia of so-called justice with armed militia in the background, and if that was not enough, the Federal army of the United States. The churches, too, and the professions, the trained intelligence of the nation stood with the robbers. The foreign workmen, on the other side, were unarmed, rent apart by differences of race and language, without a leader, rallying-point, or settled policy. If might is right they had no chance; yet right is always in process of becoming might, even in this confused welter of a world—that is hardly to be denied. What, then, will be the outcome?

One incident threw light, as from a red flare, into the sordid arena. There was at that time a store selling drugs and groceries in the very centre of the foreign population. This store had a telephone, and was therefore much frequented by quick American reporters eager to get messages to and from their papers. The foreign workmen believed, with good reason, that this telephone had been used on more than one occasion to call down the police on them. Naturally they regarded the reporters with hatred and suspicion; were they not the eager tools of the capitalist press?

One night a band of Polish and Bohemian workmen got together, headed by a hot young Jew who spoke both tongues; he led the mob to the drug store, entered with a bound, seized and tore down the telephone; the others following the brave example, rushed in and began to wreck the store, drinking, meanwhile, whatever wine or spirits they could lay their hands on. Fortunately, or unfortunately, the grocer man, it appears, had two gallon jars of wine of colchicum. These were seized, uncorked, drained in an instant, and so some ten poor wretches paid for their petty fling-out with their lives. Nature is nothing if not prodigal. I recall the incident to show that the workmen were not always in the right; but whether in the wrong or in the right, they always paid the bill, and it was generally heavy.

Curiously enough, Parsons, of "The Alarm," showed himself in his true colours at this time. The wrecking of the drug store turned a fierce, unfriendly light upon the reporters. Again and again men with notebooks were attacked by strikers or passing workmen. On several occasions Parsons intervened and saved the unfortunates from the violence of their enemies. As I have said before, Parsons was by nature and upbringing a moderate reformer, and was neither a rebel nor a revolutionary. He had a gift of speech, but not of thought.

The winter had been long and bitter. For weeks together the thermometer registered from ten to forty degrees below zero, and Chicago is exposed to every wind that blows. Great frozen lakes surround it to the north, and gales sweep the town, tornadoes of fearful violence, blizzards raking the streets with icy teeth. Not a place to be out of work in during the winter. And all through the winter strikes were of weekly occurrence. This firm or that trying to squeeze down their employees or to weed out the worse ones, brought about lockouts or bitter strikes, and at once the police patrols went galloping to the threatened point, and used their bludgeons on the unarmed and hungry strikers. But the police were too few for this additional work; they were unwisely directed, too, overdriven and harassed to exasperation. All the elements here piled ready for the final conflagration.

As the winter broke into spring, Spies and Parsons revived the agitation for eight hours' work, and set about organizing a great demonstration for the first of May. This exasperated the American population, and encouraged the foreigners. At this moment, as the destinies would have it, the small strikes were swallowed up in a great strike.

The factory of the famous McCormick harvester and reaper works was situated on the far west side of the city. Close by to the east were the teeming foreign quarters of Germans, Poles, and Bohemians. Nine out of ten of the McCormick workmen were foreigners, and were engaged in simple hand-work which anyone could do. The McCormick managers attempted therefore to fill the places of the strikers at once, for summer with its renewed demand was coming on; this caused riot after riot. The strikers picketed the streets, tried to prevent the new men from going to work, sometimes, it is said, used force. Immediately the police were called for and intervened vigorously. Women and children attacked the patrol wagons and threw stones at the police. Men, women, and even children, were savagely clubbed in return. Meetings were held nightly on every corner throughout the district to express sympathy with the strikers. The police broke up these meetings in a sort of frenzy of rage. Again and again perfectly orderly and unobjectionable gatherings were dispersed with the bludgeon. The guardians of law and order used violence on every possible occasion, even when it was clearly unnecessary, and this exasperated the foreign workmen.

The first of May dawned. All day long

the police scurried from point to point breaking up this meeting with threats, and dispersing that with force, plainly showing themselves everywhere masters of the situation. The American newspapers had talked so loudly of what the strikers were going to do, that when the first of May passed without any dangerous revolutionary attempt, nine out of ten American citizens were ready to believe that they had been mistaken, that the whole thing had been exaggerated by their newspapers, which was, indeed, the bare truth. Every one hoped now that the excitement would subside, that the angry passions would gradually settle down, and that quiet and order would once more be established. But in spite of temporary setbacks everything was hurrying to a dreadful climax.

On one side of the McCormick works at this time was a large, open field; in and about this field the strikers gathered daily in crowds. It was the second of May, I think, that the "Arbeiter Zeitung" called a meeting on this field for the afternoon of the third. There was a railroad switch on the field, and on it an empty freight car. From the roof of this car Spies opened the meeting with an enthusiastic, fiery speech. The men who listened to him were strikers, two or three thousand in number. As soon as he had finished his speech this mob, armed with sticks and stones, started for the works to attack the new men taken on in their places, the "strike-breakers," as they called them. These men hid themselves in the tower of the main building: the strikers searched about for them everywhere in vain, breaking the windows, meanwhile, with showers of stones. In the midst of this riot half a dozen police wagons came charging up. They were received with stones, thrown principally by women. The police at once drew their revolvers and began to fire at the crowd. The majority of the mob broke and fled. A few of the strikers made a stand, and were clubbed and shot down. Forty or fifty people were wounded, seven or eight killed outright by the police bullets.

This dreadful deed aroused the worst passions of both parties. The American newspapers upheld the police, applauded their action, and encouraged them to continue to enforce the law and maintain peace and order. On the other hand, those of us who were in any sympathy with the strikers condemned the police as guilty of monstrous and causeless murder.

The leaders of the strikers called meetings for the next evening, the fourth, to denounce the police for shooting unarmed men. Of these the most important was called by Spies and Parsons, and was to be held in Desplaines Street, a shabby street soon to be made memorable for ever.

I had been with the strikers in the attack upon the McCormick works. Lingg came late upon the scene; but he it was who tried to make a stand against the police when they fired on the crowd. After the riot was over, I helped him to carry away one of the wounded women. She was only a girl, eighteen or nineteen years of age, and was shot through the body. When I saw Lingg lifting her I ran to his aid. The poor girl tried to thank us. She was plainly dying; indeed, she died just after we reached the hospital with her. I never saw Lingg so wrought up before; yet he was quite calm, and spoke even more slowly than his wont; but his eyes were glowering, and when the doctor dropped her wrist with a careless "She's dead," I thought Lingg was going to fly at him. I was glad to get him away and into the streets again. There I had to leave him, because I had to go home and write my daily article. I found that even Engel had been at the riot, and had come back beside himself with indignation. Poor, gentle, kindly Engel was absolutely maddened by the brutality of the police.

"They dare to shoot women!" he cried.

"The brutes!" I could only clench my teeth.

As soon as I had finished my work I made my way to Lingg's rooms. He lived a good way from me, a couple of miles, and the walk in the beautiful summer-like air did something to quiet my nerves. On the way I bought an evening paper; I found in it a travesty of the facts, a tissue of lies from beginning to end, and a brutal tone.

When I knocked at Lingg's door I did not know what to expect; but as soon as I entered I was conscious of a new atmosphere. The reading-lamp with its green shade stood lighted upon the table. Lingg sat beside it, half in the light, half in the shade. Ida had been sitting on the other side, completely in the dark. As she opened the door I saw she had been crying.

Lingg said nothing when I came into the room, and at first I, too, had nothing to say. At last I managed to ask him lamely—

"What did you think of it, Lingg? Terrible, wasn't it?"

He looked at me for a moment.

"It's the parting of the ways."

"What do you mean?" I asked.

"Either the police must be allowed to do whatever they please, or we must strike back. Submission or revolt."

"What do you intend to do?" I asked.

"Revolt," he replied on the instant.

"Then count me in, too," I cried, the wild indignation in me flaming.

"Better think it over," he warned me.

"There's no need to think," I returned; "I have done all the thinking necessary."

He looked at me with the kindly searching eyes.

"I wish we could get at the master-robbers," he said, half to himself. "It seems absurd to strike the hands and let the directing brains go free; but the police-wrong is the more manifest, and we have no time to pick and choose."

"It's the police I'm down on," I cried hotly; "the brutes!"

"What about the meeting to-morrow?" Lingg asked. "Will they try to disperse that —I mean the meeting in the Haymarket?"

The first time I heard the word was then from Lingg's lips. Knowing the place better than he did, I began to explain that it was not in the Haymarket, but a hundred yards away, in Desplaines Street. He nodded his head; yet in some way or other he had found at once the name that shall in all future time be given to the place.

The next thing discussed was the amount of money I had. Lingg had made up his mind that I was to escape and hide in Europe; he was glad to find that I had nearly a thousand dollars put by. I had been saving for my marriage. He promised to call next morning. I was not to make up my mind then, or think of what I should do; the strain of long thinking on one subject was exhausting, he said, and proceeded to show his wonderful self-control by putting the whole of the occurrences out of his head.

He talked a little about himself, laughingly. "When it comes to my turn," he said, "and they catch me, they will give me an awful character. They'll say I am a rebel and anarchist because I'm illegitimate; but that's not true. I had the best mother in the world. I was always perfectly content with my birth. Of course I despised the wretched creature who seduced my mother and then abandoned her; but such animals are not rare among the German aristocracy. No, I grew bitter when I came to understand the conditions of a workman's life. Yet it was always pretty easy for me to get a living,' he added.

His talk that evening was curiously impersonal, for the most part, and so to speak, detached. Some phrases of it, however, were illuminating.

"The writer," he said, "tries to find a characteristic word; the painter some scene that will enable him to express himself. I always wanted a characteristic deed, something that no one else would do, or could do. One should be strong enough to bend and constrain deeds to one's service, and they are more stubborn than words, more recalcitrant than bronze. . . ."

His forecast of what would happen was astonishingly correct, though now for the first time he began to speak passionately, and his phrases stand out in my memory as if blazoned with fire.

"If a bomb is thrown the police will arrest hundreds; they will accuse a dozen innocent men, and more. I want to go into their court-room, the court-room of this robber society, and when the venal judge gives sentence, I mean to stand up and say, 'You have pronounced sentence on yourself, damn you!' and with my own hand execute my verdict.

"I have had enough," he said, speaking with indescribable intensity, "of the whole damned hypocritical society, where the greedy thieves are exalted, and those that steal and plunder and murder, judge and punish their betters. . . .

"Besides," he went on, "in my soul I'm glad to make an end; I never did mean to die in my bed, to stand upon the stage of life talking or acting and suddenly to be pulled off backward by the hair, so to speak, and thrown on the dust-heap. By God," and the deep voice was appalling in its passion, "I will pull down the curtain with my own hands, and shut off the lights when I please. I'll be my own judge and executioner. It is something to die like a man and not like a sheep. . . ."

What more was there to be said? I was merely drinking in draughts of courage from Lingg's spirit. When I went out of the room I was treading on air, filled with his desperate resolution. I, too, would pull down the curtain with my own hands, and shut off the lights. So astonishing was the man's influence, so intense the virtue that came out of him, so absorbing the passion, that I went striding through the streets wildly, without a moment's misgiving, and, finding Engel was out, went straight to bed and slept like a log.

True, I woke up next day gasping with fear, as if some one had been seated on my heart, preventing it from beating; but as soon as I came to myself and thought of Lingg the discomfort passed, and I got up and dressed. While I was having my breakfast about eight o'clock, with Engel, Lingg came in, the steady eyes shining. We had a little talk, and went out together. He accompanied me to the bank, where I drew out my money. Afterwards we went, according to his advice, to three different changers, and changed it for gold, and then he took me away to dinner with Ida.

Ida was very white and very still; we dined together in a room all by ourselves. Somehow or other this comparative solitude, or the enforced companionship with Lingg and Ida, who talked in monosyllables about different things, began to weigh upon me. At the end of dinner I said—

"Look, Lingg, I want to be by myself. I'm going back to the house."

His eyes searched me.

"Don't think you have gone too far to retreat," he said quietly. "If you feel you would rather not do it, don't mind saying so a bit, Rudolph. You have a happy life before you, and you are a dear, good fellow; I don't want to drag you into the maelstrom."

"No, no!" I cried, catching fire again from his immutable purpose. "I am going on, but I must be alone for a little while first; I must think and and make final arrangements, that's all."

"I quite see," he said. "Do you wish me to come for you to-night, or would you rather put it off?"

"Come for me," I said, "at eight," and I held out my hands. He took both my hands in his, and involuntarily I bent forward, and we kissed, for the first time, kissed as comrades and lovers. As I passed out of the restaurant I was consecrate, giddily exalted. I went to my rooms filled with intense resolution. I packed a grip with just my best things, a suit of clothes, a flannel shirt or two, a dozen collars—bare necessaries—and then lay down on the bed to face my own soul. But the exaltation of Lingg's love still held me.

"So this is the end of your high ambitions," I said to myself; "the boundary and limit of all your hopes and fears, the goal of life for you?"

"Yes," my deeper self answered with strong resolve, "this is the meaning of the struggle, and my part in it is clear. I know what the weak suffer; I know how the poor are tortured; I know the forces against them, yet I stand for the weak, and for justice and right to the end—and beyond." There was thrilling exultation in me; but no fear, no doubt.

After sitting a while by myself, I heard a little noise down below in the shop, then footsteps on the stairs, and a timid knocking at the door.

"Come in," I said; and to my astonishment Elsie came in. I could not have been more surprised if the Governor of the State had entered.

"Why, Elsie," I cried, "what are you doing here?"

"You don't answer my letters," she said, "and you did not come yesterday to see me, though it was our day, so I came to find you, sir. Are you cross with me?"

"No, indeed," I said, putting a chair for her. "Won't you take off your things?"

"I will stay a little while if I may," she said, "though it seems strange and not quite right to be here; but I must have a talk with you." She went over to the glass, took off her hat, smoothed her hair, laid aside her little jacket, and came back for the talk; and the talk, if you consider it, was curious enough.

The majority of men believe, or profess to believe, that women are insidious, sly, deceptive, or else crack-brained creatures who prefer crooked paths to straight, and would rather miss their ends by cunning than compass them by honesty. I have known only this one woman intimately, but I found her absolutely frank and simple, obeying every impulse of her feelings, like a child, or rather as she had only one dominant passion, giving, herself to that with inconsiderate abandonment, as a ship obeys her helm.

Elsie drew up a chair, sat down beside me, and began—

"I hardly know how to say it, Boy; but I

must; ain't you too much with Ida Miller?" (This direct approach was simply to surprise me; but my genuine look of astonishment checked her.) "Oh, I don't mean that you are in love with her *yet*; but she has a great influence over you, hasn't she?" and she fixed me with narrowing eyes.

I could only shake my head and repeat—

"'In love with Ida'; however did you get that into your head? Why, she's devoted to Lingg, and I never thought of her except as a friend. Your little roof must have a slate off," and I tapped her on the forehead, laughing.

"No, no; I'm sane enough," she went on impatiently; "but if it isn't Ida, who is it?"

"It's Elsie," I replied gravely.

"Don't make fun of me," she said, dimpling. "What has changed you? You know, it makes me angry to think of it. Just as I have yielded to you, you seem to have drawn into yourself and grown colder and colder. It makes me mad to think I should have given myself, and not be wanted."

The pity of it! I gathered her into my arms at once, crying—

"Elsie, Elsie, of course you're wanted just as much as ever; more than ever—much more. I cannot touch you without thrilling. If I restrain myself, it is for your sake, dear."

She looked at me through her tears, one question in her eyes.

"How can that be, Boy? You didn't restrain yourself before; nothing would stop you!"

"You have grown dearer to me, more precious," I cried. "Your frankness has been extraordinary. At first I just loved you; now I admire you and honour you beyond every one. You are such a great little personality. You have made all other women clear to me, I think, and I honour them all for your sake."

"Who has taught you to pay all these compliments?" she asked, with her head on one side, smiling.

"Elsie," I said, "and my love for her. All roads lead to Rome; all words bring me just to that one word, 'Elsie,'" and after kissing her I put her back on her seat again.

"There, you see!" she cried; "you used to hold me in your arms for hours and hours; you were never tired of kissing and caressing me; and now, as soon as possible you put me away from you!" and her eyes filled with tears.

"Because I am flesh and blood," I returned, "and do not want to yield to the desire that is driving me crazy."

"But suppose I let you yield to it," she

replied, looking down. "As you say you have changed, suppose I have changed, too; if you asked me now to marry you, I should say 'yes' instead of 'no'? Doesn't that alter everything?" And she looked up at me with the clear eyes alight, and a little hot flush in her cheeks.

I caught at any straw. I saw that if she pressed me much more I should be sure to confess that I had changed for some reason, and in this way might put her on the track.

"If we are going to be married," I said, "it would of course be different; but one would be a poor fool, then, not to wait, wouldn't one?"

Her eyes searched me again, and she shook her head slowly, as if unconvinced or suspicious.

"I suppose so," she said at length; "but it doesn't matter so much, does it?"

I was forced to admit that, so I said, "No, you sweet," and put my arms round her and kissed her lips, and felt her whole supple body thrilling, yielding to my embrace.

How I controlled myself and dragged myself away, I don't know; but I did, though the conflict was hot enough to rob me for some minutes of any power even of thinking. As in a dream I heard her telling me that she thought much more of me for my self-control, that she would have a man too strong to yield to anything, unless his reason told him it was right. And so she went on praising me until I closed her sweet lips with kisses.

"Oh," she said, after a while, looking into my eyes; "at least you have taught me what love is, Boy, and I want your love to be boundless, like mine, to stifle all considerations, and hesitations. I am willing to yield to you, Boy, my boy, now. . . ."

And she held my forehead in her tiny hands and looked bravely at me with the great shining eyes.

"You men think we women have no curiosity, no desire. It is not the same desire as yours, dear; but it is stronger, I think. Yielding means more to us than to you, and therefore we are a little more cautious than you, more prudent; but not much more, considering all things. . . .

"You tempt us with desire, with the pleasure you give, and we can resist; but tempt us with tenderness, or self-sacrifice, ask us to do it for you, and we melt at once. We women love to give delight to those we love. We are born with breasts, Boy, to give. Ask us to enjoy, and we can refuse; ask us to give joy, and we yield at once. . . .

"That is why the tempting of men is so ignoble. Oh, of course, not in your case;

you'd marry me, I know. It is different; but still the woman's is the nobler part. You ask for yourselves, and we yield for your sakes. It is more blessed to give than to receive. But you, Boy, don't accept the gift, and I don't know whether to be proud of you or angry with you. What silly things we women are!"

Elsie always startled me. There was such insight in her, such understanding. As regards love, at least, she knew more than any man. I began to wonder whether I was right in concealing anything from her. A moment's thought convinced me that I had been wrong; I ought to have told her everything; but it was too late now, far too late. I felt that she would be against me, against Lingg, passionately, terribly. I could not make a long fight with her this last afternoon; it was impossible, and besides, my secret was not mine alone; my only hope was to remain on the surface, not to get to deep, self-revealing levels; so I began to talk of our marriage.

"Where can we live, Elsie? Won't your mother be afraid, and are you quite sure you will never regret, you delight?"

"I don't think a woman ever regrets what she does for love's sake," she said; "at any rate, I'm sure she never regrets so long as she is loved. It is only when *his* love dies that *she* regrets."

"I am a little afraid," I broke off, "that my attitude to these strikes will do me harm on the American papers; it has already damaged me. Wilson says he finds socialism now even in my account of a fire; and yet I try to stick to the bare facts."

"I hate that old socialism anyway!" cried Elsie, "and the frowsy meetings. Why should you bother about the poor? They wouldn't do anything for you, and even if they knew what you were doing for them they would not be grateful to you. Besides, they're no good anyway. Why should you spoil your future for a set of common men who are nothing to you at all?"

I shook my head. "We don't do things always for the rewards, Elsie, but because we must. . . ."

"It is just silly," she said. "I wonder is it Lingg who influences you? He's quite mad. You can see madness in those burning eyes of his. When he looks at me, I get cold. He frightens me, and not a nice sort of fright, either. He scares me half to death. Oh, I wish you'd leave him and Ida to get on as they please, and never see either of them again. I am sure you would be a great deal better, and a great deal sweeter, and I know I'd just love you for it. Come! Won't you?—for my sake?" and she knelt down at my feet, and threw herself against my knees, and put up her hands and drew my head down. What a temptress she was, and what a face! I could not help taking her in my arms; I lifted her up, held her close to me, body to body. Dear God! Was I to have nothing? The next moment the other thought, the awful one came, of what I had promised to do.

I got angry, and putting her from me, rose. At once she stood opposite me.

"What is it?" she asked sharply. "I know there is something. What is it? Tell me, tell me, at once," all the old imperiousness in tone and manner. Love may soften; but it does not really change us.

I sat down on the sofa and shook my head. "There is nothing, dear; but that I love you terribly, and must not yield to it."

"Silly boy," she said, coming over and seating herself beside me, and putting her arm round my neck. "You silly boy. You shall do whatever you want to, and you shall not be annoyed by anyone." And she threw herself down on the couch. As I turned to her she said, "I will just kiss you, little bird-kisses." (When we first knew each other I used to call her kisses bird-kisses, because she kissed me, I said, like a bird pecking a fruit.) But now she knew better, and her lips dwelt on mine.

What was I to do? Was ever a man in such a position, torn two ways? Every time she touched me I went mad; my mouth parched with desire; I trembled from head to foot, and yet I knew I must not let myself go. It would be dastardly.

"After all, why not?" I asked myself. "Why not? Why not?" My blood raced in my veins, so that I was incapable of reason.

I put my hands on her, and she smiled in my eyes that divine smile of passionate abandonment. As I touched the round limbs and felt the warm flesh, her hands slid round my neck, and drew down my lips to hers. While she thrilled under my touch and her lips clung to mine, I was suddenly broken with love and admiration. I could not accept the sacrifice; I dared not leave that exquisite child with the risk and suffering; I could not. But I would kiss and caress her to the limit of my resolve, and I did. . . .

At length I felt my purpose melting.

"Oh, Elsie," I groaned, "help me, help me. It's not fair, and I must be fair to you."

She got up at once, and shook her skirts straight, with the old proud gesture that I knew so well.

"Your wish shall be done," she said: "but

there is something I do not understand, which makes my heart ache. Can't you tell me, Boy?" and she looked right into my eyes.

"There is nothing to tell," I said, "sweet mine."

She shook her head contemptuously.

"I swear, Elsie, that if I restrain myself it is simply for your sake. You must believe me, heart's delight! you must."

"I will try to," she said. "Good-bye, Boy."

"Are you going?" I cried in wildest despair, stretching my hands out to her. "Good God! Good God! I can't let you go!" and my heart choked me.

Was I never to see her again? to lose that bewitching sweet face? Never to hold the exquisite figure in my arms again, never to hear her voice in my ears; never again? The tears gushed from my eyes.

"There," she cried, putting her arms about me, "that is the first time you have been absolutely yourself since I have been in the room. That look and cry convince me that you still love me, and I'm glad, heart-glad."

"How could you ever doubt it!" I cried.

She shook her head. "Oh, Boy; I'm convinced now; but what has altered you—what is it? I cannot understand. There is something."

"You will understand one day, sweetheart,"

I said, trying to smile. "You will understand that I love you with my whole heart, that I have never loved any other woman, that I shall never love another"; and we were in each other's arms again, and our faces were wet with our tears.

"Now I am going," she said, dashing the tears from her eyes, "going at once. Good-bye, Boy." At the door she turned and came back quickly, took my hands and kissed them one by one, and then put them against her little firm breasts.

"I love you, Boy, with all my heart, my boy!" and she was gone.

I dropped into the chair, unable to restrain myself. The waters of bitterness seemed to go over my head. Nothing mattered now; nothing could ever matter after this, nothing. The pain was too bitter. I dared not think of her, my lost love. . . .

I felt I must not give way like that; I must be a man and pull myself together; but how? There was one infallible means. I called back to memory the image of the man shot on the vacant lot, and gasping out his blood as he cried to his wife and children. I reminded myself of the poor girl we took to the hospital, the sweet face of her growing greyer and greyer. I thought of the man blinded by the explosion, and his pathetic stumblings;

the horrible, maimed creature proud of his phosphorous poisoning; the great Swiss giant, writhing about like a wounded worm; and my tears dried of themselves, with indignation and rage, and I was ready. With one big sigh for all that was Elsie stifled in my throat, I set my face towards reality, and as I pulled myself up out of the chair with the hot blood running through me I heard eight o'clock strike, and a moment later those swift, steady steps on the street outside, Lingg's steps. I took a deep breath. Thank God! I was ready!

Chapter IX

AS Lingg came into the room and our hands met and he looked into my eyes with that steady light in his, I was glad, jubilant that I was ready. With a great thrill I felt for the first time that I could meet him as an equal. Death has this strange power over men, that when you are willing to walk within his shadow you feel yourself the equal of anything that lives.

"I see," said Lingg quietly, "you've made up your mind. I was hoping you had changed."

"I have packed, and am ready," I remarked, as equal to equal now. He went past me to the window, and stood looking out for a minute or so. I went over to him; he turned, and our eyes met.

"I often wonder, Rudolph," he said, putting his hand on my shoulder, "whether this world of ours will be a success or a failure. . . . After all, it's quite possible that man will never realize the best in him. There must have been countless failures before in other worlds; why should this mud-ball of ours bring it to a consummation?" And then the return. "Yet why not? It's always young, the old world, and breeding youth; always trying! Why should we fail? In any case, the attempt is something—something, too, the motive!" And his eyes lit up; I smiled. His intimate kindness to me, the comradeship even in his doubts gave the supreme touch to my resolution.

"Have you the bomb?"

"Here it is," he said, and took it out of his right-hand pocket. He always wore short coats, generally double-breasted, with large pockets. The bomb was not larger than an orange; but it was ten times the size of the bullet that he had tried on the lake, and I knew its power must be enormous. On one side of it there hung out a little piece of tape-like stuff.

"What's that?" I asked, pointing to it.

"This bomb has a double action," he said; "if you pull that tape it will set fire to something inside; the explosion will then take place in a third of a minute, exactly twenty seconds, so that you should pull it first, then wait five or ten seconds, and then throw the bomb; but it will also explode on impact, so be careful of it."

"What's it made of?" I asked, taking it in my hand. It was surprisingly heavy.

"Leaden piping on the outside," he replied; "lead is so easy to work. The composition inside is a discovery of mine—a chance find."

"I'll put it in my trousers' pocket," I said, "because there nothing can hit it, and it will be held tightly, so that I can pull the tape when I like. I suppose it won't burn outwardly?"

He shook his head.

"You may see the spark when you throw it; but there will be nothing to burn your clothes, if that's what you mean."

There was a feverish haste on me. I was impatient to have done with the work, to get it over.

"Hadn't we better go to the meeting now?" I asked.

Lingg was as quiet as ever, and spoke just as slowly as usual.

"If you will," he said; "it is a mile to the Haymarket, and the meeting is called for nine o'clock; they won't begin till eight or ten minutes past, and even if the police break up the meeting they won't do it before nine-thirty or a quarter to ten. We have lots of time. . . . Before we go, Rudolph, I want you to promise me one thing. I want you to escape; it is part of our plan for spreading terror that the thrower of the first bomb should go scot-free. Nothing spreads terror like sequence and success. I want you to promise that whatever happens you will keep away, and not give yourself up."

"I promise," I replied hastily. "Shall I throw it in any case?" I asked, feverishly passing my tongue over my dried lips, and longing, I suppose, for even the chance of a respite.

"If the police do not interfere," he said, "we are too glad to keep quiet; but if they come to break up a quiet meeting, if they draw their clubs and begin to bludgeon, I should throw it; and if you can remember as you throw it, throw yourself down on your hands and knees, too; the shock will be tremendous."

"Shall we go, then?" I asked, and turned to look for the grip; but Lingg had picked it up. Of a sudden he put it down again and put his hand on my shoulder; his eyes on mine were full of kindness.

"There's time, Rudolph," he said, "even now, to turn back. I cannot bear to think of your being in it. Leave it to me. Trust me; it will be better."

With that strange feeling of equality still thrilling in me, I exclaimed, "No, no; you mistake me. I am more than willing; all those injured and murdered people are calling to me. Don't let's talk, man. My mind is made up. From head to foot I am one purpose."

He threw back his head, then picked up

my grip, and we left the room. As we passed through the little shop, the boy told us that Engel had gone to the meeting half an hour before, and we set off at a good round pace. So wrought up was I, so excited, I had not noticed that the beautiful day was all overcast, that a thunder-storm was clouding up, till Lingg drew my attention to it.

A minute afterwards, as it seems to me now, we had reached our goal; we were in Desplaines Street, between Lake Street and Randolph Street. Desplaines Street is a mean thoroughfare on the west side, three or four hundred yards from the river, and fully half a mile from the edge of the business centre downtown. The Haymarket, as the place was afterwards called, is nearly a hundred yards away. As we came up from the south we passed the Desplaines Street police station, presided over by Inspector Bonfield; there was already a crowd of police at the door.

"They mean business," said Lingg, "to-night, and so do we."

When we got to the outskirts of the meeting we saw the mayor of the city, with one or two officials; the mayor was an elderly man called Carter Harrison. He had been asked to prohibit the meeting, but was unwilling to interfere with what might be a lawful assembly;

he attended in person to prevent any incitement to rioting.

The speakers' stand was a mere truck-wagon, placed where a blind alley intersected the street, in the centre of the block. We were at the rear of the building occupied by the Crane Brothers' great elevator factory. I should think two or three thousand people were already gathered together.

Spies had finished speaking as we came up. He was followed by Parsons, who rose to the height of the argument if ever a man did. He began by asking the crowd to be quite orderly; he assured them that if they kept order, and simply gave expression to their grievances, the American people would hear them with sympathy, and would see that they had fair play. He really believed this claptrap. He went on to say that their grievances were terrible; unarmed men, women, and children had been shot down. Why were they shot? he asked, and then began his reform speech.

The mayor listened to everything, and evidently saw nothing in the utterances to object to. "Parsons's speech," he said afterwards, "was a good political speech." After Parsons had made an end, the Englishman, Samuel Fielden, with his bushy beard, stood up and began to prose. Some rain-drops fell, a lull came in the rising wind; darkness began to overshadow us. Evidently the storm was at hand.

The crowd began to drift away at the edges. I was alone and curiously watchful. I saw the mayor and the officials move off towards the business part of the town. It looked for a few minutes as if everything was going to pass over in peace; but I was not relieved. I could hear my own heart beating, and suddenly I felt something in the air; it was sentient with expectancy. I slowly turned my head. I was on the very outskirts of the crowd, and as I turned I saw that Bonfield had marched out his police, and was minded to take his own way with the meeting now the mayor had left. I felt personal antagonism stiffen my muscles. It grew darker and darker every moment. Suddenly there came a flash, and then a peal of thunder. At the end of the flash, as it seemed to me, I saw the white clubs falling, saw the police striking down the men running along the side-walk. At once my mind was made up. I put my left hand on the outside of my trousers to hold the bomb tight, and my right hand into the pocket, and drew the tape. I heard a little rasp. I began to count slowly, "One, two, three, four, five, six, seven"; as I got to seven the police were quite close to me, bludgeoning every one furiously. Two or three of the foremost had drawn their revolvers. The crowd were flying in all directions. Suddenly there was a shot, and then a dozen shots, all, it seemed to me, fired by the police. Rage blazed in me. I took the bomb out of my pocket, careless whether I was seen or not, and looked for the right place to throw it; then I hurled it over my shoulder high in the air, towards the middle of the police, and at the same moment I stumbled forward, just as if I had fallen, throwing myself on my hands and face, for I had seen the spark. It seemed as if I had been on my hands for an eternity, when I was crushed to the ground, and my ears split with the roar. I scrambled to my feet again, gasping. Men were thrown down in front of me, and were getting up on their hands. I heard groans and cries, and shrieks behind me. I turned round; as I turned a strong arm was thrust through mine, and I heard Lingg say—

"Come, Rudolph, this way"; and he drew me to the side-walk, and we walked past where the police had been.

"Don't look," he whispered suddenly; "don't look."

But before he spoke I had looked, and what I saw will be before my eyes till I die. The street was one shambles; in the very centre of it a great pit yawned, and round it men lying, or pieces of men, in every direction, and close to me, near the side-walk as I passed, a leg and foot torn off, and near by two huge pieces of bleeding red meat, skewered together with a thigh-bone. My soul sickened; my senses left me; but Lingg held me up with superhuman strength, and drew me along.

"Hold yourself up, Rudolph," he whispered; "come on, man," and the next moment we had passed it all, and I clung to him, trembling like a leaf. When we got to the end of the block I realized that I was wet through from head to foot, as if I had been plunged in cold water.

"I must stop," I gasped. "I cannot walk, Lingg."

"Nonsense," he said; "take a drink of this," and he thrust a flask of brandy into my hand. The brandy I poured down my throat set my heart beating again, allowed me to breathe, and I walked on with him.

"How you are shaking," he said. "Strange, you neurotic people; you do everything perfectly, splendidly, and then break down like women. Come, I am not going to leave you; but for God's sake throw off that shaken, white look. Drink some more."

I tried to; but the flask was empty. He put it back in his pocket.

"Here is the bottle," he said. "I have brought enough; but we must get to the depôt."

We saw fire-engines with police on them, galloping like madmen in the direction whence we had come. The streets were crowded with people, talking, gesticulating, like actors. Every one seemed to know of the bomb already, and to be talking about it. I noticed that even here, half a mile away, the pavement was covered with pieces of glass; all the windows had been broken by the explosion.

As we came in front of the depôt, just before we passed into the full glare of the arc-lamps, Lingg said—

"Let me look at you," and as he let go my arm, I almost fell; my legs were like German sausages; they felt as if they had no bones in them, and would bend in any direction; in spite of every effort they would shake.

"Come, Rudolph," he said, "we'll stop and talk; but you must come to yourself. Take another drink, and think of nothing. I will save you; you are too good to lose. Come, dear friend, don't let them crow over us."

My heart seemed to be in my mouth, but I swallowed it down. I took another swig of brandy, and then a long drink of it. It might have been water for all I tasted; but it seemed to do me some little good. In a minute or so I had got hold of myself.

"I'm all right," I said; "what is there to do now?"

"Simply to go through the depôt," he said, "as if there were nothing the matter, and take the train."

I pulled myself together, and we entered the depôt; but when we came in sight of the barrier shutting off the train for New York, we saw that some news must have got through, for already there were two policemen standing beside the usual ticket-collectors. Lingg, with his hawk's eyes, saw them first, a hundred yards away.

"You'll have to speak, Rudolph," he said. "If you're not able to, we'll go back and take the train outside Chicago. Your name is Willie Roberts; but you will have to speak for us both, because your accent is so much better than mine. Can you?" (I nodded.) "Now, your very best," he said, as we reached the barrier.

The next moment, "Where for?" called out the official.

"New York," I answered, and stopped in front of him, while Lingg produced my ticket.

"Your name?" he said.

"On the ticket," I replied, yawning, "Willie Roberts."

"Thought you were one of those Dutchmen," he said, laughing. "There has been an explosion, or something, on the East Side, hasn't there?"

"I don't know," I returned; "but there'll be no peace, I guess, till we've had a good scrap."

"That's so," he said, and we all laughed.

The next moment he had checked my ticket, and handed the long strip back to me. I said—

"My friend is just coming with me; he'll be back in a minute."

Lingg bowed to him, smiling, and took my arm as we went on.

"Splendid," he said; "nobody could have done it better. They are without a trace of suspicion, and it is rather well for them that they did not suspect."

"Why?" I asked.

He looked at me with a quizzical smile on his face.

"Because," he said, "I have another bomb in my pocket, and they should not have taken either of us alive."

I don't know why, but the mere mention of another bomb set me trembling again. Again I could hear the infernal roar; I shivered from head to foot, and my heart stopped.

How I got into the train I don't know.

Lingg must have almost lifted me in; but when I came to myself I was in a first-class carriage, in the corner. Lingg had put my grip in front of me on the seat, and was sitting beside me. Suddenly I felt deadly sick; I told him so. He took me out to the cabinet, and I was sick as I have never been sick in my life, throwing up again and again and again, feeling the while wretchedly weak and ill, as if every atom of strength had been sucked out of me. He gave me a drink of cold water, and then some water with a dash of brandy in it, and threw open the window, and soon I felt a little better.

"I cannot sit up, Lingg. I'm sure to give myself away. I'm so weak and ill; I don't know how or why," and all broken up I began to cry weakly.

"That's all right, Rudolph," said Lingg gently. "I will sit with you till you're better. Can you be alone for five minutes while I send a telegram?"

"Yes," I replied; "but I wish you wouldn't go."

"All right," he said in the cheeriest tone. "I will sit with you and write the telegram; but if you show yourself ill, people will remark you. Pull your soft hat down over your forehead, and we'll go back to your seat; I'll write the telegram there, and remember, I'm going to sit with you till you are all right. All I ask you to do is to speak when need is, because my wretched accent will give us away as Germans. Say you've had too much to drink."

A few minutes afterwards the train started. I told the conductor as he passed that my friend was coming to the next station with me, and gave him a dollar bill. I said we wanted to talk; we had not met for a long time; I was just passing through Chicago, and we had had a drink together.

I noticed that Lingg had opened the window on my side; the fresh air and the rain were beating on my head and face. In a few minutes I began to feel better, and strange to say, almost as soon as I began to get better I became conscious of being inordinately hungry.

"I am famished," I said to Lingg. "Shivering with cold and famished; but I'm all right."

"I'll get you a basin of soup," he said, "at the next station. I'm glad you're all right. Thank God, the colour is coming back to your cheeks; we've had luck."

"I'm ashamed," I said, "breaking down like this, and putting you in danger."

"Nonsense," he returned. "Don't think that. You're the more to be honoured for having done what you did, in spite of the body's weakness."

I felt better after that.

All this time there were only a couple of women in the car, and they were at the other end of it; they did not like the open window, I suppose.

In twenty minutes we stopped, and Lingg got out and got me a basin of soup; as soon as I had taken it, I felt stronger. I realized then that I had a terrible, racking headache, and was very weary.

"Go to sleep," said Lingg, when I told him, and he shut the window, and settled the grip in front of me so that I could put my feet on it. "Go to sleep; I will sit by you," and in a moment, as it seemed to me, I was asleep. When I woke, two or three hours afterwards, the train was stopping again. We had just reached ——

"Do you feel better?" Lingg asked. "I ought to get out here, if you can go on alone; or shall I stay the night with you?"

"I am quite well, now," I replied bravely.

"Well," he said, "you will reach New York in thirty hours, and you sail the next morning; your berth is taken on the Cunarder, 'Scotia,' second cabin, still under the name of Will Roberts; don't miss her, and get off at Liverpool. Ida will communicate with you at the post office in Liverpool and Cardiff, and Will Roberts can write to her to Altona, under the name of Jane Teller. Do you understand? Here in this book everything's put down, together with a code which I have made out for you; the book to which the code refers is here, too. Nobody on earth can read that script; but if I were you I should write nothing for some months, not for many months if things go badly; but you will be the best judge of that. Remember, prudence is always best in case you are in doubt, and remember, too, I have your promise to escape; you must not be caught; you will remember?"

I nodded. "We did right, didn't we?" I asked weakly.

"Sure, Rudolph," he answered. "Sure. Have no doubt. I am going to tread the same path, you can bet on that." His eyes were shining like a god's.

"I have no doubt of you," I said; "but I begin to doubt whether the path is the right one."

"That's because you are shaken and ill," he replied gravely. "If you were well, you would not doubt. Think of what they did; the girl they shot, and the little boy! And now good-bye, dear friend, good-bye!" Once again, and for the last time, we kissed.

The next moment he had left the train, and I was alone. I could not be alone! I sprang up and hurried to the door to call him; the deadly cold came back on me, but I pulled myself together. After all, to call him back would endanger him and Ida! I would not. I stood at the door and looked after him, saw him striding down the platform, the same swift, silent stride. I noticed the broad shoulders, the strong figure. I took a full breath and went back to my seat. It was half-past twelve o'clock. A new day, I said to myself. My God! a new day. . . .

In a few minutes the conductor came in and asked me if I would not like to sleep.

"I have made you up the second berth from here," he said, "number 10; your friend thought you had better not be disturbed before. Been ill, ain't you?"

I was passing through Chicago, I said, and we had had a big dinner, and I had taken too much to drink; I had not seen my friend for a long time.

"I guessed that was it," he replied. "I smelt the brandy. It isn't good to get out on the bust like that, unless you are accustomed to soak. I nearly killed myself a while back. I didn't drink very much, either, half a bottle of Bourbon, I guess; but I just got up and wanted to fight everybody. I was mad drunk; I'd have fought an elevated railroad, if it had come near me, I would."

The common talk brought me back to the common everyday life; did me infinite good.

"Sit down and have a drink," I said.

"No, no!" he replied, shaking his head. "No, I have sworn off, truth! I told the missis I never would agen, and I won't. . . . We've two children, two girls, one fair, and t'other dark. Ye never saw sich a pair of peaches! I ain't going to drink what ought to go to them, no sir. I only make a hundred dollars a month at this job; of course, now and then one gets a dollar from some one but they don't hand it out easy, the rich. . . .

"My wife's a daisy of a manager, but it costs us forty dollars a month to get along, and what with clothes, and rent, and taxes, we cannot save more than thirty dollars a month, no sir; and in twenty years that won't be a fortune, will it, not for two of 'em? The purtiest children ever you see. Here they are" (and as he spoke he took out his pocketbook and showed me the photographs). "There's Joon, and there's Jooly. We call 'em like that because they was born in those months. Ain't they cute!—What?"

Of course, I praised the children though he needed no encouragement.

"Their mother is a Kaintucky woman, I'm from about here myself—a hoosier. You're on the road, ain't you? In dry goods, I guess, from the grip?"

"Yes," I replied; "going back to New York. Come out again in a week."

"I thought so," he said; "I sized ye up right the first moment I seed ye."

The bell rang and he had to go off and attend to his duties; but not before I told him to call me about nine o'clock in the morning, and bring me coffee, as I felt real bad. He said he would, and I crawled into my bunk and tried to go to sleep. At first it seemed impossible; but I put my whole resolution to the matter. I must not think, I said to myself, I must sleep, and in order to sleep, as Lingg said, I must think of something else. But my brain seemed empty, and whenever I was alone there was the spark against the sky and I heard the roar, and saw that ghastly sight. Then I thought of Elsie, but that tore my heart. No; I would not think of the past . . . .

At last I found the way; I would think of the conductor's two children; the dark one, and the fair one. "The purtiest children in Buffalo," the one seven years old and the other five, and their mother, too, who was a daisy of a manager, and the father saving and working. The pretty "peaches." They seemed to be anything but pretty in the photographs; yet the father's praise made them beautiful to me—and I remembered no more.

The cheerful conductor woke me up in the morning with the coffee, and as he woke me, I started up and struck my head against the top berth, and fell back, shaking.

"Good God!" I cried; "how you startled me!"

"An over-night drunk on brandy is the damnedest thing the next morning. Got a bad mouth?"

"Awful," I said, "and bad nerves; I'm all ill, shaky."

"Don't I know it," he said. "You get up, and get into your clothes, and sit down here by the open window. It's just a beautiful day, warm and sweet; would bring the dead to life; and there's your cawfee, just as good cawfee as you kin git anywhere, and the milk in it'll do you good. If I were you I'd throw that brandy out of the window."

"Well," I said, "my friend told me to take a hair of the dog that bit me."

"Oh, pshaw!" he exclaimed, "there ain't no sense in that. A young man like you'll get better without anything."

"I think you're right," I said, which seemed to gratify him.

"Have you heard the noos?" he asked. I

shook my head; I was afraid my voice would shake.

"They've been throwing bombs in Chicago," he said. "Them damned foreigners have killed a hundred and sixty policemen in the Haymarket."

A hundred and sixty! I stared at him and Lingg's word again, "the Haymarket." A hundred and sixty!

"Good God!" I cried; "how awful!"

"That's right," he said. "The police have made two thousand arrests this morning. I guess they'll get the men that threw the bomb, and rope's cheap in Chicago. They'll make 'em all dance without a floor, damn them!"

"Well," I said, slipping out of my berth; "I don't feel much like dancing."

"Put on your boots," he said, "and come to the window here," and I did as I was told.

I had stood the first test, and already sleep had renewed me; the blessed oblivion had knit up the ravelled sleeve of my thoughts, and I was once more master of myself, without any fear now; but with an infinite regret. . .

I would not think of it, and in order not to think of it, I thought of Elsie; but that was too bitter to me. What would she think? What could she think? Would she try to see me? Would she guess? I feared she would. I dared not think of her.

As soon as I could I got the conductor again, and set him talking about his children. All I had to do was to put in a "Really?" or a "You don't say!" at the proper moment, and he would go off again at score, telling me his own history, and his wife's, and the whole story of the children—how he had saved Jooly in whooping cough by giving her a hot bath; how Joonie could walk before she was a year old; "yes, sir, she has the biggest legs you ever saw"—everything. I could write their family history now. . . .

But I was very sorry when he handed me over to the next conductor, a taciturn Yankee, who had hardly a word to say. I feared the small, grey, ferretty eyes of him, so I bought some books in the car, and set myself to read them; but I do not know what they were about. Still, they gave me an occupied look, and kept me from awkward questions. Dinner time came and passed, then tea time, and then time for sleep again, but I hardly dared to get into my berth. I felt sure that I should not sleep, and I was right. My headache grew acute; the chunketty-chunk of the train hammered on my nerves. I never closed my eyes; but I got peace by using Lingg's formula, and steadfastly thinking of unimportant things, and after I had done this a certain number of times I began to get confidence. So long as one is master of one's mind, I said to myself, one is master of fate, and except for those dread hours from the Haymarket till Lingg left me, I had never lost my self-control. The train went on—chunketty-chunk, chunk, chunk! chunketty-chunk-chunk! all through the night. I think I saw every hour on my watch.

But at last the night waned to an end, and as soon as I decently could, I got up, before six o'clock, and saw the sun rise in majesty over the Hudson. We were running alongside the great river to New York. I got my breakfast at seven o'clock, and at ten I was out of the train, without exciting the suspicion of any one, I am sure. I had played the game to the extent of telling the taciturn conductor that I was in the dry goods, and not very rich; but if he would have a drink with me, I should be pleased. He shook his head.

"Nary drink," he said.

"A cigar, then?" I queried.

"I don't mind," he said, and I got him a fifteen cent cigar, as if that must be a good one, and he appreciated the attention. . . .

Back in New York again! I had only been away a little more than a year; surely I had lived fifty years in the twelve months; a long lifetime! . . .

I would not go where I was known. Where

would Will Roberts go?—a second rate hotel. I walked to one, had a bath, and then in my room went through all my clothes to see if there was anything with my name on it. Nothing. I wrote one or two envelopes, addressed to Will Roberts, in different handwritings, dirtied them, tore them at the corners, shoved one in the grip, put another in my pocket, together with Lingg's precious book, which I went through hurriedly. I found in it a letter for "dear Will" which I thrust into my pocket, to read at leisure. I was eager to get out of the room into the open air, where I could be alone and at ease. I took the street car a block or two from the hotel, and rode right out to Central Park, three or four miles away.

God! What a beautiful place it is. I made my way right through the park to Riverside Drive, and sat down looking over the Hudson, and there I read Lingg's letter: here it is—

"Dear Will,

"When you read this you will be in New York, or perhaps in your own loved England again, or will it be in the Welsh hills? Wherever it is, I know that you won't forget me, and you must know I shall never forget you. We may meet again, but it is not likely. You told me you would make your home on the other side, and never return, and I think you are right, for the climate here doesn't suit you. I shall never leave Chicago. Still, our spirits have met, and have been one in purpose and love, and that seems good to me.

"Ever yours,

"JACK."

I went and had lunch in an Italian restaurant and bought the papers. There never was anything like them; they were all filled with the wildest lies of hatred and fear. For the first time I saw the phrase that the police were using "the drag-net" in Chicago. They had already arrested four thousand persons on suspicion; among them Spies and Fielden and Fischer, and were searching for Parsons. Parsons, it seems, had left the town within an hour of the throwing of the bomb. The first papers were filled with the idea that he had thrown the bomb, and the hunt after him was hot and fierce.

I walked about the whole of the afternoon; the sunlight and air calming my nerves. I had only glanced through the lying papers.

. . . .

The next morning I had to be on board by nine o'clock; that night in the hotel I slept a little. At five o'clock I got up, dressed myself, shaved clean; then walked down to the landing-stage and went on board the tender which took me to the big steamer, and found my berth. There I decided in my own mind that I was born in Pembrokeshire and was going back to my native land. My accent, I knew, would pass me anywhere as an American.

On board the steamer they were all talking of the bomb-throwing in Chicago. Every one was hoping that Parsons, who threw the bomb, would be arrested. They knew all about it now. Sixty policemen had been wounded, eight had been killed outright, seven others were not expected to live; but a great many of these wounded persons, I ascertained afterwards, had been wounded by police bullets. The accused persons, Spies, Fischer, Fielden, were already charged as accessories before the fact of the murder of Mathias J. Degan; Degan being the first of the dead policemen whose body was identified.

The accusation filled me with contempt. I knew better than any one that neither Spies, nor Fischer, nor Fielden were accessories before the fact, or after the fact; nor, indeed, were they connected with the fact in any remotest way. Of course, their innocence must appear in due course. I dismissed the accusation with a pitying smile; yet I should not have been so foolish-sure; I ought to have known better than most people the hollow mockery of American justice.

Chapter X

THAT passage from New York to Liverpool on the "Scotia" was a most blessed interlude. I went on board with jangling nerves, plagued by the incessant questionings of conscience, maddened with memories of loss never to be made good, loss of friendship and of love. I felt like one torn up by the roots and tossed out to misery and death; yet as soon as I got on board and we left the land behind us, the healing processes of nature began their divine work. There was something that appealed to me in the quiet English manners of the officers; there was rest and sympathy in the courtesy and consideration of the stewards; a sort of slow content in the lives of all these people that acted on me as a perpetual lenitive. I talked very little; but I went about where men talked, for the conversation of others took me out of my own sad and bitter thoughts, and allowed me to rest.

The very first day every one went to get weighed, and I was drawn along with the others. In Chicago I had weighed about a hundred and sixty pounds, now to my wonderment I was just under a hundred and fifty. I had lost ten pounds in three days, yet I had eaten and drunk as usual. I began to understand how terrible the strain had been.

I did not sleep well the first days on board, the sea air seemed to excite me; every hour, too, I grew more anxious about Lingg, and the conviction that I should never see Elsie again was an aching, an irremediable grief. I could not help thinking of her, wondering what would become of her, how she would take my unexpected and inexplicable absence. My thoughts ran on the same theme, from Lingg's danger to Elsie's sorrow, morning, noon and night, like a monkey in a cage, till my poor mind was all sore and smarting.

One morning the steward told me I did not look well, and when I confessed I could not sleep he advised me to see the doctor and get a draught; so I hunted out the doctor, and found one of the most charming of men, a little Scotchman, called Philip, dark and nice-looking, sympathetic, too, and quick-witted, who was something more than a master of his trade. A doctor begins by studying diseases and ends by studying his patients; that was where Doctor Edward Philip had begun, though he was still under thirty. He told me it was easy to make me sleep, and he gave me a small dose of chloral.

A sudden thought came to me, and I asked him why I could not have a dose of morphia.

"No reason," he said, "except that it has after-consequences," and he showed me a little bottle filled with tiny tabloids of morphia, one-tenth of a grain in each.

I said nothing that night; but I noted the fact, and determined to cultivate the doctor. I went off, for the present well content with my dose of chloral. Philip had told me that exercise was a good thing, so I paced the deck the whole live-long day, and at eleven o'clock I was in my berth, ready for sleep. I took a cup of chocolate, and then the chloral, and when sleep would not come, I set myself to think of my mascot, the two little children of the conductor, Joon and Jooly, and his intense pride in them, and so drifted into oblivion.

When I awoke the steward was standing by my side.

"Seven o'clock, sir! You told me to wake you at seven."

I felt a new man. What a blessed thing sleep is! I got up and dressed, and from that moment I date my convalescence.

Day after day I used to go in and have a talk with the doctor, and long before the end of the voyage, I had managed to buy from him the little bottle of morphia tablets, half of which I kept in a glass bottle in my trousers pocket, and half in a cardboard pill box in my waistcoat pocket, so that in case of arrest I could immediately swallow them. I was determined not to be caught alive; but strange as it may seem, I had absolutely no fear of being arrested. Life offered so little to me—life without Elsie and Lingg was so barren and tedious a waste—that I did not care how soon it ended, so long as it did not end in public shame, and on the scaffold. The assurance that I had with me an easy method of escape helped my overwrought nerves to rest.

As the days passed and we swung into the clear sunlight and dancing air of mid-Atlantic, my spirits began to recover their normal tone. Day by day I grew stronger, and all too soon we sighted land; about eleven o'clock one beautiful May morning we ran up the Mersey to Liverpool. I had been directed to a quiet, second-class hotel by Doctor Philip, and after thanking him for all his kindness, I went on shore. I had shaved regularly on board ship, and I had not the slightest fear of being recognized.

I had never been in England before; the houses seemed to me tiny-small, and innumerable. The railway-engines looked like toy-engines; the wagons on the railway like toy-wagons after the fifty-ton freight wagons of the American railways. But Liverpool reminded me of Hamburg, again and again, in a hundred ways; the English people, too, reminded me of Germans and my childhood. They were slighter people than the Germans, but a little taller; better-looking, I thought, and better dressed, wearing an air of greater comfort. On every side there were evidences of greater wealth; this little island was evidently the centre of a great empire.

When I got to the hotel, after my supper, I took up an evening paper, and the first thing I saw, staring at me, was a little paragraph headed "Chicago":

"The Arrest of the Anarchist Leader."

My heart sank; was it Lingg? Every word of the telegraphed account was photographed on my brain. The details were meagre; no name was mentioned; but the bare report scared me. I wanted to know more; but there was nothing to be known. The night passed for me in a whirl of excited thought. Next morning the papers had more details; but still no name; yet evidently in some dumb, instinctive way the people in Chicago had begun to realize that at last the police had caught some one worth catching. I felt sure it must be Lingg. The reporters spoke of him as a "wild beast." How did they get that idea? I plagued my brain; but there was dislike and fear in every line written about him. The new captive had made an extraordinary impression on the reporters, that was clear. I could not sleep.

I had already discovered in Liverpool a place where one could find all the American papers, and I went there day after day. About a week after my landing, the first Chicago paper came to hand; as I opened it the paragraph jumped at me: "The Arrest of Louis Lingg." My heart turned to water. I was soon able to reconstruct the whole story, and I began to understand the reporter's adjectives: "a daring terrorist," "the bomb-maker," "the wild beast, Lingg."

The assistant chief of police, a man called Hermann Schuettler, was not only a brave man, but a very powerful one; he had once killed a tough in Chicago with a single blow of his fist. When information reached the police headquarters about Lingg and where he lived, Schuettler at once undertook to arrest him. The police, provided with a full description of Lingg, surrounded the block while Schuettler went to his house. But the bird had flown. The informer's information, however, was very complete. He evidently knew the little carpenter's workshop near the river where Lingg did odd jobs when out of work. Schuettler and an assistant, Loewenstein, made their way there. It was a frame building of one story, divided up into a large working-room and two small bedrooms. The door of the workshop was locked; Schuettler put his shoulder against the lock, and burst into the room. At the sound Lingg turned from where he had been reading, on the other side of the fireplace by the window, threw down the book, and with one leap was at the policeman's throat. Schuettler talked of himself in one of the papers as about the strongest man in Chicago; in the way of business he had fought dozens of toughs; yet he admitted to the reporters that he had never had a struggle like that with Lingg. They rolled over the floor of the room, fighting like demons; Lingg steadily dragging Schuettler towards the door. They were so braided together and their movements were so quick that Loewenstein could only look on and await his opportuinty. It came at length. Bit by bit Lingg was steadily mastering Schuettler; Schuettler admitted that he was choking, when he got Lingg's thumb in his mouth and almost bit it off. In spite of the pain Lingg hung on, and in a moment more Schuettler would have been unconscious. Lingg was on top, his head exposed, and just when he had won, Loewenstein struck him senseless with a loaded club, and he was carried off to the police station before he recovered consciousness. Somehow or other everybody knew at once that the capture was important. Lingg said no word; but the great fight he had made impressed people, and the mere being of the man was so intense that every one wrote of him as "the leader of the terrorists."

Thinking over the whole story, I could not help asking myself how Lingg's name had got out. At once it flashed across my mind that he had been given away, that Raben had denounced him. I felt it to my finger tips—the white snake! I had a terrible night, reproaching myself for ever having had anything to do with Raben; a terrible night!

The next day I went again to the post office, and found a letter for Willie Roberts. It was from Ida. The letter was purposely obscure, yet plain enough for me. Ida began by telling me that her Jack had been taken ill, dangerously ill; she was frightened, though she still hoped for the best. His message to me was to keep my promise; he wished me to remember, too, that sick men often did noteworthy things. Ida went on to say that she was in the sick-room every day; her life was there, and she scarcely lived away from it.

Herewith ended the immediately personal part of Ida's letter. She told me, besides, that she had had a long visit from a young lady who was a terrible spit-fire, with an immense affection for Master Will. The girl knew why Will had run away from her; forgave him freely, and would go to him whenever he wanted her. "If I am any judge of love," Ida wrote, "this is the real thing." The girl's mother, however, seemed to think Will was a ne'er-do-weel, which only showed how little she knew him. Ida had promised to give the girl any message Will cared to send. And Jack wished to add that R. was from Kerioth.

These were the main points of the letter; I was "to keep my promise not to be caught, and expect some deed or other from Lingg." My guess that Raben was the traitor was justified. "R. was from Kerioth" bothered me a little till I remembered that Judas was from Kerioth. Elsie had forgiven me, and would come to me if I sent for her. Now what message should I send in reply? Just this—I should keep my promise to my friend, and begged my love to forget me. I could hardly bear to write it, and I was glad afterwards that Elsie did not accept my decision as final. I need hardly say I wrote my reply in such a way that it could not have excited suspicion, even if it had fallen into the hands of Bonfield himself, or Schuettler.

The more I thought of Ida's letter, the more I wondered what Lingg meant by saying that even prisoners could do "noteworthy things"; surely he was powerless there, in prison, for good or evil; or why had he fought so desperately for freedom? Even I had no conception of his prescience and courage.

My own part seemed utterly unworthy. I wanted to go back and give myself up; but there was my promise to Lingg; he had repeated it in the train, and now Ida had reiterated it. Well, I would go on to London and see if I could not influence the English press a little, for clearly the English newspapers on this matter were merely copying the American newspapers; they repeated the sensational adjectives of the Western reporters, only giving less space to the accounts, because the matter was not of such interest in England.

One thing appeared clearly from all the Chicago papers, that the whole American population was scared out of its wits by the Haymarket bomb. Every day the Chicago police found a new bomb. I thought they had started a special manufactory for them, till I read in the "Leader" of New York that the same piece of gas-piping had already served as a new bomb on seven different occasions. Captain Bonfield and his satellites were very busy; they had used the "drag-net" to some effect. In ten days they had arrested over ten thousand innocent persons, nearly all foreigners, on one pretext or another, and not an anarchist, except Lingg, in the whole crowd. Every day there were illegal arrests by the hundred; every day hundreds of innocent persons were thrown into prison without a shadow of evidence; the policemen who could denounce and arrest the greatest number of people got the quickest advancement. The whole town was frightened to idiocy.

I went off to London the same day and took lodgings in Soho. A quiet sitting-room and bedroom cost me fifteen shillings a week, and my breakfast each morning, a cup of tea and a roll, cost me only three shillings and sixpence a week more. I could easily live for a couple of years, even if my press work brought me in nothing.

It was well that I had not reckoned too much on my pen. I wrote an account of what I called "The Reign of Terror in Chicago," about a column in length, and took it round to the London newspapers; but I never could find an editor; not one of them ever kept any office hours; or, more probably, not one of them would see a stranger without an introduction. It is harder to have a talk with an English editor in London than with a Secretary of State in America, or the President himself.

Tired out with calling and seeing no one, I made fair copies of the article, and sent them to five or six papers. I received no answer. I thought the article might be too descriptive, so I wrote one full of personalities, giving little pen-pictures of Spies, and Fielden the Englishman, and Engel. I hoped that if this article were accepted I might follow it up with a pen-portrait of Lingg; but I need not have worried myself; not one of the papers published the article; not one of them even returned it to me. I began to see that what I had regarded as the dulness of English papers, was a sort of mental twilight which suited the eyes of the readers.

But there is everything in London, every quality of thought and talent. I went out one day to a meeting of the Social Democratic Federation, and found people something like the men I had known on the other side. None of the speakers, however, seemed to me extraordinary, There was a thin, hatchet-faced man, called Champion, who had been, I was told, an officer in the army, and who talked wild communism which he did not understand. There was a Mr. Hyndman, however, a stout, prosperous-looking Jewish gentleman, who had read a good deal, and who spoke excellently, though he had not, perhaps, got hold of the heart of the matter;

still, he was honest and earnest, with a perfectly clear understanding of the organized social swindle, and that's a good deal to say of anyone. Another man made a deep and pleasant impression on me. He was below middle height, a squarely-built, stout little man, with a good round head, ample forehead, handsome features, and beautiful, lovable blue eyes. I was told he was William Morris, the poet, and I listened to him with a good deal of interest, though his ideals seemed to be rather mediæval than modern; still, he was a charming, unaffected personality. He reminded me of Engel and Fielden; in essential kindliness and goodness these three men were very much alike.

It was while attending one of the meetings of the Social Democratic Federation that I heard of "Reynolds' Newspaper," and I at once sent the editor copies of both my articles. He rejected "The Reign of Terror in Chicago"; but accepted the personal article, in which I described Spies and Fielden and Engel. He altered some of my epithets, however, and cut out some entirely, so that the effect was that of a water-colour sketch on which a blurring wet sponge had been freely used.

I should like to speak well of England, for it gave me rest and shelter when I was in sorest need. But it was quite plain to me that England is still, as in Heine's time, the most stubborn upholder of the established fact in the whole world. Individualism is pushed even further there than it is in America, and the remains of a feudal aristocracy petrify extravagant inequalities of possession and privilege. Poverty is treated as a crime; the poorhouses degrade men by the exaction of useless work, and by the distribution of incredibly bad food. A hundred thousand persons are sent to prison annually because they can't pay small fines; thousands more are imprisoned each year for debt—the last survival in Europe of chattel slavery. The bankruptcy laws are as barbarous as the Inquisition. By inflicting savage terms of imprisonment for trifling offences against property, English judges have manufactured a class of habitual criminals who are hardened beyond brutality by the semi-starvation and the floggings of the gaols. It is now proposed by some authorities to imprison these tortured wretches for life. The lower animals are treated better in England than in any other country in the world; the poor are treated like horses in Naples or dogs in Constantinople.

As I got to know the Englishman better, I grew to like him as a well-meaning person who wears the biggest fig-leaf he can find;

but with time it has slipped out of place, and is now worn boldly on the wrong side.

I spent the whole of June in London, and managed to get two or three articles accepted by the advanced section of the press. They were fairly well paid for, and I lived so cheaply that I was not forced to dip into my savings. Every mail-day I read the Chicago papers, and every mail I was more astounded by the lunk-headed bungling of the Chicago police, and by the curious effect their own cowardice had on the American population. The police acted on the principle of arresting every foreigner they could lay their hands on, and by the middle of June they had from twelve to fifteen thousand innocent men and women in jail, and still continued to discover bombs and rifles and anarchist clubs every day.

When the State Attorney got to work, however, to frame a coherent case, he soon found that nearly all these arrests were utterly illegal and silly; prisoners, in spite of the protests of the police, had to be released literally by the thousand; there was not a scrap of evidence procurable against them. The best the prosecution could do was to fix on the people connected with the two advanced papers, and their friends, and try to make out a case against them. Spies, of course, was charged, and his assistant, Schwab; Fischer, too, and Fielden, on the ground of certain speeches they had made; Lingg, as the founder of the Lehr and Wehr Verein, and poor Engel because he had always gone to the advanced meetings, and was a convinced admirer of Spies. Parsons was charged, too; but he could not be found for the moment.

The attitude of the accused served as a contrast to all this cowardice and stupidity. Not a single one of them turned State's evidence, or tried to lay the blame of his position on any one else, or attempted to deny the beliefs he held. And at length came the dramatic climax to this quiet, unacknowledged superiority of the prisoners. The police had not been able to find Parsons; but suddenly a letter from Parsons appeared in the press, declaring that as he was innocent, he would give himself up and be tried with the others, and one day, to the general wonder, he quietly took train to Chicago, and walked into a police station.

The surrender of Parsons, which was wired to London and appeared in the London papers, had several results. First of all it caused a certain sympathy to be felt towards him and his fellow-prisoners. A number of Americans began to doubt in their hearts whether a man who was guilty would give himself up, and if Parsons was not guilty, none of the eight could be convicted. Yet the bomb had been thrown, and some one must be punished for throwing it. The second effect of Parsons' surrender touched me; it would surely force the police to look again for the actual thrower of the bomb; clearly he was not the man, or he would not put his head in the lion's mouth. And this entailed the further consequence that the informer who had given Lingg away would probably again be put to use. If Lingg and I were right in taking Raben to be the informer, he would now certainly denounce me to the police, and my prolonged absence must confirm his suspicion that I was the actual thrower of the bomb.

Two days after the dramatic surrender of Parsons came the statement that the thrower of the bomb was a German writer named Rudolph Schnaubelt, who had made his escape and returned to Germany, and was now being searched for, especially in Bavaria, by the German police. Raben was the informer; of that now I had no doubt; but fortunately he knew nothing precisely, his suspicions were incapable of proof. I wrote, however, at once to Ida saying that I was quite well, and very eager to see Chicago again. I should like to come out at once if I could do any good, or be of any service. Would she let me know what Jack thought? Ever yours and his, "Will."

Ten days after I had sent this letter I recieved a note from Ida, written evidently after Parsons had given himself up, and I had been denounced to the police. In this note she begged me not to leave London; Jack was a little better,would recover, the doctors thought; but in all cases, hoped I would make myself a home in my own land. Ida added that she saw my little friend frequently, who sent me a thousand loving messages.

I did not answer this letter. I could say nothing to Elsie, except that she ought to forget me as soon as she could, and the line of conduct marked out for me did not become more pleasant on reflection. I felt I ought to be in Chicago making a full confession which would free the innocent; but my promise bound me, and the feeling that Lingg was sure to be right in claiming its fulfilment. Besides, my confession even would not free Lingg, though I took all the blame and guilt on myself, for the latest Chicago papers stated definitely that materials for bombs had been found in Lingg's rooms, and chemistry books containing a new formula for a high explosive written in his own hand. Gradually it seemed even the purblind public and the newspapers were beginning to recognize that Lingg was really the storm-centre. Here is a comparatively fair description of him; it is from the pen of an American eye-witness who had studied him. I reproduce it in order to let my readers see how Lingg struck the best sort of reporter.

"The strange figure in the group, the strangest man I have ever known, and the least human, is Louis Lingg. He is a kind of modern berserker, utterly reckless of consequences to himself, driving on in a sustained fury of vengeance upon the whole social order. Little of his abnormal physical strength is apparent when he is in repose. He is slightly under average height,* very compactly built, with tawny hair, a strong face and the most extraordinary eyes I have ever seen in a human head, steel-grey, exceedingly keen, and bearing in their depths a kind of cold and hateful fire. His hands are small and delicate; his head large and very well shaped; his face indicates breeding and culture. It is when he walks, as I often see him striding to and fro in the jail corridor, that he seems most formidable; for then his lithe, gliding, and peculiarly silent step, and the

*It is curious to notice here how even careful observers are often utterly mistaken on important points. The writer of the above sketch declares that Lingg was "slightly under average height"; the truth is that Lingg was rather above the "average height," being nearly five feet eight in his stocking feet. Schaack, the police captain, stated afterwards in print that Lingg was "tall." —*Note of Editor.*

play of muscles about his shoulders, suggests something cat-like, or abnormal, an impression heightened by the leonine wave of hair he wore when he was arrested, though when I saw him he was closely cropped and clean-shaven. After all, for a small man, he is the most terrific figure I have ever met. To any question or remark he is wont to respond with a disconcerting stare, and I think few people observe him without a feeling of relief that he is on the other side of the steel bars. . . ."

Chapter XI

THE trial in Chicago was a startling, a horrible revelation, even to me, of man's innate brutality. It seems only natural to expect human beings to be at their best in a trial where life and death hang in the balance. It shocks the onlooker to discover that the great issue does not affect in any way the character or even the conduct of ordinary people.

All through that year the capitalist papers in Chicago had been shamelessly one-sided. Day after day their columns had been filled with furious encouragement of the police; again and again they had called upon Bonfield and his helpers to "use lead" against us; but I had hoped that now this would all cease, that the hireling partisans of the established order would hold their hands, at least for a time. They could feel pretty confident that the judges whom they had appointed and the machinery of the law which they had instituted would act as they had designed them to act. At the worst, I thought, there will be a show of fairness, and I comforted myself with the reflection that if there was any fair-play at all, it would be impossible to convict seven out of the eight accused persons; for those seven had had nothing on earth to do with the throwing of the bomb, and, in fact, knew nothing whatever about it. Poor fool that I was! I still imagined that innocence insured acquittal in a court of justice.

But already when I thought of the trial I began to grow indignant, for strong as their case was I began to fear, and this was the heart of my fear. The police had already asserted that they had found bombs in Lingg's rooms. I knew Lingg well enough to know that that was almost certainly untrue; he would never have implicated Ida in his crime. From the description of the place, too, where he had been captured, I knew that he had been trapped in his little carpenter's workshop, and bombs would have been discovered there if anywhere. Besides, the police description of the bombs found in Lingg's rooms was altogether wrong; they had not the same shape as Lingg's bombs, and, above all, the explosive used was declared to be dynamite, which Lingg never used. For these reasons I felt certain that the bombs were of police imagining, or police manufacture. And if the police could manufacture lying evidence against Lingg, what was to hinder them manufacturing lies about the others? I began to fear for the result and, as it turned out, with good reason.

The next batch of Chicago papers showed me that the police had discovered bombs in Parsons's desk, and rifles by the dozen in Spies's house, and a little later bombs in Engel's shop. I had no need to read further; even the Chicago police had surpassed themselves, and reached the limit when they attributed bomb-making to kind old Engel. The papers treated all these so-called discoveries quite seriously; published pictures of the bombs; pictures of the fulminating caps, anything and everything to prejudice the case, to excite horror and detestation of the accused. Evidently the established order, the robbers in possession, were determined at all costs to strike down their enemies. Why should I hesitate to call them robbers? When writing of the Paris Commune, did not Ruskin say that "the capitalists are the guilty thieves of Europe . . ."? Did he not attack, as it should be attacked, that "occult theft; theft which hides itself, even from itself, and is legal, respectable, and cowardly, which corrupts the body and soul of men, to the last fibre of them"? And if you dispute the authority of Ruskin, will you be convinced by Carlyle, or by Balzac, or by Goethe, or by Ibsen, or by Heine, or by Anatole France, or by Tolstoi, by any or all the leaders of modern thought? On this subject they are all agreed. And agreeing with them, I mean to show how this conspiracy of legalized thieves in Chicago defended themselves, and at length rid themselves of their opponents. I beg my readers to believe that I expose this shameless vengeance of theirs not in anger, but simply as a warning and a lesson to the class I represent. It is well for working-men to know how the middle classes prostitute justice in the most democratic country in Christendom.

The trial was a cruel farce; from beginning to end a mockery of justice. For weeks before it began the papers, as I have said, had been poisoning the minds of the people in Chicago with every imaginable police lie and slander—any stick seemed to the journalists good enough for the anarchist dog. At the time the trial commenced some thousands of men were still in prison in Chicago on suspicion; held there in defiance of law, as a ready means of terrorizing any witnesses that might be called for the defence.

Day after day the court-room was packed with friends of the established order; well-dressed citizens who showed their feelings, now by cheers, and now by groans, in most unmistakable fashion. The proletariat, who outnumbered the wealthy ten to one, were not allowed to have any of their representatives in court; some who came there were arrested and dragged off to prison without any pretence of legality, in order to encourage the rest. What a disgraceful, pitiable farce it all was!

First of all, the trial was held too soon after the offence to be in any way fair to the accused, much less impartial. It began on the twenty-first of June, within six weeks of the bomb-throwing. Then, too, it was held on the very scene of the crime where men were still too frightened to think of justice, and though a change of venue was asked for, it was peremptorily refused. But not only was the court-room packed; the jury was packed also. Out of the thousand odd talesmen on the list, only ten came from the fourteenth ward, the working-class quarter, yet this ward alone had a population of 130,000, whereas the whole population of Chicago was only five hundred thousand. And to make security doubly sure, the ten talesmen who were taken from the fourteenth ward were all carefully selected by the police; they all lived, indeed, within a few yards of the police station. It was quite in vain that Captain Black, the counsel for the defence, used his right of challenge on such men; he challenged all of them he was allowed to challenge, a hundred and sixty for the eight defendants; but all the talesmen were of the same class, so that he was powerless. A single instance will establish this. He challenged one juror, and appealed to the judge against him; for when questioned this juror admitted that he had made up his mind from the first that the accused were guilty—even before he had come into court. The judge, in order to flaunt his prejudice, or rather in order to discover his complete sympathy with the capitalist class, allowed this juror to serve.

Pontius Pilate was an infinitely fairer judge than Judge Gary; Pilate had some misgivings; now and then tried to show fairness; but Gary was proof against any such sympathy. From the beginning to the end of the trial he always supported the State Attorney Grinnell, and opposed the prisoners' counsel. Take one instance: he allowed a work of Most, the half-mad anarchist, to be put in evidence against the prisoners, though there was no evidence whatever, no particle of presumption even, that any of the prisoners had ever seen the book, and though it was written in a language which neither Fielden nor Parsons could understand. With a hostile public filling the court, with hostile papers whipping prejudice to madness, with a packed jury of bitter opponents, with a judge who over-rode the most ordinary forms of law in order to prejudice the jury against the prisoners, there was not much chance of a decent verdict. In spite of all this, however, the case against the prisoners was so weak that it seemed again and again as if it must break to pieces of its own rottenness.

The chief witnesses for the police were Captain John Bonfield and Messrs. Seliger, Jansen and Shea. They all contradicted themselves and contradicted each other on vital points. Bonfield was asked whether he had ever used the words, "If I could only get a thousand of those Socialists and Anarchists in a bunch . . . I'd make short work of them." He admitted that he had used them, and declared that he was justified. Seliger lived in the police station, and admitted that he had received large sums of money from the police. Jansen and Shea confessed that they had joined Socialist clubs and had made speeches to incite the members against the police—confessed further that they had been paid for those services; and yet Judge Gary held that their evidence was admissible, and asserted that on the main points it had not been shaken in cross-examination. Yet these witnesses were on their own admission *agents provocateurs*. This travesty of justice dragged on for two months; but long before it came to an end I was sickened with the conviction that the jury would find every one of the eight guilty, and yet there were moments when it seemed impossible for even that jury to commit such a crime.

Captain Black did his work splendidly as advocate for the defence; he tore the whole indictment of the State Attorney to pieces. He showed that at first the eight men had been put on trial for murder, and for weeks the police had tried to prove that they were the makers and throwers of the bombs, or at least privy to the throwing (for the one bomb I threw had become three, according to the police testimony). This case, Captain Black pointed out, had absolutely broken down; there was not a tittle of credible evidence to connect any one of the prisoners with the throwing of a bomb. Then he showed how the State Attorney Grinnell, recognizing this, had begun to change his ground, and charge the accused as anarchists. "The whole prosecution now rests," he said, "on the attempt to prove that these men have incited to murder by their speeches and writings." He went on to ridicule the idea that any connection had been established between the strong language used by the defendants and the throwing of the bomb. He made his final appeal to the jury to treat the case as a political case, as a case in which the hot words of speakers on either side were not to be taken seriously; but the packed class jury were above argument, and beyond appeal. They brought in a verdict of "Guilty" against every one of the eight.

The value of the verdict appears from one fact. Among the eight was one man, Oscar Neebe, against whom nothing had been proved, whose language had always been moderate, who was not even at the meeting in Desplaines Street; but the jury, thinking it a pity to make an exception, brought in Neebe guilty with the rest. Then the prisoners were asked whether they had anything to say why sentence should not be passed upon them.

One after the other got up, and made better speeches than I should have believed them able to make. Parsons, of course, used the occasion magnificently; according to all accounts surpassed himself. He began by drawing attention to the fact that this trial was simply an incident in the long conflict between capitalism and labour. "It was well known," he declared, "that the representatives of the millionaire organization, known as the Chicago Citizens' Association, had spent money like water in order to buttress up the case against the accused at every weak spot. These millionaires had at their disposal the capitalist press—'that vile and infamous organization of hired liars.' . . . The trial was instituted by the capitalist mob, prosecuted by the mob, conducted amid the cheers and howls of the mob, and had resulted in a mob verdict. . . .

"You are now asked," he went on, "to enter a verdict against us as anarchists. Why not consider first the writings of the capitalist press which came first in time, and which we only answered? When the sailors in the docks were striking to obtain higher wages, what did 'The Chicago Times' say? 'Hand-grenades should be thrown among them; by such treatment they would be taught a valuable lesson and other strikers would take a warning from their fate. . . .' What did 'The New York Herald' say? 'The brutal strikers can understand no other meaning than that of force, and ought to get enough to remember it for many generations.' What did 'The Indianapolis Journal' say? 'Give the strikers a rifle diet for a few days, and see how they like that kind of bread.' What did 'The Chicago Tribune' say? 'Give them strychnine.'

"Are these editors and writers on trial for inciting to murder? Yet murder came again and again as a result of their incitement. I have quoted you 'The Chicago Tribune's' article; three days afterwards seven unarmed strikers were shot down by the police, murdered in cold blood. Was the editor or the writer of the article in 'The Chicago Tribune' arrested and charged with murder? There is evidently in America one justice for the rich, and another for the poor. We anarchists are to be treated as murderers; every hot or unconsidered word we have used is to be brought up against us, yet there might be some mitigation of the hatred you feel towards us if you considered our position. Do you think it easy for us to see workmen starving who are willing to work? to watch their wives and children getting thinner and weaker day by day? All this winter thirty thousand workmen have been out of work in Chicago, or, taking a family of three children to each head, nearly a third of the whole population of Chicago has been for months on the brink of starvation. When we see little children huddled round the factory gates, the poor little things whose bones are not yet hard, when we see them torn from the fireside, thrown into the bastiles of labour, and their frail little bodies turned into gold to swell the hoard of the millionaire or to bedeck the form of some aristocratic Jezebel, it is time to speak out.

"Judge Gary has declared that resistance to the execution of the law is a crime, and that if such resistance lead to death it is murder; well, Judge Gary is mistaken. Our Declaration of Independence is a higher authority than Judge Gary, and it asserts that resistance to tyranny, to unlawful authority, is right; and what could be more unlawful than for police to use bludgeons and revolvers on unarmed men exercising the American right of free speech in an open meeting? The Judge Garys pass away and are forgotten; but the Declaration of Independence will remain as a monument of human wisdom. . . .

"The prosecuting attorney has tried to excite prejudice against me personally by calling me 'a paid agitator.' Well, I am paid, and I have been paid. I receive the wages fixed by myself, eight dollars a week, for editing 'The Alarm,' and all my other work. Eight dollars a week, that is what my wife and I live on—'a paid agitator'; it is for the world to judge whether the sneer is deserved . . . .

"Do not think, gentlemen of the prosecution, that you will have settled this case when they have carried my lifeless body to the potter's field. Do not imagine that this trial will be ended by strangling me and my colleagues! I tell you there will be another trial, and another jury, and a more righteous verdict."

I have only given a few extracts from Parsons's speech, taking a bit from this newspaper and a bit from that; for though he spoke for two days, the whole of the reports I could get would have gone into a column. The same papers, "The Chicago Tribune," and "The Chicago Times," which gave the police evidence verbatim, minus the contradictions, and reported the speech for the prosecution at full length, scarcely deigned to give one word in a hundred of Parsons's speech; yet even these prejudiced papers admitted that his speech was a great one, and had a great effect.

But to my mind, knowing the man, and reading at a distance, the speech of Engel was just as effective, and even more touching in its transparent honesty. He did not carry the war into the enemies' camp as Parsons did; he simply showed what the poor had suffered, and confessed that his sympathies were naturally with all those who laboured and starved, and who were treated always with harshness and contempt. Everything Engel said reached one's best sympathies. But the sensation of the trial was the speech of Louis Lingg, though it was very short.

"It is a pleasant irony," he began, "to call

this a fair trial in open court, with a packed jury, a prejudiced judge, and crowds of hired police witnesses; but the irony becomes sharp when we are asked, after being brought in 'Guilty,' whether we have anything to say why we should not be hanged, it being perfectly well understood that if we spoke with the tongues of angels we should still be hanged.

"I had intended," he went on, "to defend myself; but the trial has been so unfair, the conduct of it so disgraceful, the intent and purpose of it so clearly avowed, that I will not waste words. Your capitalist masters want blood; why keep them waiting?

"The rest of the accused have told you that they do not believe in force. I may tell you that they have no business in this dock with me. They are innocent, every one of them; I do not pretend to be. I believe in force just as you do. That is my justification. Force is the supreme arbiter in human affairs. You have clubbed unarmed strikers, shot them down in your streets, shot down their women and their children. So long as you do that, we who are Anarchists will use explosives against you.

"Don't comfort yourselves with the idea that we have lived and died in vain. The Haymarket bomb has stopped the bludgeonings and shootings of your police for at least a generation. And that bomb is only the first, not the last . . .

"Now I have done. I despise you. I despise your society and its methods, your courts and your laws, your force-propped authority. *Hang me for it!*"

According to all accounts this speech of Lingg had a tremendous effect; the coolness of it, the detached impartiality of the beginning, the bold avowal of his belief in force, the noble declaration that he alone was guilty, the daring of the whole thing, affected everybody. Above all the threat that the Haymarket bomb was not the last. But, of course, the speech had no influence on the judge.

Judge Gary, in giving sentence, began by saying that he was sorry for the unhappy condition . . . of the accused; "but the law holds that whoever advises murder is himself guilty of the murder that is committed pursuant to his advice. . . ." He went on to say that "the defendant Neebe should be imprisoned in the State Penitentiary at Joliet at hard labour for the term of fifteen years, and that each of the other defendants, between the hours of ten o'clock in the forenoon and two o'clock in the afternoon of the third of December next, in the manner provided by the statute of this State, be hung by the neck until he is dead. Remove the prisoners."

The whole spirit and meaning of the trial can be understood by any impartial person from an article which appeared in "The Chicago Tribune," welcoming the verdict and the sentences with indecent and shameless delight. The article was headed "Chicago Hangs Anarchists," and the writer proposed that a hundred thousand dollars should immediately be subscribed for the jury who had so nobly done their duty.

I cannot describe the alternations of hope and fear which I experienced in the two months the trial lasted. For sixty days I was on the rack. I speak figuratively, because this English language is figurative; it has all been made by poets and romance writers, by people with imagination, and not by people with open eyes and clear judgment; but new experiences demand a new telling, and the language of plain fact is sufficiently impressive. Before the trial was half over I had got into a habit of sleeplessness which first came to me after I left Chicago. At the beginning I paid no attention to this insomnia. When I was tired out, I thought I should sleep; but as the conviction grew in me that these men would all be sentenced—Parsons, who had given himself up, Spies, the lovable Fielden, dear old Engel, Lingg—the sleeplessness grew on me, and however tired I was I could not sleep without chloral or an injection of morphia. Even when I went out of London to Richmond Park, and walked all day in that beautiful place, and returned tired out, I could not sleep; or if I dozed away for a few minutes I began to dream hideous dreams, which woke me in spite of myself, shaking with fear.

As my anxiety grew greater the hallucinations became more distressing. One that I remember most acutely used to take the form of an eye, which seemed to stare and stare at me till I awoke. The eye would often in my dream grow luminous, and in its light I would see again Crane's Alley, and the truck, and the speakers, and the little red light, as of a falling star, and then the pit in the street, and the red shambles, and I was awake, shivering in a cold sweat.

In another of these dreams a point would appear and turn quickly into a beak and furnish itself with wings, and swoop down nearer and nearer till I realized that it was trying to tear out my eyes, and then it would come close and suddenly change into the dreadful street, and again I was awake, gasping with terror.

Even when I merely closed my eyes, all the colours of the kaleidoscope would paint themselves in bars and rings upon my eyelids.

Sometimes I saw nothing but crimson, and then orange, and then bars of alternate crimson and orange. How could one sleep with one's nerves playing such tricks?

The sleeplessness made the strain intolerable; I lost appetite and lost strength. One day I went to a doctor, and he told me I was suffering from nervous breakdown, and if I did not take a rest the consequences would be serious. I asked him how I should rest. He shook his sapient head, told me not to think of anything unpleasant, to go out, and live in the open air, much as one might tell a hungry man to pay a thousand pounds into his balance at the bank.

I reached breaking point just before the trial. I had been out reading the papers, and had forgotten to get anything to eat. When I returned to my lodging I ran up the stairs two at a time as was my custom. As I got into my room and closed the door everything swayed about, and I fell against the bed, and then slid down on the floor in a faint. When I came to I felt very weak and ill; but somehow or other I managed to crawl into bed, where I lay for an hour or so. As luck would have it, the servant came up to fill the water-jug, and I asked her to bring me some cocoa and bread and butter. The food revived me; but I was too weak to get up, and next day the weakness continued, and I was surprised to see how pale and drawn my face was, that used to be rather round and well covered.

Days passed, and I got gradually stronger; but my nerves were all ashake for months. I used to sit in the chair by the window for hours without moving, while the tears poured weakly from my eyes.

Strange to say, when the verdict came and the anxiety was over, I began to recover a little. I at once made up my mind to go back to Chicago and give myself up, and this resolve having laid my cruel doubts, I began to sleep better. But a few days afterward I received another letter from Chicago, which turned my resolution into an entirely new direction.

It was this letter which brought me back to life and life's purpose again: "Jack seems very anxious about you," Ida wrote; "he hopes you will write the story of his illness and your exile. 'Tell him,' he says again and again, 'he was born a writer, and one good book is worth a thousand deeds. I rely on him to write and do nothing else. . . .'"

Perhaps Lingg was right; at any rate, his advice held me, and I began at once to write the story as I have set it forth here, and the writing of it—the purpose and the labour—brought me slowly back to life.

At first I wrote merely as a reporter, and found that after a hundred pages I was still writing about my own boyhood. I tore up all I had written and began again, determined to leave out everything which did not illustrate the main theme, and this determination, in spite of my want of talent and painful inexperience, is pulling me through; but no one could be more painfully conscious than I am how unworthy the writing is of the subject. I am acutely aware, too, that this book is only interesting when I am dealing with great persons, with Lingg, and Ida, and Elsie, and Parsons, so I will return to them, and my story, for the greatest and most terrible things are still to tell.

All this time I was not able to get the notion out of my head that Lingg would not go sheep-like to the scaffold. To the very last I had expected him to execute justice on his justicers, and end the trial in open court with a bomb. If he had not done this it was because it was impossible. He had probably been kept under the strictest watch. But now I felt sure the watch would be relaxed, and Lingg's daring and resolution were so extraordinary that he would probably do something yet to strike terror into his opponents.

Meanwhile hope that the sentence might be

mitigated was not abandoned. An application for a new trial was made to Judge Gary and was refused; but that was only what might have been expected.

About this time my heart was buoyed up by the fact that a change in popular feeling seemed to be taking place in Chicago. In the late summer the people began to prepare for the elections, and to the astonishment of the capitalists, the Labour Party went from triumph to triumph. No doubt, as a consequence of these successes, the judicial aspect of the case altered for the better. On Thanksgiving Day, the twenty-fifth of November, Captain Black got a *supersedeas* or stay of execution of the vile sentence. This *supersedeas* allowed an appeal to the Supreme Court, which Captain Black began at once to prepare.

The fogs of November and December drove me from London, in spite of the fact that the prospects of my friends were brighter; in spite, too, of the fact that I was beginning to make some little progress with my book. Work in the gloom and grime and dirt had become almost impossible to me. I was terribly depressed; my nerves seemed to give way utterly in the semi-darkness and filth. So I seized the first opportunity and took steamer for Bordeaux. The passage cost very little, a couple of pounds for the four days. We had a very stormy passage; but that was to be expected in the Bay of Biscay, and long before we got to Bordeaux the air was clear and light, and the wind had blown away all the depressing fogs. I found a room in a little lane on the vine-clad outskirts of the town, and lived there cheaply for the winter. I managed almost to cover my expenses by what I wrote for "Reynolds'," so that everything I did on the book seemed to me clear gain. The worst of my sojourn in Bordeaux was that I was almost completely cut off from the American world. The papers held no foreign news worth talking about; the French, indeed, seem to believe that the smallest thing which happens in France is more important than the greatest thing which happens in any other country. There is an insularity of mind about them which is astonishing. They have lived so long with the idea that they are the first nation in the world, and their language the most important language, that they have not yet awakened to the fact that they are only a second-rate nation, and English and Russian, and even German, are incomparably more important tongues than French. They are like men in a class of growing youths; they imagine themselves stronger and wiser, whereas they are only older and more vicious.

Early in March I made my way to Paris, and from Paris in a few days I went on to Cologne; there I got in touch with the world again, and learnt that on the thirteenth of March Captain Black's appeal had been laid before the Supreme Court. Judgment, however, was not expected for some time.

I found a socialist club in Cologne, and, indeed, in every German town which I visited. I was afraid to go freely to the meetings; but from time to time I attended some of the lectures and found that in Germany, at least, the new creed was every day making new converts.

In the course of that summer I wrote a good deal for the advanced German papers, esepcially for the socialist sheets; but I found that Lingg's idea that a perfect modern State should embrace both socialism and individualism was not acceptable to socialists. They insisted that co-operation would have to take the place of competition altogether as the motive-power in life, which I could not at all bring myself to believe. Again and again I pointed out that all the evils of our society arose from the fact that the individual had combined with others and so increased his own strength, and was thus enabled to gain control of great departments of industry which he had no business to control, and thereby annex profits which should have gone into the coffers of the State. The world seemed to me gone mad. Seven out of ten people one met believed in unrestrained individualism, and declared that the gigantic evils of it were only accidental and unimportant, whereas the other three were certain that competition spelt nothing but waste and fraud and shameless greed, and declared that with co-operation the millennium would come upon earth. I stood between these two parties, and for my moderation was regarded as an enemy by both. The individualists would not have me because I could not accept their extravagant lies; the socialists would not have me because I could not go the whole way with them. Again and again I was forced to see the truth of Lingg's saying that the modern State was not complex enough: there should be many more Government appointments at small salaries for people with extraordinary peculiarities or gifts which enabled them to see and do things that other men did not see and could not do. Progress in society comes usually from what scientists call "sports," men or women of some extraordinary gift, and the "sports" in a democracy, I noticed, have little chance of survival.

The vast body of brutal public opinion, as I had found in America, overwhelms them, hates them, or at least is impatient of their superiority, and indeed of their mere existence, and so the feet of progress are clogged.

Chapter XII

As the months went on I began to look for a good issue, but towards the end of the summer my hopes were suddenly blasted. On the twentieth of September the Supreme Court gave its judgment, affirming the judgment of Judge Gary's Court with one voice. When I was able to read the "opinion" of the Supreme Court in the American papers I gasped with astonishment; it was simply manufactured. Statements were assumed as indisputably true which were absolutely false, which were never even mentioned in evidence in the lower Court. The higher one went, the worse one fared; I ought to have divined it. The better the judges were paid, the higher their position, the more certain they were to be on the side of the established order; on every single point the Supreme Court judges warped the law to suit their prejudices.

As was to be expected, the Labour Party did not accept this infamous verdict as decisive. The "opinion" created intense excitement among the labour leaders, and the labour organizations in Chicago prepared to agitate boldly. The capitalists, however, were ready for the fight. A labour meeting of protest was called and well attended, but was boycotted by the capitalist press. That was not enough; stronger measures, therefore, were at once adopted. Mrs. Parsons was going about exciting sympathy by distributing copies of that part of her husband's speech at the first trial which contained an appeal to the American people, based on the Declaration of Independence. She was arrested and thrown into prison, and immediately on top of this, all meetings in favour of the condemned men were forbidden in Chicago. Evidently the capitalists were not only straining but degrading the law in order to take vengeance upon their enemies. Then I learned tardily that Captain Black had gone to New York to take counsel with General Pryor, the ablest counsel in America, on the best method of appeal to the Supreme Court of the United States. He could not, however, get evidence to lay before the Supreme Court; the use of the "record" of the Court below was refused to him, for the first time in American history. When I read this I knew that matters were desperate, and that whatever I could do must be done quickly.

At once I went back to London and began to stir up the Radical clubs. Every one of them heard me with sympathy and acted on my advice. I found, too, some notable English men and women working in the same cause, particularly Doctor Aveling, and Eleanor Marx Aveling. Mr. Hyndman, also, was indefatigable, both speaking and writing in favour at least of a fair trial, and William Morris imperilled his reputation in America quite cheerfully by writing an impassioned appeal on behalf of the condemned men. Two or three Americans, too, distinguished themselves in the same way, especially William D. Howells and Colonel Ingersoll, the famous lecturer, who showed his accustomed courage by writing against what he dared to call "a judicial murder."

The Supreme Court had fixed the eleventh of November for the execution, and I began to fear for the first time that these men would indeed be executed on that day, for the extremity of need only discovered the weakness and want of organization of the proletariat, the overwhelming strength of the capitalist established order. In London the protests of the Radical clubs were scarcely noticed by the middle-class papers. Every one of the great sheets, like "The Times" and "The Telegraph," simply announced the date of the execution and the finding of the Supreme Court as ordinary facts which must have been expected. Justice was to be done, they all said, and the sooner the deed was accomplished the better; and that was the spirit in America, too, only there it was intensified by a certain amount of fear and rage. "At last we are coming to the end," said "The Chicago Tribune," "and we shall soon be quit of monsters who are better out of life."

That seven out of the eight men were entirely innocent seemed to concern no one, and interest no one in particular. If one spoke about it in a public-house or in the street, one met simply cold looks, unwilling attention, shrugging shoulders. I was forced to the conclusion that the number of people in this world who care for justice or right, apart from their own interests, is very small. Now, as in the old days, there were not five righteous to be found in a city. Anger and rage seemed to give me back some of my strength. Again I wrote to Ida, saying that I was eager to return to Chicago. I pleaded with her as I knew she would plead with Lingg, and again our letters crossed; for in the last days of October I received a letter from her in which Jack thanked me for having kept my promise and bade me watch the end carefully, for "a good witness would be needed." I could hear him say the words, and at once I set myself to get every particle of information I could about the condemned men and their treatment. What I learned, and what came of it, and the terrible end, I must now tell as best I can.

The so-called anarchists had been confined for the fifteen months in what was called "Murderers' Row" in the Cook County Jail. Their cells were small, square rooms, with one heavily barred window, high up, and a heavy door. Outside the ordinary door there was another door made up of bars of iron, which was used in summer for purposes of ventilation.

The head jailer's name was Folz, a veteran in the service, who was careful, watchful, yet considerate. From time to time the prisoners were permitted to talk with their friends; but then only in the so-called "Lawyers' Cage," a cell ten feet by sixteen, the door of which was not only made of iron bars; but was covered, too, with a close network of wire. Outside this stood the person talking to the prisoner; inside, the prisoner with his death-watch in close attendance. As soon as the Supreme Court had given its judgment and fixed the date of execution, the harshness of the prisoners' treatment was sensibly mitigated. The wives of the condemned men were permitted to visit them nearly every day, and Miss Miller was allowed to see Lingg as freely as if she had been his wife.

In the early days of November Captain Black strained every nerve to get some at least of the prisoners pardoned; he was convinced of their innocence, and laboured as only an able and kindly man could labour on their behalf. At length he got Schwab and Fielden and Spies to sign a petition for pardon. The petition was based on several reasons: the first was that they were innocent of the bomb-throwing; the second was like unto it, that they had no knowledge whatever of the bomb-throwing; and the third was founded on the fact that at the Haymarket meeting they had advised peaceable measures. This petition was forwarded to the Governor, and every one hoped that Governor Oglesby would do something to mitigate the terrible sentence.

Every effort was then concentrated on the attempt to get Parsons, Engel, and Fischer to petition at least for their lives. Mrs. Fischer and Mrs. Engel did what they could, while Mrs. Parsons would not consent to try to influence her husband in any way. Parsons absolutely refused to sign any petition that did not contain a demand for unconditional pardon and absolute liberty. At length the three signed this petition, and Captain Black brought it and laid it before Lingg, who first of all pointed out that it was quite useless, and then declared that even if it were thinkable that such a pardon would be granted, he would not ask for it. It was only when Mrs. Engel came and implored him to do it for her husband's sake that Lingg at last yielded, and that petition, too, went to the Governor. The Governor's answer was reserved till the tenth of November; but it leaked out that he would remit the death sentence on Schwab and Fielden at least. It was not to be expected that he would take into account the petition for an unconditional pardon which had been addressed to him by the other four men.

While these things were going on an event occurred which once more lashed the passions of men to fever heat. In spite of a good deal of laxity in the management of the prison, Jailer Folz had the cells searched from time to time. Fortunately, or unfortunately, he had the cells searched on the Sunday morning, the sixth of November, the first day of the fatal week. Nothing was found in any of the cells except Lingg's, and in Lingg's cell three bombs were found, it was said, by an accident.

The accident was peculiar enough to carry conviction with it. Lingg, it seems, had asked again and again for oranges all through the summer, and Miss Miller brought him oranges, which he kept in a little wooden box by his bedside. When the cell was opened to be searched he was asked to step into the "Lawyer's Cage." He got up at once, and asked quietly—

"May I take my oranges with me?"

"No," replied the jailers; "please leave everything; you don't need to eat oranges for two minutes."

Lingg had already taken the little wooden box in his hand; as they refused him he tossed it carelessly on the bed and went out into the "Lawyer's Cage." The policemen paid no attention at first to the little box; they searched the whole cell till they came to the bed; then Deputy-Sheriff Hogan took up the box, opened it, and shoved it along outside the door into the corridor. As luck would have it the box went too far, went through the railings of the corridor and fell on the floor beneath; there it burst, and the oranges rolled all over the place. Hogan, seeing the result of his push, went to the railings of the corridor and looked over, and noticing that all the prisoners were concerned with these oranges, called to them to bring them up; but just as he was turning away, he saw one of the prisoners had stripped the yellow skin from an orange and discovered a layer of cotton-wool underneath. At once he sprang down the stairs and seized the box. On closer examination, according to the police report, three bombs were found among the oranges, concealed in orange skins.

After this discovery Lingg was removed to a separate cell, number eleven, altogether apart from the others, and watched night and day by his death-watch. Had he meant to blow the jail up, or to use bombs on the very place of execution? I could not divine.

The discovery in Lingg's cell set all America in a quiver of rage and fear. Chicago was given over to panic; the governor of the prison was attacked in the press; the conduct of the jailers blamed, and the sheriffs condemned on all sides. Too much licence had been allowed. These anarchists were fanatics—murderers and madmen—and must be watched like wild beasts, and killed like wild beasts. The press was unanimous. Fear dictated the words that rage penned; but what manner of men these anarchists were was soon to appear, beyond all doubt, from their deeds. They were not to be painted by the lies and slanders of terrified enemies, but by their own acts in the light of day to all men's wonder.

Chapter XIII

OF the seven accused men only one was an American, Albert Parsons, and it seemed as if the higher the tide of execration rose against the other anarchists, as foreigners and murderers, the more the American mob desired to make an exception in favour of Parsons. It is the tendency of masses of men to praise and blame at haphazard and extravagantly. Their heroes are demi-gods, their enemies fiends. As I have shown, public opinion had turned Louis Lingg into a devil, a monster, a wild beast, and this same public opinion now tried to turn Parsons into an angel of light. It must be confessed that he touched the sympathies of Americans on many sides. He was not only a native-born American, but a Southerner who had fought as a boy for the Confederate States, and who after the war had approved the conditions imposed by the North. In '79 he was nominated as the Labour Candidate for the Presidency of the United States, and declined the honour.

This man's past proved beyond doubt that he was absolutely disinterested; a fanatic, if you will, but a man of highest principle; a good man, that is, and not a bad one. It was impossible even for malice to condemn Parsons as a murderer, as Lingg, Spies, Engel, Fischer, and the others were condemned. Besides, he had not been caught by the police; with singular magnanimity he had given himself up, and of his own impulse faced the danger. The sincerity of his motives, his noble character, the eloquence of his defence, had made a deep impression on the people. Governor Oglesby, who was already minded to reduce the sentences of Fielden and Schwab to imprisonment for life, could not overlook the claims of Parsons. Every one wanted to condemn the foreign anarchists as a body, and not to excite further sympathy with them by forcing Parsons to share their fate. Accordingly, on the Wednesday morning, the ninth of November, Captain Black was informed that if Parsons would sign a petition for mercy without any further words, the Governor would grant it in view of his past life.

Captain Black, who was of high character and greatly esteemed by the people of Chicago, hurried at once to the prison, and used every argument that he could think of to induce Parsons to sign a colourless petition, merely asking for mercy. To his eternal the reflection that "the only fine man of the crew was a native-born American." They were soon to be undeceived, soon to be taught that among the despised foreigners was one man, in character and courage, head and shoulders above his fellows.

All the while, since the discovery on the Sunday morning of the bombs, Lingg had been kept by himself in cell 11, and had been denied to every one. The jail clerk, Mr. B. Price, took turn in looking after him, with his death-watch, Deputy-Sheriff Osborne. Captain Osborne seems to have been very kind to Lingg, who naturally responded to sympathy as a watch to its main-spring.

Early on the morning of the tenth, Osborne communicated to him the decision of the Governor, and told him, too, how in spite of every temptation Parsons had refused to ask for mercy or place himself in an exceptional position. When Lingg heard it he cried—

"That's great, great! Well done, Parsons, well done!"

Shortly afterwards Lingg took a ring from his finger, handed it to Mr. Osborne, and desired him to keep it as a memento of his kindness to him.

"Take it to the window," he said, "and look at it. It is not worth much, but perhaps on that account you will prize it the more."

Had he succeeded in cheating the gallows? There was no time to answer the question. Aided by the deputies the jailer carried the body to the door of the cell, out into the cage, and into the office. A bloodstained trail marked the way. It was an awful sight. The features of the criminal were bathed in blood. The entire lower jaw was gone, and part of the upper. Ragged strips of flesh hung down below the eyes. His chest seemed to be stripped of flesh to the very bones. The eyes were closed, and the right hand convulsively clutched the jailer's coat. But not a groan escaped him. . . .

"Doctors were sent for in every direction. Dr. Gray, the assistant county physician, responded almost immediately. By his orders Lingg was taken to the bathroom, back of the jailer's office. Here he was laid upon two small tables hastily pushed together. A couple of pillows were placed under his head. In an instant they were dyed a deep crimson, and a dark pool of blood formed on the floor below. The physician, bending over him at work with a glistening knife and needles, cut away the shattered pieces of bone and shreds of bleeding flesh. It was the work of a few minutes only to tie the severed arteries. The doctor fills a small sponge with some liquid, and plunges it down the awful-looking cavity that leads to the throat. The dying man's big chest slowly begins to rise and fall. He was not dead yet. His heart and lungs still performed their functions. Up and down, up and down, heaved the chest, and at each motion torrents of blood poured from the torn palate into the throat. Unceasingly the doctor and his assistants, who had arrived in the meantime, continued to apply the sponge. At last the hand of the unfortunate man moved. It clutched the blanket thrown over his body. His whole frame trembled for a moment, and then he raised that terrible head and the face mangled out of all semblance of humanity. For a moment he opened his eyes and coughed a hoarse, gurgling cough, and with it up came again a stream of blood. It was a horrifying sight. . . .

"The Sheriff at last arrived. His face blanched as he glanced at the spectacle before him, and then he turned away. Hot blankets were brought, and hot water applied to the feet of the fast sinking man. Presently the flow of blood was stopped, and the bandages round the lower part of the face gave the distorted features a more human appearance. Hypodermic injections of ether were given every few minutes. Their bare arms covered with blood, the physicians continued their frightful task. At last they were rewarded for their labours.

"The mangled body gave tokens of life; the signs of returning consciousness were unmistakable.

"'Open your eyes,' said County Physician Mayer. Lingg slowly opened his eyes.

"'Now shut them,' said the doctor. They closed mechanically almost.

"In the midst of the operations upon him the anarchist raised his hand to the doctors. They paused. He essayed to speak. It was impossible. The tongue, torn at the roof, falls back into the throat. He makes a motion as if desiring to write. Paper and pencil were laid at his side. Slowly, but with a firm hand, he traced the words—

"'Besser anlehnen am Rucken. Wenn ich liege, kann ich nicht athmen.'

"'Better support to my back. When I lie flat, I cannot breathe.'

Was there ever such superhuman resolution?

"He slowly turns upon his right side. His eyes become glassy. A pallor overspreads his features. It is evident that the end is near.

"'Are you in pain?' asks the physician.

"A nod of the head is the only answer; but not a groan, not a sign of suffering. . . .

"At half-past two the County Physician went to the telephone in the jailer's office and sent the following message to the Sheriff—

"'Lingg is sinking fast; he cannot last much longer.'

"Already there began the stertorous breathing. The pallor deepened. The eyes resumed their glassy stare. A tremor passed through the body. There was a quick and sudden upheaval of the breast. For a minute or so the breathing continued, Then everything was quiet. The doctor looked once more upon the face, and then said—

"'He is dead.'

"Jailer Folz took his watch out and compared it with the timepiece on the wall. It was exactly nine minutes to three o'clock. The dead anarchist lay upon the table with his breast bared. The doctors left the room. There were only a turnkey and a reporter to close his eyes. The latter attempted to do it, but they would not close. He finally attempted to do it with some pennies which he had in his pocket, but they were not heavy enough. A policeman at that moment entered the room. It was with satisfaction almost that he looked upon the murderer of his comrades.

"'Have you some nickels with you to close his eyes?' he was asked. He fumbled with his hand in his pocket; but presently drew it away. 'Not for that monster,' he declared resolutely.

"Opinions differ as to the means employed by Lingg to end his miserable career. Theories are plentiful; but evidence is scarce. Proof is wholly wanting. One thing can be accepted with safety; it was a high explosive did the work."

This terrible occurrence threw the whole prison into disorder. The jailers ran about like maniacs; the prisoners screamed questions; the prison was in an uproar. Parsons pushed to the bars of his cell and, when he heard what had happened, cried out, "Give me one of those bombs; I want to do the same thing."

The news of the explosion quickly spread beyond the prison walls, and a crowd collected demanding information—a crowd which was soon swollen by reporters from every paper in the city. The news got out in driblets, and was published in a dozen prints. The city seemed to go mad; from one end of the town to the other men began to arm themselves, and the wildest tales were current. There were bombs everywhere. The nervous strain upon the public had become intolerable. The stories circulated and believed that afternoon and night seem now, as one observer said, to belong to the literature of Bedlam. The truth was, that the bombs found in Lingg's cell and his desperate self murder had frightened the good Chicagoans out of their wits. One report had it that there were twenty thousand armed and desperate anarchists in Chicago who had planned an assault upon the jail for the following morning. The newspaper offices, the banks, the Board of Trade building, the Town Hall, were guarded night and day. Every citizen carried weapons openly. One paper published the fact that at ten o'clock on that Thursday night a gun store was still open in Madison Street, and crowded with men buying revolvers. The spectacle did not strike any one as in the least strange, but natural, laudable. The dread of some catastrophe was not only in the air, but in men's talk, in their faces.

There has never been seen anything in any part of America like the spectacle Chicago presented on the morning of the eleventh of November. For a block in each direction from the jail, ropes were stretched across the street, and all traffic suspended. Behind the ropes were lines of policemen, armed with rifles, all the way to the jail the sidewalks were patrolled by other policemen armed to the teeth; the jail was guarded like an outpost in a battle. Lines of policemen were drawn round it, and from every window armed policemen looked forth; the roof was black with them.

At six o'clock in the morning reporters were admitted to the prison; after that, entrance was denied to every one. From six till close upon eleven o'clock some two hundred reporters stood there, cooped up in the jailer's office, waiting. Wild stories were whispered from one white face to another, stories that tried the strongest nerves. Two of the reporters fainted under the strain and had to be taken outside. "In all my experience," writes one of those present, "this was the only occasion on which I ever saw an American reporter break down under any punishment, however terrible, to be inflicted on somebody else."

"It is hard," says the same eye-witness, "now to understand the power of the infectional panic that had seized upon the city and the jail; perhaps some idea of our feelings may be gained from the fact that while we waited there a Chicago newspaper issued an extra, seriously announcing that the jail had been mined, and at the moment of the hanging the whole structure and all in it were to be destroyed."

Lingg's forecast of the result of the second bomb was more than realized.

Some time afterwards this same honest reporter and eye-witness gave a description of the judicial murder which should be read here.

"The word came at last; we marched down the dim corridors to the courtyard appointed for the terrible deed; we saw it done; we saw the four lives crushed out according to the fashion of surviving barbarism. There was no mine exploded; there was no attack; the Central Union did not march its cohorts to the jail nor elsewhere; no armed or unarmed anarchists appeared to menace the supremacy of the State. In all men's eyes there was something of the strain and anxiety that made all the faces I saw about me look drawn and pallid; but there was nowhere the lifting of a lawless hand that day. It sounds now a horrible and cruel thing to say, yet visibly, most visibly, all men's hearts were lightened because those four men's hearts were stilled in death.

"One other strange scene closed the drama, for who that saw it can ever forget that Sunday funeral procession, the black hearses, the marching thousands, the miles upon miles of densely packed and silent streets; the sobering impression of the amnesty of death; the still more sobering question whether we had done right? Lingg's self-immolation and the astounding courage with which he had borne his horrible sufferings had brought every one to pity and to doubt. The short November day closed upon the services at the cemetery: in the darkness the strangely silent crowds straggled back to the city. There was no outbreak at the graves or elsewhere; everywhere this silence, like a sign of brooding thought."

And so the long tragedy came at length to its end. I can never tell what I felt on reading these reports. How I could see it all! How well I understood Lingg and the reason of his desperate act. What the four bombs were for I could not imagine at the time, though I was soon to learn; but surely he had used the bomb on himself in order to get the terrorizing effect he wanted without hurting any one but himself. Think, too, of his courage and iron self-control! How he found perfect words to prevent Osborne from suspecting him, and how when called back to life and exquisite torture by the surgeon's skill, not a groan escaped him, not a cry. Tears poured from my eyes. Such power lost and wasted, such greatness come to so terrible an end! There was something dreadful to me in the idea that even the policeman could speak of Lingg, lying there dead, as a "monster." All he had to do was to ask the death-watch, Osborne, and he might have got a fairer opinion of him, for Osborne after the catastrophe was not afraid to speak the truth. This is what he said of Lingg: "I have the highest opinion of Louis Lingg; I believe him to have been misunderstood; as honest in his opinions as it is possible for a man to be, and as free from feelings of revenge as a new-born babe. I only wish that every young man in America could be as strong and good as Louis Lingg, barring his anarchism."

Even his jailers were won by him to pity and to reverence.

Chapter XIV

MY long task is nearly done, and I am not strong enough to linger over the last sad happenings. Ten or twelve days after I received at Cologne the telegraphic news of Lingg's death, I got the newspaper accounts of the whole occurrence, which I have used in the last chapter, and with the same post a long letter from Ida, containing four leaflets covered with Lingg's clear script. He had written them and given them to Ida to be sent to me on her last visit on Saturday, the fifth of November, just before the bombs were found in his cell. Here is the letter—

"DEAR WILL,

"You have followed my lingering illness, I know, and will be glad as I am that the doctors are going to allow me to get up within a week. I have suffered and must still suffer; it has taught me that no one should inflict suffering who is not ready to bear it cheerfully; I am ready. Our work's nearly finished, Will, and it is good work, not bad, as you once feared. The First Factory Act passed in the State of New York, preventing children under thirteen being worked to death, is dated 1886. The only thing that remains for one of us now is to do what Jesus did with the cross, and by sheer loving-kindness turn the hangman's noose into a symbol of the eternal brotherhood of men. My heart burns within me; we won the Children's Charter and it was cheap at the price; good work, Will; never doubt it.

"It is good, too, that you and I got to know and love each other. Be kind to Ida; marry Elsie; get on with your great book, and be happy as men are happy who can work for themselves and others.

"Your loving comrade to the end,

"JACK."

I don't wish to put too high these hasty lines scribbled in jail almost at the last minute; but it is impossible to read them without recognizing the noble courage and generous thought of others which breathe through them: "out of the strong came forth sweetness."

So far as I was concerned this letter lifted me out of the slough of despair. Determined to do as Lingg asked me, I got work on the papers in Cologne and did my best to take up again the burden of life.

Ida's letter to me explained everything, and I read it with tears dropping from my eyes. She forced herself to give me Lingg's last thoughts:

"'Tell Will,' he said, 'that it seemed to me wrong to strike subordinates or instruments more than once, and I was prevented striking principals or the court as I had intended.

"'Besides, we were being misunderstood: men of the baser sort said we struck out of greed or hate: it was necessary to prove that if we held the lives of others cheap, we held our own cheaper. Men do not kill themselves for greed or hate; but for love, and for an ideal. My deed will teach the wiser among our opponents that their police are of no use against us; authority must be one with right and love to win a man's reverence.'

"He was mad, Will," Ida wrote on, "as those are mad who are too good to live. I begged him for my sake not to touch the thing; but he got me to bring it in on my fingers and in my hair, bit by bit; he wanted enough for the others as well as himself—'the key,' he called it, 'of our mortal prison.'"

The rest of her letter was very simple and very touching; it was evidently written after the final scene and the quiet burial. Mrs. Engel had been very kind, she said, and had insisted that Ida should go to live with her.

They were together now in the shop, Ida helping to take care of the three children. The youngest is just like Engel himself, Ida added, so chubby and kind and strong; and then she went back to Lingg:

"He told me not to think of the past, and I am trying to do as he wished; but it is very hard; often I forget, and Johnny pulls my dress and says, 'Don't twy, Auntie Ida! don't twy.'

"Elsie comes to see me every day; she is loyal and true. Write to her; she is prettier than ever, and in her mourning looks angelic. Write often, Will; we must draw closer now —ah, God! . . ."

I wrote by return to Ida telling her of my loving sympathy, and begging her to let me know if I could help her in any way, and inclosed a letter to Elsie, asking her if she were willing to marry me. She replied that she was willing to come to Germany or France, and marry me at once; might she bring her mother? The letter was all sweetness. The dear baby phrases in it were as balm to my heart. "I wish I were with you, dear, to nurse you; you'd soon get well. You have taught me love; I am a better woman for having known you, and so proud of my boy. I am longing to start, and yet the thought of meeting you makes me very shy. . ." The sweetheart!

I wrote back that I hoped for nothing better on earth than her companionship, and that I would begin at once to get a house ready and would send for her as soon as possible.

But it was not to be. One evening I had wandered about trying to coax myself to hope, or at least to work; but in vain. All my thoughts turned to melancholy brooding and sadness. It seems to me now, looking back, that something in me broke when Elsie left my room on that fatal afternoon in May. I was not strong enough for such tremendous, conflicting emotions; something else snapped when I threw the bomb and realized what I had done, and the last strand that bound me to life gave way when Lingg died. Nature treats us as we treat stubborn children. We cling to the bough of life as long as we can, and Nature comes and strikes our fingers one after the other, till, unable to endure the punishment any longer, we loosen our hold and fall into the void.

My punishment had broken my will to live; it had probably undermined my strength also, for a simple wetting brought me down. Next morning I could scarcely breathe with bronchitis, and was ill. I wrote to Elsie and told her that I had caught a bad cold; begged her to wait for me, I should soon get better;

but I knew even then that I was more likely to get worse.

I continued to work at my book feverishly, determined to finish my task; but at the end of ten days in bed, the kindly people of the house called in a doctor, who looked very grave and advised me to go to Davos Platz, and when pressed told me that I was in a consumption, and that both lungs were affected. The truth was, I suppose, that my frame was too weak to resist any attack, and I looked forward to the end with a sigh of content; one gets so weary of this hard, all-hating world! I redoubled my efforts to finish the book. As soon as I had had two fair copies made of it, and had sent one off to Ida and one to Elsie, I felt considerably better; only this short, last chapter remained to be done. Somehow or other I thought that if I could get back to the air of my native Alps again I should get quite well, so I came back to Munich and then here to Reichholz, close to the homeland, for a visit; it will be a long one. Before I began to write this chapter yesterday I wrote long letters to Ida and Elsie, taking an eternal farewell. I think, I hope, I shall get a reply from Elsie; and if I do, I will add it to this last chapter, and the whole book shall be sent off to her after my death to do with as she and Ida may direct,

And now, what is the end of the whole matter? I went out into the world and fought and laboured in it, and have come back to my birthplace. A journeying and fighting—a sweet kiss or two and the clasp of a friend's hand—that's what life has meant for me. One starts out with a certain capital of energy, and whether one spreads it over threescore years, or exhausts it in three, matters nothing. The question is what one has done and achieved, and not whether one suffered or enjoyed, much less how long it took one to do the work.

There is something in our case, I feel sure, to the credit side. As Lingg said, the bomb thrown in the Haymarket put an end to the bludgeoning and pistolling of unarmed men and women by the police; it helped, too, to win the Children's Charter, and to establish "Labour Day" as a popular festival. The effect of Lingg's desperate self-murder was prodigious. Chicago took his teaching to heart; such a death has its own dignity and its own virtue. In some dim way the people in Chicago came to recognize that Lingg and Parsons were extraordinary men, and all confessed in their hearts that there must be something very wrong in a social state which had driven such men to despair.

One fact exemplifies the change of feeling.

Near the spot where the policemen fell in the Haymarket, a monument was erected in memory of them with a statue of a policeman on top. But after a very short time it was removed on some convenient pretext to be erected again, miles from the scene of the unhappy event, in a wooded park, where no one sees it or knows what it commemorates. Somehow or other it was generally understood that the police were not the heroes of the occasion.

In the same way, I remember, after Marat was killed in the French Revolution, he was given a gorgeous state funeral; his body was interred with all ceremony in the Pantheon; men and women went mad over him, wore Marat hats and Marat ties and Marat coats to do him honour; but in a year it was found that Charlotte Corday was justified, that she was a great woman and not an assassin; and so before the months had run full circle, Marat's body was taken out of the Pantheon, his coffin broken open, and his dust scattered to the winds. Justice has its revenges.

The outcome and the result in our case is perhaps uncertain. Was the work well done? Is revolt best, or submission? I'm afraid the more I seem to have paid in pain and misery for what I did, the more certain I feel that we were right.

One thing is past doubt. Louis Lingg was a great man, and a born leader of men, who with happier chances might have been a great reformer, or a great statesman. When they talk of him as a murderer, it fills me with pity for them, for in Lingg, too, was the blood of the martyrs: he had the martyr's pity for men, the martyr's sympathy with suffering and destitution, the martyr's burning contempt for greed and meanness, the martyr's hope in the future, the martyr's belief in the ultimate perfectibility of men.

What have I to say more? Nothing. He that has ears will hear, and the others do not matter. Nearing the end I begin to see that the opinion of one's fellows is not worth much, and another saying of Lingg's comes to help me here. "The law of gravitation," he said, "is the law of the ought; it would be easy to put oneself in perfect relation to the centre of gravity of this world; would be easy and safe and pleasant. But, strange to say, the centre of gravity, even of our globe itself, is always changing, moving towards some unseen goal. Stars beyond our ken draw us and change our destinies. And so Mr. Worldly Wise comes to grief. Our only chance of being right is to trust the heart, and act on what we feel."

One word about myself. Here at the end

I am fairly content. I have not had much happiness in life, except with Elsie; but through knowing Elsie and Lingg, I came to a fuller, richer life than I should ever have reached by myself, and whoever has climbed the heights is not likely to complain of the cost. I am only sorry for Elsie and Ida; I wish, I wish—but after all, even the roughest men do not trample on flowers.

I cannot believe that in this world any unselfish deed is lost, that any aspiration or even hope dies away without effect. In my own short life I have seen the seed sown and the fruit gathered, and that is enough for me. We shall no doubt be despised and reviled by men, at least for a time, because we shall be judged by the rich and the powerful, and not by the destitute and the dispossessed for whom we gave our lives.

Afterword

TO "THE BOMB" WRITTEN IN 1920

FLAUBERT exclaimed once that no one had understood, much less appreciated, his "Madame Bovary." "I ought to have criticized it myself," he added; "then I'd have shown the fool-critics how to read a story and analyze it and weigh the merits of it. I could have done this better than anyone and very impartially; for I can see its faults, faults that make me miserable."

In just this spirit and with the self-same conviction I want to say a word or two about "The Bomb." I have stuck to the facts of the story in the main as closely as possible; but the character of Schnaubelt and his lovestory with Elsie are purely imaginary. I was justified in inventing these, I believe, because almost nothing was known of Schnaubelt and as the illiterate mob continually confuse Socialism and Free-love, it seemed to me well to demonstrate that love between social outcasts and rebels would naturally be intenser and more idealistic than among ordinary men and women. The pressure from the outside must crush the pariahs together in a closer embrace and intensify passion to self-sacrifice.

My chief difficulty was the choice of a protagonist; Parsons was almost an ideal figure; he gave himself up to the police though he was entirely innocent and out of their clutches and when offered a pardon in prison he refused it, rising to the height of human self-abnegation by declaring that if he, the only American, accepted a pardon he would thus be dooming the others to death.

But such magnanimity and sweetness of spirit is not as American, it seemed to me, as Lingg's practical heroism and passion of revolt. In spite of Miss Goldman's preference for Parsons, I still believe I chose my hero rightly, but I idealized Lingg beyond life-size, I fear. No young man of twenty ever had the insight into social conditions which I attribute to him. I should have given him less vision and put in a dash of squalor or of cruelty or cunning to make the portrait lifelike. But the fault seems to me excusable.

The whole book is probably too idealistic; but as all rebels—socialists and anarchists alike—are whelmed in these States in a flood of furious and idiotic contempt and hatred, a certain small amount of idealization of the would-be reformers is perhaps justified. On the whole I'm rather proud of "The Bomb" and of Elsie and Lingg.

In a pamphlet published by the police, shortly after the execution of the Anarchists, it was stated that "Lingg's father was a dragoon officer of royal blood, but he only knew his mother for whom he always showed a passionate devotion. Four years after her liaison with the handsome officer, his mother wedded a lumber-worker named Link. When Louis was about twelve his fosterfather got heart-disease through exposure and died. The widow was left in poverty and had to do washing and ironing in order to support herself and a daughter named Elise who had been born of her marriage.

"Louis received a fair education [I continue to give the gist of the police record] and became a carpenter at Mannheim in order to help his mother. In 1879 he was out of his apprenticeship and went to Kehl and then to Freiburg.

"Here he fell in with free-thinkers and became an avowed Socialist. In '83 he went to Luzern and thence to Zurich where he met the famous anarchist Reinsdorf to whom he became greatly attached. He joined the German Socialist society "Eintracht" and threw his whole soul into the cause.

"In August 1884 Mrs. Lingg married a second time, one Christian Gaddum, in order, as she said, to find support for her daughter; she herself being in poor health; she asked Louis to return home if only for a visit.

"But Louis had now reached the age for military service and as his whole being revolted against German militarism he decided to emigrate to America.

"After the wayward boy had taken ship at Havre he and his mother corresponded regularly. All her letters breathed encouragement; she sent him money often and concluded invariably by giving him good counsel and urging him to write frequently.

"That Lingg had a great love for his mother is shown by the fact that he kept all her letters from the time he left home till he killed himself.

"His illegitimate birth appears to have annoyed the youth; he worried his mother to give him his father's name. In one letter she says: "It grieves me that you speak of your birth; where your father is I don't know. My father did not want me to marry him because he did not desire me to follow him into Hessia and as he had no real estate he could not marry me in Schwetzingen according to our laws. He left and went I don't know where."

"A little later Louis appears to have asked her to get him a certificate of birth, for a later letter from her satisfies this request. I reproduce it word for word as characteristic of their relations:

MANNHEIM, June 29, 1884.

DEAR LOUIS: You must have waited a long time for an answer. John said to Elise that I had not yet replied to your last letter. The officials of the court you cannot push. For my part I would have been better pleased if they had hurried up, because it would have saved you a great deal of time. But now I am glad that it has finally been accomplished. After a great deal of toil, I put myself out to go to Schwetzingen and see about the certificate of your birth. I know you will be glad and satisfied to learn that you carry the name of Lingg. This is better than to have children with two different names. He [the first husband] had you entered as a legitimate child before we got married. I think this was the best course, so that you will not worry and reproach me. Such a certificate of birth is no disgrace, and you can show it.

I felt offended that you took no notice of the "confirmation." Elise had everything nice. Her only wish was to receive some small token from Louis, which would have pleased her more than anything else. When she came from church, the first thing she asked for was about a letter or card from you, but we had to be contented with the thought that perhaps you did not remember us. Now it is all past. . . .

I was very much troubled that it has taken so long [to procure the certificate], but I could not help it. Everything is all right, and we are all well and working. I hope to hear the same from you. It would not be so bad if you wrote oftener. I have had to do a great many things for you the last eighteen years, but with a mother you can do as you please—neglect her and never answer her letters.

"The certificate sent him read as follows:

CERTIFICATE OF BIRTH

No. 9,681.

Ludwig Link, legitimate son of Philipp Friedrich Link and of Regina Von Hoefler, was born at Schwetzingen, on the ninth (9th) day of September, 1864. This is certified according to the records of the Evangelical Congregation of Schwetzingen.
SCHWETZINGEN, May 24, 1884.

(Seal.) County Court: CLURICHT.

"One thing appears from the above, and that is that at home Louis' name was Link. Other documents, some of them legal, also found in his trunk, show that his name was formerly written Link. He must have changed it shortly before leaving Europe or just after reaching the United States. The thought of his illegitimacy [according to the police report] helped to make him in religion a free-thinker, in theory a free-lover, and in practice an implacable enemy of existing society. His mother's letters show that she wished him to be a good man, and it was no fault of her early training that he subsequently became an Anarchist.

"No sooner had Lingg reached Chicago than he looked up the haunts of Socialists and Anarchists. . . . Lingg arrived here only eight or nine months before the eventful 4th of May, but in that short time he succeeded in making himself the most popular man in Anarchist circles. No one had created such a furore since 1872, when Socialism had its inception in the city.

"Lingg had not been connected with the organization long before he became a recognized leader and made speeches that enthused all the comrades. While young in years, they recognized in him a worthy leader, and the fact that he had sat at the feet of Reinsdorf as a pupil elevated him in their estimation. This distinction, added to his personal magnetism, made him the subject for praise and comment. . . .

"His work was never finished, and never neglected. At one time he taught his followers how to handle the bombs so that they would not explode in their hands, and showed the time and distance for throwing the missiles with deadly effect; at another he drilled those who were to do the throwing. . . . He was not alone a bomb-maker; he also constituted himself an agent to sell arms. This is shown by a note found in his trunk addressed to Abraham Hermann. It reads as follows:

> *Friend:*—I sold three revolvers during the last two days, and I will sell three more to-day (Wednesday). I sell them from $6.00 to $7.80 apiece.
>
> Respectfully and best regards,
>
> L. Lingg.

"In truth, he was the shiftiest as well as the most dangerous Anarchist in all Chicago.

"The Haymarket riot proved a most bitter disappointment. Lingg was fairly beside himself with chagrin and mortification. The one consuming desire of his life had utterly and signally failed of realization." [Here occurs the police account of his arrest which I have reproduced in "The Bomb." I now continue it]:

"During the time Lingg remained at the station his wounded thumb was regularly attended to; he was treated very kindly, had plenty to eat, and was made as comfortable as possible.

"One day I asked him if he entertained any hostility towards the police. He replied that during the McCormick factory riot he had been clubbed by an officer, but he did not care much for that. He could forget it all, but he did not like Bonfield. He would kill Bonfield, willingly, he declared.

"Lingg was a singular Anarchist. Though he drank beer, he never drank to excess, and he frowned upon the use of bad or indecent language. He was an admirer of the fair sex, and they reciprocated his admiration, his manly form, handsome face, and pleasing manners captivating all.

"There was one visitor he always welcomed. It was his sweetheart, who became a regular caller. She invariably wore a pleasant smile, breathed soft, loving words into his ears through the wire screen that separated the visitor's cage from the jail corridor, and contributed much toward keeping him cheerful.

"She simply passed with the jail officials at first as "Lingg's girl," but one day some one called her Ida Miller, and thereafter she was recognized under that name. She was generally accompanied by young Miss Engel, the daughter of the Anarchist Engel, and during the last four months of her lover's incarceration she could be seen every afternoon entering the jail. She was always readily admitted until the day the bombs were found in Lingg's cell. After that neither she nor Mr. and Mrs. Klein were admitted. While it has never been satisfactorily proven who it was that introduced the bombs into the jail, it is likely that they were smuggled into Lingg's hands by his sweetheart. She enjoyed Lingg's fullest confidence, and obeyed his every wish.

"It is not known whether Miller is the real name of the girl, but it is supposed to be Elise Friedel. She is a German, and was twenty-two years of age at the time, her birthplace being Mannheim, which was also Lingg's native town. She was tall, well-made, with fair complexion, and dark eyes and hair."

Here ends the police account so far as it concerns us or throws light on the characters of "The Bomb." It is informative and fairly truthful but plainly inspired by illiterate and brainless prejudice. Still it proves that in my story I have kept closely to the facts.

FRANK HARRIS